PRAISE FOR *THE*

"Take the classic Gothic element of a spooky old house, add a dash of modern #MeToo seasoning, and let everything simmer in the warmth of timeless maternal love, and you have Beth Castrodale's deliciously clever new novel. *The Inhabitants*, dream-drenched and mysterious, tantalizes and satisfies to the final pages. A remarkable read."

—Chauna Craig, author of *The Widow's Guide to Edible Mush-rooms* and *Wings & Other Things*

"Beth Castrodale's wonderful new novel is an engaging read that incorporates art, architecture, herbal medicine, #MeToo, and the supernatural. After breaking up with her longtime partner, Nilda Ricci embarks on a new life when she and her daughter move into an architecturally significant house with its own history and secrets. There, Nilda, a painter, encounters an attractive, intriguing neighbor who might not be what he seems; unsolved issues from the past; the resurfaced traumas of a childhood friend; and mysterious apparitions. The result is a page turner of a novel about deciding what's real or imagined, making sense of the past, and looking to the future. Richly grounded in physical details and keen psychological insights, this superbly crafted novel delivers on many levels."

—Jan English Leary, author of *Thicker Than Blood*, *Skating on the Vertical*, and *Town and Gown*

"Beth Castrodale's moody and atmospheric new novel, *The Inhabitants*, will have you looking twice at gifts from neighbors and considering locks for your closet doors. The protagonist and her daughter arrive at Farleigh House, the eccentric construction of a nineteenth-century architect, for a new beginning. Instead, they're met by mysterious forces from the past—a fireplace that erupts in faces, an unseen weight at the foot of a bed, and a wave of rage on a feeding frenzy. *The Inhabitants*, a modern-Gothic novel, reminds us not only that there is a place for the past in the present but also that going back must often precede moving forward."

—Cynthia Newberry Martin, author of *The Art of Her Life*, *Love Like This*, and *Tidal Flats*

"In her beautifully paced new novel, Beth Castrodale gives us a fresh take on the classic haunted-house tale. *The Inhabitants* guides Nilda Ricci, a newly single mother, and her daughter through the strange and disconcerting Farleigh House, into which the two of them have recently moved, and also through the corridors of the past—through fear, regret, and memory that sit in the quietly beating hearts of not only the house but also in sculptures and paintings and even lullabies. Eventually, all these passageways converge, with Nilda at the epicenter, in a way that is both inevitable and surprising. Ultimately, *The Inhabitants* asks which is more terrifying: the spirits and the strange house they haunt, or the monsters that walk among us every day? Masterfully told and beautifully balanced, *The Inhabitants* is a terrific read."

—Jim Naremore, author of *American Still Life* and *The Arts of Legerdemain as Taught by Ghosts*

"From the idiosyncratic house the novel's artist-mother heroine, Nilda, inherits, to the mysterious housekeeper she also inherits, to the eccentric neighbor who invents 'creativity' tonics for Nilda, to the revelation that the man whose portrait Nilda is commissioned to paint poses a danger that must be stopped, dread and fascination permeate Beth Castrodale's fiercely feminist modern-Gothic novel. But while *The Inhabitants* is heady and menacing, it's also a tender story about the undying devotion of motherly love."

—Michelle Ross, author of *They Kept Running*, *Shapeshifting*, and *There's So Much They Haven't Told You*

"The deceptively innocuous spell cast by *The Inhabitants* is like walking in a pleasant wood and encountering a coiled rattle-snake. This well-crafted book is highly recommended for those who love tales of the supernatural. The otherworldly elements are finely blended with life's challenges, the lure of romance, magic potions, and the life-altering presence of evil."

—Morgan Howell, author of *The Moon Won't Talk*

Also by Beth Castrodale

I Mean You No Harm
In This Ground
Marion Hatley

THE INHABITANTS

Beth Castrodale

Regal House Publishing

Published by
Regal House Publishing, LLC
Raleigh, NC 27605
All rights reserved

ISBN -13 (paperback): 9781646034963
ISBN -13 (epub): 9781646034970
Library of Congress Control Number: 2023950834

All efforts were made to determine the copyright holders and obtain their permissions in any circumstance where copyrighted material was used. The publisher apologizes if any errors were made during this process, or if any omissions occurred. If noted, please contact the publisher and all efforts will be made to incorporate permissions in future editions.

Cover images and design by © C. B. Royal

Regal House Publishing, LLC
https://regalhousepublishing.com

The following is a work of fiction created by the author. All names, individuals, characters, places, items, brands, events, etc. were either the product of the author or were used fictitiously. Any name, place, event, person, brand, or item, current or past, is entirely coincidental.

Printed in the United States of America

For all of the friends who have sustained me,
with love and gratitude

With its gabled and turreted roof, bay windows, and patterned shingles, Farleigh House appears from the outside to be quite the ordinary Victorian. Certain features of its interior, however, push back against the typical tastes and conventions of that time, just as the home's architect and original owner, Nathaniel Farleigh (1809–1881), was known to have done with his other designs and constructions. Some have found these features disquieting.

—From *Vermont Homes of Note*, 1971

1

Farleigh House. The name had struck Nilda as self-important, and ironic given that no Farleigh had lived in the place for nearly a century.

Now, because of what felt like some cosmic mistake, the house was hers.

On her knees in its back yard, she was pulling weeds in a name-only flower bed, trying not to think of the much more important tasks she didn't have the energy, or the money, to tackle: patching the failing roof, upgrading the dodgy, underpowered electrical system, re-mortaring chimneys that threatened to send bricks tumbling. That all these things were now Nilda's responsibility might never cease to bewilder her.

Sidney was closing in from the left, holding out her maybe-kitten/maybe-bear plushie.

"Fuzzy's tummy hurts."

"Awww, I'm sorry. Does she need a kiss?"

Sidney shook her head, still pouting.

"What about a cookie?" For Fuzzy, invisible cookies usually did the trick.

Another headshake. "She doesn't like it here. She wants to go home."

Since they'd moved here two weeks earlier, Sidney had

said she wanted to go home at least five times, and now she was bringing Fuzzy in on the case. There seemed no way of getting across that they would never return to their beloved but cramped and bank-account-busting apartment in Boston, which within hours of their departure was occupied by the next tenant.

"*This* is home now, sweet pea. Remember?"

"No, it's not."

Nilda tried another argument for this place, knowing it was a reach. "Angus likes it here." The last time she saw him he was on the couch, sleeping.

"He likes everywhere."

She was right.

"Come here," Nilda said, out of ideas.

She drew Sidney close and rocked her, rocking being the one thing that almost always soothed her. Going through the usual motions, humming the same wordless tune into her daughter's hair, Nilda realized she was only encouraging Sidney's clinginess, which had picked up after the death of Nilda's mother— Sidney's only remaining grandparent—and worsened since the move here. Once a remarkably independent child, she seemed to have slipped back in time, as if she were six years old going on three.

I'll set more limits, soon, Nilda told herself once again, knowing she'd break this promise as soon as Sidney needed her to.

A sound stopped her humming: a chattering—no, clucking. Looking to the source she saw a chicken emerge from a break in the fence that separated their yard from the neighbor's—the only other neighbor in sight.

Nilda knew that Nathaniel Farleigh had built the place next door for his eldest son, but, like Farleigh House, it hadn't remained in the family. The most recent occupant, apparently, had been some lone, elderly doctor who'd lived in the home for years, until his death a few months before. Supposedly, his former caretaker was still checking in on the place, including the chicken coop at the edge of the property. But the trespassing bird reminded Nilda that she hadn't seen him for days.

She, and now Sidney, watched the creature strut along the fence line. Looking both puzzled and dauntless, it jerked occasional glances their way, prompting giggles from Sidney.

"Hi, chickie!" she said at first. Then "Come *here*, chickie!"

No, Nilda thought. *Go home, chickie.*

Usually a hardcore animal lover, she couldn't deal with one more needy thing at this time in her life. That included the rotting fence, which evidently was her responsibility. For now, she felt capable of nothing more than finding some object to block the breach—after she got the chicken back through it.

"*Here,* chickie!"

The bird shifted course and started strutting in their direction. Nilda waited, knowing if she went for it too quickly, she'd spook it out of reach.

Down the fence line a rustling and crackling sounded from the hedges along the neighbor-facing side of the house. As Nilda tightened her hold on Sidney, the rustling stopped.

"All right if I come through?"

A male voice, friendly sounding.

"Uh, okay," Nilda called.

Seconds later, a tall, lanky man emerged from the greenery: not the caretaker, at least not the one she'd seen before. This guy was younger-looking, and something about him—maybe the black T-shirt and vintage Converse, or his mop of dark curls—telegraphed *musician*. Surely, a misperception born of masochism.

He crept forward, holding out some dowsing-rod-like wire contraption: a repurposed coat hanger, Nilda realized. As if noting her confusion, he paused and held her gaze, then chicken-flapped his arms, grabbed one wrist.

I'm here to catch that bird, was the message Nilda took.

In Sidney his movements set off another round of giggles. He put a finger to his lips, quieting her.

As he closed in on the chicken, the creature picked up its pace and clucking. Then it stopped, started pecking the grass. Behind it, step by cautious step, the man crept closer and extended the hanger, the end of which was bent into a small hook.

With a lunge and swoop, he hooked the chicken by one ankle and grabbed it by the other, letting the hanger drop to the grass. After taming the flapping, squawking chaos into something manageable, he held the bird close to his chest, looking pretty pleased with himself.

"Nice work," Nilda said. She rose to her feet, keeping hold of Sidney's hand. Up close, she saw that there was a chemical symbol on the front of his shirt. She had no idea what it meant, if anything.

"I'm sorry it was necessary," he said. "I gotta fix that door to the coop. And that gap in the fence."

Nilda decided to keep her mouth shut about the fence being her responsibility. If he was up for fixing it, she'd be happy to let him.

"Well, thanks for coming to get him—*her?*"

"Her. Fortunately, there's only hens in the coop. No roosters to wake us at dawn."

"Are you the new caretaker?"

"In a manner of speaking." He shifted the chicken to free a hand, which he extended to Nilda. "I'm Graham. Graham Emmerly, your new neighbor."

Emmerly. If she was remembering correctly, that had been the doctor's last name.

She gave him an awkward, left-hand shake, not letting go of Sidney. "I'm Nilda Ricci. And this is my daughter."

She knelt and murmured to Sidney, "You wanna tell our neighbor your name?"

Sidney turned away from him, buried her head in Nilda's shoulder.

Sorry, Nilda mouthed to him.

It's okay, he mouthed back. Then he knelt to their level.

"Hey," he said to Sidney. "This chicken needs a name. Would you like to give her one?"

Sidney gave him her grouchiest face. "I already said it. She's *Chickie*. And I'm *Sidney*."

"Chickie it is. And pleased to meet you, Sidney."

As Sidney melted back into Nilda, he headed for the gap in the fence and got the chicken through it.

"I just tossed out some feed," he called back to Nilda. "That should keep her on my side of the fence for now. The rest of them too."

He headed for the dropped hanger, then folded it up, crammed it into his back pocket.

"How many are there?" Nilda asked.

"Six? Seven? If you want one, it's yours."

Sidney turned her *Gimme* look on Nilda. "Can we, Mommy? *Please?*"

Since the death of Nilda's mother, such pleas had become harder to resist. But this time Nilda was going to hold her ground. She didn't need another pet to take care of. And the one they already had, Angus, was as untested on farm animals as they were. Who was to say that a chicken wouldn't trigger some heretofore dormant bloodlust in the typically gentle mutt-hound, leading to a scene of carnage no six-year-old should have to witness?

"No, we can't. But maybe Mr. Emmerly will let us visit Chickie on occasion."

"Any time," he said. "And, please, call me Graham."

It seemed to Nilda that he'd appeared out of nowhere. But the fence was high and the hedges overgrown, and the shed that functioned as the neighbor's garage was on the other side of the property. Given how busy she'd been with setting up the house and studio, and trying to get that new portrait started, he could have been coming and going for days without her noticing.

Nilda ran her fingers through Sidney's hair, an apology for

the chicken deprivation. "Are you related to the guy who used to live next door?"

"I'm his son."

She wondered whether the late Mr. Emmerly had been this tall, his eyes this dark.

"I'm sorry for your loss."

"I appreciate that. But as they say, his time had come. And I'm glad I'm able to start taking care of what was important to him, chickens and all."

"So the chickens were a longtime thing?"

"Ohhh yeah. My parents kept laying hens for years, got me trained early in caring for them, which I did until I left for college. After my mom died and my dad got too frail to manage things himself, the caretaker took over. And did a half-assed job in my opinion. But there's nothing that can't be put to rights."

She wondered whether he had a partner or kids. He wasn't wearing a ring. "Do you have any other relatives in town?"

"Nope. I'm here for the house. And a teaching gig at the community college."

"What in?"

"Chemistry."

That explained the symbol on his shirt.

"I'm impressed that you can teach chemistry. In high school I barely passed it." Noticing the look that had come over him, Nilda smiled. "Do I detect an air of disappointment?"

"Not in you. I'd lay a bet that your teacher was to blame."

"That's very generous of you."

"It's not generosity. What I mean is, chemistry is its own fascinating world, full of mysteries and revelations. But most instructors, especially in high school, make a stultifying business of it. And that's *such* a disservice."

He smiled, as if to check his turn to the serious. "Enough of my soap-boxing. Let's talk about you. What do *you* do? And what brought you here?"

The first question wasn't hard to answer, and she did. What brought her here was a far more complicated story.

Nilda had no blood connection to the Farleighs. She hadn't even met the great-aunt who'd willed the place to her mother, Jo, only as an afterthought. "Her first choice was the Farleigh Animal Clinic," the great-aunt's lawyer explained to Nilda. "She wanted them to move their operations to the house and dedicate a wing to her two favorite Yorkies, now in the Great Beyond. But then she learned they might tear the place down or sell it as soon as they got their hands on it. And that was it."

For months the great-aunt's death notice, will, and an explanatory cover letter from the lawyer had sat in an unopened envelope on Jo's notoriously messy, mail-covered desk—until Jo died, leaving Nilda to sort through all the piles, discover the letter and will, and eventually call the lawyer. The understanding that the house would be hers, should she choose to accept it, had warped the grief she'd been immersed in, added a sickening thrill. A thrill of new possibilities. Still, she might have passed on the deal if not for one big incentive: a dear friend from college, Toni, happened to live just a short distance from this place.

Now she gave Graham the briefest version of this story, and the two of them laughed over the coincidence that they'd both inherited, at roughly the same time, homes so closely connected to Nathaniel Farleigh.

"I wish I knew more about him," Nilda said. "I checked out his Wikipedia page and it's, uh…"

"Lame-o?"

Nilda laughed. "Yeah." The entry included a photograph of Farleigh and a list of some of the homes, businesses, and institutions that his architecture firm had designed. Little more.

"Well, I've got a few stories about him."

"*Really?*" Nilda said.

"Really. As a matter of fact, that room up there?"

She followed his gaze to an upper window, belonging to Sidney's room.

"That used to be his study. And apparently the place where he turned out hundreds of architectural models, after he was ousted from his firm."

"What happened?"

"It's a long story. But let's just say his designs were getting stranger and stranger, and—"

"And what?"

"It appears he…he wasn't well. And in some of the later entries in his journals, he claimed this house had something to do with that. He said he felt like the walls were closing in on him."

Great, Nilda thought.

"But he was okay with that study. Apparently, he spent hours there, working."

Graham seemed to sense that Nilda wasn't loving all these details. "I'm sure that whatever he was struggling with had nothing to do with this house. I'm just glad he had the model making to take his mind off his troubles, real or imagined. To maintain some feeling of control."

Sensing Fuzzy traipsing across her bare feet, Nilda glanced down at Sidney and waved. When she turned her attention back to Graham, he looked remorseful.

"I'm sorry I brought up such dark stuff. Not a great way to make you feel at home."

"It's fine, really."

"No, it isn't. It's one of the drawbacks of being a history buff. Sometimes I get carried away."

In truth, Nilda was ready for a change of subject. "What about Eula Joy. You have any memories of her?"

She'd explained that it was Eula Joy who'd left her mother the house.

He brightened up. "Of course I remember Mrs. Austerlane, and Mr. Austerlane. They were great people, and great neighbors. Summer nights, my folks used to hang out with them on this very lawn, sometimes for hours. They'd knock back more than a few 'twilight daiquiris,' as my mom used to call them."

Somehow, this didn't square with what Nilda's mother had told her of Eula Joy, who, according to Jo, preferred her Yorkies to all of human society, including her late husband. The pictures Nilda had seen of her great-aunt seemed to capture this attitude better than any words could have. Several of them caught her smoking in a lawn chair, a Yorkie—or Yorkies—in her lap, and glaring at the intruding photographer. As Jo once said of her aunt, "It would have been hard to find a more ironic middle name for her."

Sidney tugged at Nilda's T-shirt. "I'm hungry, Mommy."

"Okay. Let's get you some lunch." Nilda looked to Graham. "Would you like to join us?"

"No, no, no. I've taken up enough of your time. But thanks."

Nilda felt a quiver of disappointment. Then she checked herself. This wasn't the time to invite more complications into her life.

"But listen," he said. "I'd love to have you two over soon. As soon as I get things a bit more sorted out over there." He nodded toward his place.

"That would be nice."

"All right, then. I'll be seeing you soon."

He started turning away then paused, spotting something in Nilda's hair. Slowly, he reached for it, then stopped.

"May I?" he asked.

She nodded.

Looking into her eyes, he plucked whatever it was from her hair and held it before her: a maple seed. He let it spin its way to the ground, then turned away. Watching him retreat to the hedges, Nilda wondered whether the shiver he'd sent through her had been the slightest bit intentional.

"Hey!" she called, before he vanished. "What's with the symbol on your shirt?"

He stopped and turned back to her, smiling. "It's the formula for dopamine, one of my favorite molecules." Then, with a wave, he was gone.

Dopamine. Was it good or bad, or a little bit of both? Nilda couldn't remember.

As she and Sidney headed back to the house, Nilda felt her phone buzz in her pocket. Against her better judgment she took it out, saw that Clay was calling—as if he'd sensed the intrusion of a handsome stranger. He, who'd enjoyed more than his share of pretty strangers, on tours and off them.

She dismissed the call.

"Is it Daddy?"

Nilda didn't want to lie to Sidney. "Yes. We'll call him back after lunch."

When they were halfway back to the house, Nilda stopped. "Hey. Where's Fuzzy?"

Sidney dropped Nilda's hand and ran back to where they'd visited with Graham. There, she retrieved Fuzzy from the ground.

The plushie had become Sidney's favorite, perhaps because it had been Jo's last present to her. For that same reason, Nilda had formed her own attachment to the toy. She couldn't bear the thought of it being lost or abandoned, even in this yard she now owned.

Grow up.

In this new reality she was one hundred percent mother, no longer anyone's child.

A final word: My longtime housekeeper, Helen Thurnwell, may stop by as she's able to clean or perform other small household chores that need tending to. She has been ailing recently, and so has cut back on her hours. But it seems that she continues to find comfort from her routines here, which she's observed for many years.

Though she has never expressed this outright, I believe she feels close to her late son in this place, for he accompanied her here every time he could and often played in the house, the yard, and anywhere else he could roam. That she lost him, especially when he was so young, has never ceased to weigh upon her, understandably.

I'm informing you of this tragedy only to help you understand the situation with Helen, and I'm trusting that you won't be so insensitive as to mention it in her presence. Because of the comforts she takes from this place, and the kindness she's shown to me over many years, I ask that you never tell her that her services are no longer required.

—From a memo by Eula Joy Austerlane, dated November 3, 2010. To: Inheritor(s) of My Property in Hitchfield, Vermont. Subject: Home Maintenance

2

Nilda had spent much of the past five years immersed in the stares of strangers, which in Boston had cluttered her studio walls. She'd met none of these people before finishing their portraits, never wanted to. Never wanted to read about the ones who'd made the news. She wanted nothing more than what she could discern from their photographs, collecting telling clues—first from the eyes then from everything else.

Her best portraits conveyed these clues to canvas, giving the sense that the subject was present. Her worst portraits, which she dubbed "photo repros," made her feel like a con artist, doing nothing more than trading brushstroke tricks for money.

So far, the three photographs of William Fletcher Tenneman, the newly appointed headmaster of the Fairmoore School, were yielding nothing to her: WFT at his desk at Fairmoore; WFT in sunlight, in golf wear; WFT with one arm around his wife, the other around his daughter.

Dedicated. Athletic. Loving.

Surely, these were the character traits Nilda's contact at the school was hoping she'd take from the photographs. But they were up against her preconceived judgments of the man.

Rich. Privileged. Out of touch with reality as most people know it.

Stop it.

Even as headmaster, Tenneman probably wasn't making the big bucks. The real issue, she realized, was her longstanding public-school-kid grudge against Fairmoore, a prep school whose annual tuition had been nearly double what her mom had made in a year. She reminded herself that she stood to make far more money from this job than she'd gotten for any other portrait—if she didn't let her personal baggage get in the way. And once it was done, she could turn back to her own art and never accept another portrait commission, thanks to the inheritance from her mom, and Eula Joy. Though it wasn't a lot of money, it would allow her a bit more freedom.

Nilda traded WFT's family photo for her coffee mug and tossed back what was left in it. As she returned to the coffee pot, she wondered whether this new space was part of her problem with getting the portrait started. The unfamiliarity of it, or maybe something else.

Though someone—Eula Joy's lawyer?—had described this outbuilding as a "shed," it was far bigger than Nilda's cramped studio in Boston, offering ample room not only for her easels, canvases, and other supplies but also for her mom's glass-blowing tools: the furnace, annealer, pipes, jacks, etc. Nilda hadn't been able to bring herself to get rid of these things, in which her mother was as physically present as she'd ever be again.

But maybe they were more a distraction than a comfort, more a reminder of loss than a balm for it.

"Ms. Ricci?"

Nilda jumped, splashing the coffee pot's contents across her mug and the table. Looking left, she saw a shadow in the light from the half-opened door.

She replaced the pot and went to the door, opened it wide.

Before her stood a woman in a blue shirtwaist dress and matching tennis shoes. Another neighbor? No, she guessed. This visitor's expression was neutral, almost businesslike.

"I'm Nilda Ricci."

The woman nodded curtly. "I'm Helen Thurnwell."

Nilda struggled to connect the name with a memory. "The housekeeper?"

"Yes."

That didn't seem possible. Eula Joy's heads-up about Helen Thurnwell had been written nearly ten years ago, a time when the housekeeper was supposedly slowing down, "ailing." Nilda had assumed that Helen was elderly, maybe even dead. But this woman looked about forty. Was this the original Helen's daughter? It felt rude to ask, right now at least.

"I went to the house first, but no one answered the door. So I thought I'd swing by here."

Nilda thought she remembered Angus barking, just briefly.

"How'd you know I moved in?" Nilda restrained herself from asking, *And how did you know my name?*

"Ms. Lehrer told me."

The name rang a bell, but Nilda didn't know why. With all the people she'd had to deal with over the past few months—the lawyers, the person who'd been managing the property since Eula Joy's death, and everyone the manager had working for her—she couldn't keep track of who was who.

"Come in, please."

Nilda stepped aside, inviting Helen into what any experienced tidier would surely regard as chaos. Half-unpacked moving boxes littered much of the space, and the only things she'd unloaded were the supplies she needed for the portrait, and the curtain of glass baubles her mother had made for Nilda's old studio. Now installed in the shed's east-facing window, its teardrops, bulbs, and icicles cast colors across the floor.

"Can I get you a cup of coffee?" Nilda didn't have anything else to offer, not even a chair.

"No, thank you. I won't be long." Helen glanced about the shed, her face revealing neither judgment nor surprise. "I've just come to see if you have need of my services."

Although Nilda had many needs, nothing in the cleaning department sprang to mind. In truth, keeping things tidy had never been a priority for her. When the property manager told her the house would be "broom clean" before she moved in, Nilda replied—not as a joke—that things would be all downhill from there.

Helen broke Nilda's silence. "The house is long overdue for its spring cleaning, Ms. Ricci."

Nilda pictured the dusty surfaces of her recently expanded collection of furniture. She'd asked the property manager to leave all of Eula Joy's behind, suspecting that otherwise, she and Sidney would feel as if they were living in an abandoned home. The possessions from their Boston apartment filled maybe an eighth of the space.

"Please. Call me Nilda."

Helen nodded. "If it's agreeable to you, Nilda, I could begin with that. Then I could give those kitchen cabinets a thorough going-over. I can't remember the last time they had a good polishing."

Nilda wiped up the coffee she'd spilled, then took another shot at filling her mug. "When was the last time you were here?"

Helen stared off for a moment, thinking. "I can't recall exactly, but it wasn't long before Mrs. Austerlane's death. And those last times I saw her, it was—" Her voice broke, and she took some time to collect herself. "It was as if I wasn't even here. She didn't recognize me. Had no memory of me at all."

Eula Joy's lawyer had told Nilda about the dementia, which

had eventually required that a 24/7 medical crew be installed at the house.

"She thought the world of you, I'm told."

Helen glanced aside, as if uneasy with the compliment.

"At some point I'd love to hear your stories of her better days. I never got to know her myself."

Now the silence was on Helen's end. After a moment she said, "I'm afraid my stories wouldn't amount to much. Mrs. Austerlane kept a certain distance from other people, including me."

The sunlight brightened, intensifying the purples, reds, and golds splashed across the floor. The colors caught even Helen's attention.

"But I can tell you one thing with absolute certainty: she was nothing but good to me and my husband. Even bought us our own place. That's why I'll never accept any payment for my services."

This didn't feel right to Nilda, who over the years had worked far too many crappy jobs for too little money. "I don't think I'd feel comfortable with that."

More silence from Helen. "Then try to consider this from my point of view. Helping to maintain this place in the way Mrs. Austerlane would have wished, it would be a way for me to honor her memory. And I'd rather not mix money with—with personal concerns."

Nilda wasn't going to argue the point any further, for now. "How often would you like to come by?"

"Would two or three days a week suit you?"

"Of course. Set your own schedule."

Helen took another, more pointed look around the shed, as if starting to think through what she might accomplish here. As she did, Nilda studied her up-swept, neatly pinned hair. Like her shirtdress, it seemed to have come straight out of 1960.

"I'll need to work evenings, if you don't mind. The car's tied up with my husband most days."

"That's fine."

"And I'll be sure to keep out of your way."

"I'm sure you won't be in my way. But I can't promise my six-year-old will stay out of yours. She's been on something of a tear lately."

As soon as she spoke, Nilda thought of Helen's son, hoping she hadn't resurrected the sadness of his loss. But Sidney was a reality that Helen would have to face, sooner rather than later, and she showed no sign of being troubled by the mention of her.

"Where is she now?"

"At a friend's place." A reminder that it was time for Nilda to pick Sidney up from Toni's.

"I look forward to meeting her when I return. On Wednesday, if that's all right."

"Sounds good to me."

"I'll see you soon, then." Helen turned to leave.

"One other thing, while I think of it. Have you ever heard any of those stories about Nathaniel Farleigh?"

Helen cast her a wary glance. "Which ones?"

Just how many of them are there? Nilda wondered. "The ones about this house affecting him, mentally."

Helen arched a brow. "I've never put much stock in fantastical stories, or hearsay."

"I'm guessing you don't put much stock in the ghost stories either."

Two nights before, during another bout of insomnia, Nilda googled Nathaniel Farleigh and turned up a Reddit thread with multiple claims that his spirit stalked an old building on Main Street: once the location of the architecture firm from which he'd been ousted, now a dentist's office with apartments upstairs.

Helen seemed to be staring through her. "I think—"

Nilda waited a beat. "You think what?"

"We have far more to fear from the living."

A breach in anything—in a wall or a fence or our own guardedness—can leave us open to danger, or to new possibilities.

—From "Unexpected Gifts" by Martha Gadway

3

He hammered the last nail into the wood, then sat down before what remained of the gap in the fence. One panel down, one to go.

Though it was a good hour from noon, the heat had pervaded the shade, soaking his T-shirt with sweat. He drank most of his water and set the bottle aside. Then he stared into the gap and remembered his first sight of her. Beauty in that blighted yard. Beauty that seemed to have risen from the rough, like chicory flowers along a highway.

Dirt from that yard had been swiped across her T-shirt, and more of it clung to her knees. But she seemed to care no more about this than chicory cared about the grit it emerged from. She just kept her eyes on him, their green deepening the longer she looked at him.

That she was a painter hadn't surprised him. He'd always felt a special connection to artists, because he was one too, in his own way. In his best days in the lab, he was all about the work, everything else having faded to insignificance. Surely, Nilda understood that feeling, maybe even prized it.

Chloe certainly had.

In his mind Chloe glanced up from a contact sheet, as if annoyed by the interruption. A look that had become more and more common, toward the end.

All for the best that she was gone.

He drank the rest of his water and looked back through the gap, eyeing those old hydrangea bushes, the only flowering thing in the yard. They looked just like they had all those years ago, back in the time of the Austerlanes. Now, as then, their leaves were as spotted and withered as Mrs. Austerlane had been, dogs at her feet or in her lap as she lounged in a lawn chair. The only place he'd seen her was in that yard, usually as he passed through the woods behind it.

Too often, she'd spied him too, one night with those binoculars, trained on him for as long as he glanced her way, until vanishing from her sight. As if she knew what he was up to in the woods, and maybe she did.

He got to his feet and shoved the other panel into the gap, blotting the yard from his sight. Then, nail by nail, he hammered Mrs. Austerlane from his mind.

When he finished, his thoughts returned to Nilda. She hadn't been wearing a ring, and he'd seen no sign of a man—or woman—coming and going. Even if there was someone else, he knew what was behind that look in her eyes. And that was all he needed, really.

In time he'd have her. About such instincts he was never wrong.

Although I don't believe in ghosts per se, it might be said that every living space is "haunted" by the builder's or architect's choices: about the placement or size of windows, for example, or about the openness or compartmentalization of interior spaces. Often, these choices seem to exist in the background and draw little, or limited, notice from day to day. Yet there is no doubt that they affect every occupant, sometimes deeply, even if these effects are beneath one's level of awareness.

—From *Constructed Reality*, by Eden Fallowe

Obviously, everything I make is breakable, sculptures being no exception. But this one looks indestructible. In fact, it looks like a destroyer.

—Part of a letter from Jo Ricci to her mother, July 7th, 1979

4

Of all the glassworks Nilda's mother had made, this had been Jo's favorite, one she'd said she'd never sell.

Now Nilda snatched a stray foam peanut from the sculpture, which she and Toni had carried into this bay-window nook just yesterday, after it had spent nearly a month in its moving crate. It had taken her that long to decide on this location for the piece: a well-lighted spot in this vault-ceilinged dining room, at a reasonably safe remove from foot traffic and airborne toys—Sidney's or Angus's.

The problem was, there was only one right place for the sculpture, for Nilda: in front of the picture window in her mother's living room, where it had stood for years. But there was no moving it, or herself, back in space and time to that room as she'd known it, a place where her mom might round the corner at any moment, with a question or random thought, or her cry of "Coffee's ready!" (Like Nilda, Jo drank coffee from waking until well into the afternoon and seemed incapable of functioning—creatively or otherwise—without it.) That living room, and the rest of Jo's rented house on the North Shore, was now occupied by strangers, Jo's things replaced by theirs.

To Nilda the sculpture had always been something of a mystery, shaped in heat her mom had stoked long before she was born. In her childhood she'd seen it as a huge red Slinky, stomped flat then twisted by an angered giant. Later, after she'd learned the story behind it—or as much of the story as her mom would tell her—she saw it as a wave of rage, frozen just before breaking. When the sun struck the sculpture at just the right angle, as it was doing now, it spilled blood-red light across the floor.

Nilda learned the sculpture's official name, *Revenge in Glass*, when she was in middle school and asking more questions about her mother's work than she ever had. Mainly, because she'd just discovered her own drive to make things, drawings and paintings, outside of school or art camp.

"Revenge against who?" Nilda had asked.

Jo paused at the annealer, where she'd placed new pieces to cool. "Someone from long ago, before I met your dad. Not a nice guy."

Nilda's dad *was* a nice guy, or so she'd been told. He died before she turned two, so most everything she knew of him— his talent with the banjo, his penchant for falling asleep in the middle of movies, his love for mutts like Angus—came from her mom.

"What did he do?"

Jo didn't answer. Not this question anyway. She mopped her forehead with her handkerchief and pushed that ever-straying curl from her eyes. "I made that piece instead of killing him. It was almost as satisfying, and it kept me out of jail."

These words brought Toni to mind.

Nilda had never told her the story behind the sculpture, so much as she had one. Because Toni had a hit-list-worthy man in her own past and seemed just as reluctant to speak of him. She'd mentioned this man, one of her high school teachers, back in college, while she and Nilda shared beers on the porch of their off-campus rental. As Toni put it, he'd "cornered" her during office hours, "cornered" suggesting something far worse. But she didn't say anything more about what had happened, and she looked as if she'd take those words back if she could. Why, Nilda never knew. Maybe the wound had been too fresh back then, high school having ended for them just a few years before. Yet in all the years since, Toni never raised the subject, nor did Nilda, fearing she'd open that wound again.

Nilda ripped tape from the last box of her mom's glass-works: tiny things, all but lost in foam peanuts. She might have unpacked them—and all of Jo's works, large and small—sooner if their new home didn't confound her so. It seemed that nothing of hers or Jo's or Sidney's—nothing that mattered—looked quite settled here, and she feared they never would. Why? Nilda kept trying to put her finger on it, and not place all the blame on the house.

After all, it didn't lack for what the former manager of the property had called "Victorian charm," with its gingerbread porch detailing, seahorse-topped newel posts, and ceiling medallions sculpted with fruits and vines and lily pads, to name just a few of the ornaments. But now and then, the charm bent toward the strange: in narrow, doorless nooks—too small to be of any use that Nilda could discern; in porthole and eyebrow windows set in strange places—near the ceiling of one bedroom, near the floor of another. Then there were the mantels and pillars of the house's three fireplaces. In the living room and dining room, they were carved with faces of the sleeping or the dead—not cherubs or gods but mere mortals, it seemed, with jowls, stitched brows, and bags beneath their closed eyes. In the carvings around her bedroom's fireplace, weathered hands grasped laurels or pointed upward, in the direction of a fire's flames or smoke, or of heaven.

When the property manager first walked Nilda through the house, she'd talked up its "potential" and "good bones," as if willing Nilda to see past the scuffs and wear in the oak and fir floors, the yellowed paint and wallpaper, the leak-suggesting ceiling stains—and toward a less depressing, if not *House & Garden*–worthy, future.

In the living room she'd noticed Nilda's gaze lingering on the faces around the fireplace. "Quirky, huh? That's classic Nathaniel Farleigh."

Quirky was something that Nilda, and some of her more abstract paintings, had been called more than a few times, enough for her to know it as left-handed praise. Most likely, Farleigh had heard this type of reaction, and worse, to his work and been asked to explain it. The truth was, Nilda herself wished she knew the thinking behind those fireplace carvings, those nonsensical nooks and windows.

As it was, they remained a mystery, overlaid with still more of the unfamiliar: the rummage-sale-worthy assortment of Eula Joy's furniture, mixing styles from the fifties to eighties. Among the pieces: a Swedish-modern sofa and end tables, a kitchen table topped with boomerang-patterned Formica, twelve mismatched kitchen and dining room chairs, sixties-era queen and twin beds, and a corduroy-covered recliner. Collectively, the Victorian detailing, the Farleigh peculiarities, and the rummage-sale furniture, now coexisting uneasily with her and Sidney's possessions, made Nilda feel as if she were surrounded by an orchestra's worth of instruments that would never get to the point of performing together, destined instead to remain in the tuneless state of a pre-concert warmup.

Nilda took the first glasswork from the box. Peeling away the bubble wrap, she uncovered the first piece she'd made under her mother's tutelage, when she was seven or eight: a palm-sized blue egg with green swirls. Until that time she'd never gotten that close to the heat of the glory hole, to the orange glow of molten glass; fright kept her at a distance. But that day, her mom urged her ahead, guiding Nilda's hands as she turned the pipe, shaped the glowing bulb on its end. Jo's voice was low, encouraging.

Keep turning, keep turning. Good! Now back to the hole. Nice!

That day, Jo got her past her fear of that heat, of the molten glass. And for the first time, Nilda got more than a glimpse into what had been, for as long as she could remember, her mother's secret world. At her former distance from that world, usually from the door to her mom's studio, Nilda sometimes watched Jo while she was immersed in her work, under some spell Nilda knew she wasn't to interrupt, not only because that would spark her mother's impatience but because Nilda understood, even from an early age, that the spells were private, a part of Jo that could never be shared.

All Nilda could do was observe, feeling everything from fascination to bewilderment to envy, until her drawing and painting took a more serious turn, and she fell into spells of her own. At that point it seemed that a new, unspoken understanding developed between her and her mother, and a new bond. And it seemed to Nilda that no one grasped her work, or what she was trying to do in a certain drawing or painting, better than Jo did.

Sometimes, Jo would take Nilda's hand as she studied one of her new pieces, now and then offering her highest praise: "Oh, honey, I *feel* this." Always, she'd squeeze Nilda's hand at "feel."

Nilda turned back to the box, unwrapping miniature studies of *Revenge in Glass* and setting them on the fireplace mantel. Unwrapping the last bundle, she discovered the bright yellow fish that, back in Boston, had stood on three fins on Sidney's nightstand, its tail swished to suggest swimming.

Thank goodness.

For some reason Nilda thought she'd packed the fish with Sidney's toys, but on the unpacking end, it wasn't in any of the boxes labeled for Sidney's room. Since then, Sidney had asked about the fish—one of the last things Jo had made for her—countless times, but Nilda hadn't had the heart to tell her it might be lost.

Now she held it fast in her hand, warming the glass. Then she headed for the stairs.

Halfway up them, she heard the contented, one-sided chatter that Sidney had started up a week or so ago—or, rather, it was one-sided to Nilda. The other conversationalist, according to Sidney, was a red-haired boy who at various times between breakfast and bedtime, found his way to Sidney through the closet of her room.

"Yes," Sidney was saying now. "Chocolate chip cookies are her favorite."

The *her*, presumably, was Fuzzy.

At first, Nilda had been mildly concerned about this new development, but a stint of internet searching—and an extended conversation with Toni—convinced her that she had no reason for alarm. Apparently, imaginary friends were quite common among children Sidney's age, especially those who felt lonely or who were in need of "self-soothing" due to big transitions in their lives. Considering the recent loss of Jo, the move to this house, and Nilda's split with Clay, Sidney had more than enough reasons for self-soothing.

And so far, it seemed to be working. Since her imaginary friend had come on the scene, Sidney had been far less clingy and moody, and she hadn't asked to go "home" to Boston.

One other positive: Sidney hadn't sleepwalked once since their move here, though Nilda supposed the situation could change at any time. In Boston Sidney had had a few such episodes—nothing inherently harmful, the pediatrician had assured Nilda, though a child who wandered around in the dark certainly risked injury. As a precaution, Nilda had installed a safety gate at the top of these stairs, closing it every night after Sidney's bedtime.

"Hel-*lo!*" Nilda called, as she neared Sidney's room. Though the door was cracked open, it felt rude to interrupt her chatter without warning. She gave the door a knock as she pushed it open, finding Sidney on the floor with Fuzzy and her tea set: three cups and saucers laid out.

With a smile Nilda extended the fish to Sidney.

"Finster!" Sidney bolted up and grabbed him. "Where *was* he, Mommy?"

"Somewhere I didn't expect."

Sidney thrust the fish toward the unattended teacup. "Alex, this is Finster. My grandma made him."

Nilda wondered how Sidney had come up with the name Alex, whether it was attached to some neighborhood kid or daycare pal back in Boston.

Sidney set Finster in front of Fuzzy's teacup. "You two share."

As she prepared to leave, Nilda took a final glance about the room, which seemed rather ordinary considering that it was the place where, according to Graham, Nathaniel Farleigh devised some of his stranger architectural creations. The room had just two irregularities. The first: the deep pitch of the far wall, which followed the angle of the roof. This was interrupted by a large dormer, where Nilda imagined Farleigh's desk; it would have been bathed in light from the window, which looked out on the backyard and woods. The second: what the property manager had called a witch window and described as an occasional feature of older Vermont homes. "Don't ask me how they got that name. And don't worry, no witches are going to fly into your house."

Set into the wall perpendicular to the pitched one, the witch window also followed the roof's angle, tilting sharply. In her early days in the room, Sidney seemed fascinated by it, not only because of its odd angle but because it looked out at the fence between their place and the neighbor's. When the window was open, it now and then admitted the clucking of the chickens, prompting Sidney to go right up to it and call for Chickie—until Graham did as he'd promised and closed the gap in the fence, seeming to close himself off as well. It had been two weeks, maybe more, since he'd fetched the hen from their yard, and Nilda was beginning to assume that, going forward, their only interactions would be exchanges of waves and hellos, whenever they happened to run into each other. That was all for the best.

"There's fish near us, Mommy." Sidney was tipping a teacup to Finster's mouth.

"Really? Where?"

"In a creek, in the woods."

The creek was news to Nilda, but so far, she hadn't stepped more than a few yards into the woods, which extended a couple of miles behind them, apparently dead-ending in a housing development.

"How do you know?"

"Alex told me. Can we go there?"

Nilda wondered whether Sidney had imagined the creek, or whether she'd heard about it from someone she hadn't imagined. Perhaps the property manager had mentioned it, out of Nilda's hearing.

"Uh, sure." Nilda was glad to hear the *we* from Sidney. At least a few times, she'd told her she didn't want her wandering into the woods alone: something Sidney seemed tempted to do. "Maybe we could—"

Sidney shushed her, a finger to her mouth. "Alex is saying something."

Nilda felt a wave of impatience, then checked herself, waited for Sidney to receive the entirety of her message.

Sidney lowered her finger. "The man is coming. You should go to the door. The *back* door."

"What man?"

Sidney looked to the space above the empty teacup, as if waiting for an answer. Then she said, "Go *now*, Mommy."

Nilda thought, *I'm not about to follow commands from an imaginary friend.* If this was any sign of where the Alex interactions were heading, she was going to have to set some limits.

Knocking sounded from downstairs, setting off Angus.

Racing downstairs, Nilda realized that the knocking was indeed coming from the back door. Why? Delivery people and visitors, rare as they were, usually rang the front door bell.

"Move it, Angus."

He sat before the door, his barks echoing throughout the hallway. They had gone from something steady to a bark-and-pause pattern, the pauses rumbling with a growl. What was up with him?

"I said, *move it!*"

She nudged him with her knee, making just enough room to open the door.

In front of her stood Graham, in his same old vintage Converse, with his same old mop of curls. But this time he was wearing a plain blue T-shirt, no chemical symbols.

It was what he held before him that drew her eye: a glass vase of zinnias and snapdragons, and poppies so red the petals' edges seemed to vibrate.

"From my garden," he said, hefting the vase. "I've been meaning to bring some by."

"Awwww, they're gorgeous. Thank you."

Nilda wasn't sure he could hear her over Angus, who in decibels at least, was doing justice to the AC/DC guitarist Clay had named him for.

She stepped onto the back patio, closing the door on his barking and growling. Then she took the vase from Graham and breathed in the scent of the snapdragons: spicy bubblegum.

"Sorry about the dog. He's not used to people coming to the back door."

"I should be the one apologizing. I just wanted to check your side of the fence, make sure the patch job looked okay from this angle." He nodded toward his handiwork. "Seems it's holding up."

"It is. I really appreciate your doing that."

They'd entered that uncomfortable *What's next?* space, and Nilda knew what the best next step would be for her, at this particular time in her life: to tell him that she had to go, that she'd see him around, to make it clear that she wanted nothing more than a cordial, neighborly relationship—waves and hellos from afar.

"I don't want to keep you," he said. "But I'm wondering if you and Sidney might be free to come to my place next Friday, for dinner."

A thrill surged through her, the type she recognized all too well. There was no stopping it, or preventing it.

"That would be nice."

They set a time, and Nilda promised to bring toll house cookies: one dessert she was unlikely to screw up. Then Graham headed back to the hedges, vanished into them once again.

Nilda took the flowers into a silent house, Angus having withdrawn to some spot beyond the hallway. Her thoughts returned to Sidney, to how she'd stared ahead at her invisible friend. She'd been looking in the direction of the witch window. Surely the way she'd spotted Graham.

Among the choices that the portrait artist must make is how to approach so-called imperfections in the sitter, such as wrinkles or blemishes. Although some subjects may ask that such characteristics be removed or blurred, there is an argument for maintaining—even embracing—every aspect of the human face and form, for not shying away from how a subject inhabits the world, in every sense of that word. As Lucien Freud once observed, "I paint people not because of what they are like, not exactly in spite of what they are like, but how they happen to be."

—From "Reflections on Portraiture" by Nils Caruso

5

Yesterday, finally, Nilda had committed her rough sketch to the canvas. Now, as she laid down the first layer of paint, the major lights and darks, William Fletcher Tenneman was starting to emerge from the void: the Fairmoore School's new headmaster, at his desk.

At the request of her contact at the school, Nilda had erased the "distractions" from the photographed version of the desk—WFT's phone and laptop, a scramble of file folders and papers, an enormous iced coffee, and a Toucan Sam–colored toy parrot—and replaced them with a single open book "to suggest his long, distinguished history at the school." Apparently, he'd taught there for years.

Nilda wished that, somehow, she could connect to that long, distinguished history and convey some sense of it to the canvas. But she seemed to have reached the final stage of commissioned-portrait burnout, and the only thing that kept her going was the $20,000 payment that waited on the other end of the job.

A car door slammed, and a minute later, Toni appeared at the studio/shed, just as she'd promised an hour ago. As usual, she was more put together than Nilda would ever be, her jeans looking fresh off the rack, just like her blue silk camisole; her bob salon-sleek.

Nilda tended to wear worn jeans, leggings, or shorts, depending on the weather or occasion, or whatever happened to be clean. Her top of choice: T-shirts, unless circumstance demanded that she wear one of the dressier shirts from her thrift-store runs. Her hair? It defied sleekness. Like Jo's, it was too corkscrewed to conform to any of the styles hairdressers had tried to impose on it over the years. So Nilda had taken to cutting it herself, and keeping it out of her way with an elastic.

Toni was shouldering a bulky leather tote and cradling a rolled-up something: a blind. She hefted the blind and nodded to the window in the southern wall of the shed. "Let's hope this fixes your little problem."

At certain hours glare from the window blinded Nilda, something she'd mentioned when Toni first visited the shed.

"You're an angel." Nilda took the blind from Toni and set it by the window, while Toni made her way to the coffee-pot table and started taking things from her tote: a brown bag of goodies, paper plates, and a vacuum pack of coffee.

"Hold my wings till we're sure that thing fits. But how about a snack first?" Toni hoisted the bag in the air: "Le Sel's finest."

"Bless you," Nilda said. Le Sel, a little patisserie in town, had become a favorite of hers.

Toni started arranging the goodies on a paper plate, announcing them as she went. "We got your cheese croissants, we got your *gougères*, we got your choco drops for Sidney. Where is she, by the way?"

"Napping." Nilda wished she could do the same. Her insomnia had gotten worse since the move, leaving her wiped out during the day but unable to sleep soundly at any time. She turned a grateful eye to the coffee Toni had brought, her own supply having just run out. "Mind if I tear into that?"

"That's why it's here."

As she got the coffee going, Nilda was reminded of Toni's college nickname, The Fixer, a recognition of her preternatural

ability to anticipate the needs of her friends, and to understand when something was off in their lives—even when they
couldn't, or wouldn't, see it for themselves.

During the height of her troubles with Clay, Nilda's thoughts
returned many times to that late spring evening of junior year,
when she and Toni were drinking cheap wine on their rotting
front stairs. In a moment of silence during some immemorable
conversation, Toni took Nilda's hand, got her to look her in the
eye.

"Zack is draining your life force. Like a vampire."

Toni had sensed, rightly, that although their previous conversation had nothing to do with Zack Parell, Nilda's kind-of-
boyfriend at the time, he'd been lingering in the background
of it, ever-present in Nilda's mind. She was nonstop sick with
desire for him, always waiting for his next call, or for one of
his unannounced—and increasingly rare—appearances at her
and Toni's rented house, either late at night or just before dawn.

It seemed that in that moment of silence between her and
Toni, when Nilda was staring off into space, Toni saw that
soul-draining want in her eyes, and just couldn't take it anymore. Nilda didn't break up with Zack right away. But late that
summer she did, by phone, holding Toni's hand the whole time.

The two of them had taken to calling that time on the stairs
"the moment of truth," and they'd come to use it as code for
any time a romantic relationship had reached the point where
its doomed state could no longer be denied. Nilda had called
a moment of truth with Clay, twice: the first time, because his
touring was making him all but absent from her and Sidney's
life, the second time, because she'd caught him cheating.

But even before the first time, when Nilda was living in Boston and Toni was here in Vermont, Nilda sensed that Toni was
close to calling the moment of truth herself, in the silences that
fell between them whenever Clay came up in the long phone
conversations they used to have. Whenever Nilda mentioned
Clay's pluses to Toni—he was a kind person at heart, despite
his flaws; he was a loving father to Sidney, whenever he was

around; of all the guys she'd dated, Jo liked him the most—it felt as if she was trying to defend him not only to Toni but also to herself.

That she'd had sex with Clay the night before leaving Boston was something Nilda would probably never admit to Toni, and something that had made her all the more relieved to have fled the city.

Fortified by coffee, croissants, and *gougères*, they installed the blind, which of course fit perfectly. Toni topped off her coffee, then looked to the easel by the north-facing window, the one Nilda had been working at when Toni arrived.

"Who's your latest victim?"

"No one you'd know, I'm sure."

Actually, Toni could have afforded Fairmoore, which apparently drew students from across New England, and beyond. But she rarely spoke of anything that signaled her family's wealth, which seemed to embarrass her, especially in the company of friends like Nilda, who wouldn't have gone to college without a decent aid package and a job on the side. Toni didn't invite Nilda to her Connecticut home until well into the third year of their friendship, and as she showed Nilda around the castle-dim stone mansion, around the grounds that busied three gardeners, she seemed by turns irritated or flushed with shame.

At the time Nilda was struck less by the grandeur of the place than by thoughts of how lonely it must have been for Toni, the only child of a world-traveling and indifferent-seeming father. Her mother, whom Toni described as the opposite of indifferent, had died when Toni was thirteen.

Toni stepped around to the front of the easel. As she studied the work in progress, Nilda watched for her reactions.

A blank stare.

Then Toni swallowed, her eyes shining with tears.

"What's wrong?" Nilda asked. Whatever it was, she sensed it had nothing to do with her execution of the piece, flawed though that surely was.

No response.

"Toni?"

Toni glanced at Nilda, then looked back to the canvas. "He's really arrived, hasn't he? Portrait and all."

Nilda felt as if she, as if both of them, had ventured onto unsteady ground. "You know him?"

"It's that teacher I told you about. Or did I?"

A wave of nausea rolled through Nilda. She waited for it to pass. Then she thought back to that evening on their old porch, remembering how Toni had stared into her green bottle of beer as she spoke of the teacher cornering her. Afterward, Toni set the bottle aside, never finishing it.

"You did," Nilda said.

Tentatively, she stepped closer and laid a hand on Toni's shoulder. "You don't have to talk about this. Not if you don't want to. In fact, we can get the hell out of here."

For a long time, Toni kept silent, still staring at the canvas. Then she turned to Nilda. "I think I *need* to talk about this, if that's okay."

Maybe the sight of him had unleashed memories she didn't want to bear on her own.

"Of course it's okay."

Toni reached for Nilda's hand and led her back to the coffee table, where the week before, Nilda had set up a couple of chairs. They settled into them, sitting knee to knee.

"I had him for U.S. History, junior year. And at first, I thought he was great. I mean, he'd have us discussing and debating stuff, not just memorizing facts and regurgitating them for tests. Like he really seemed to care about making history matter to us. And when one of us made some point that really impressed him, he'd say, 'Yes!'"

Toni clapped her hands together, apparently imitating Tenneman. "When you got one of those yeses, you felt singled out, special."

She didn't look as if she were recalling a happy memory; she seemed to be holding something bitter in her mouth.

"A couple of months into the term, he had us working on

these papers where we had to connect something from the news to a historical event and make some kind of argument. And he asked to see drafts of the papers, during his office hours."

Nilda's stomach dropped.

"I don't remember much about the paper I was working on. Just that I was making some connection between affirmative action and *Brown v. Board of Education*. What I *do* remember is his office, how small and cramped it was, how unworthy it seemed of a man with the powers to make history so alive and exciting.

"And then there was this stupid toy parrot, at the edge of his desk. I remember him calling it 'history bird.' And when he pressed this button on the back of it, it rattled off dates of different wars and battles, then squawked this creepy phrase, *Doomed to repeat… Doomed to repeat.*"

Even back then, the parrot, Nilda thought. She was glad she'd put away the photograph that included it.

"As small as his office was, there was this folding partition at the back of it. And he led me behind it, to a couch."

Toni was staring off toward the work in progress, maybe seeing that couch in her mind's eye.

"He sat down and patted the spot next to him, and I knew I shouldn't sit there. But what else was I supposed to do? Just walk out?" Toni laughed dryly. "Yeah, I should have, like a brave girl. But I wasn't a brave girl. I was a *good* girl, used to doing as I was told. And he knew that. He was counting on it.

"I put my paper in the spot he'd been patting, and I sat as far away from him as I could. He didn't show any reaction at first, and the way he picked up my paper, it was like he was grabbing a newspaper someone left behind on the subway. He paged through it with this blank face, and I could tell he wasn't reading any of it. I could tell he didn't give a crap about it, or whether I succeeded or failed in his class. At some point he just tossed it on the little table in front of the couch, and he moved right up next to me."

Toni clutched her chest. "My heart was beating so fast, I thought I might pass out."

As gently as she could, Nilda laid a hand on Toni's arm. *Stop her? Let her take a break? No, let her finish.*

"I can't remember exactly what he said at this point, but I know that he called me 'an exceptional young woman,' with an 'exceptional mind.' And when he put his hand on my thigh, he started talking about everything he could do for me if we 'deepened our connection': internships in Washington, recommendations to Ivies, a bunch of other things I didn't really hear because I was so afraid of the way his hand was moving: up and up, under my skirt, into my und—"

Here, Toni broke down.

Nilda ran for the paper towels on her supply table and rushed a handful of them to Toni. As she watched Toni wipe her eyes, Nilda felt complicit in reopening old wounds: the very thing she'd feared doing for so many years. But maybe those wounds had never really closed.

Toni collected herself and went on: "I wanted to scream, but I couldn't. It was like he stole my voice. But I managed to shove him away and run out of there. I left my paper behind, and his class behind. Started skipping my other classes too, until I was put on probation."

Nilda knew how uncharacteristic skipping class would have been for Toni, who'd been an honors student in college.

"Did you—" Nilda stopped herself.

"Did I what?"

"Did you tell anyone? I mean, someone who could have done something?"

Toni worked the damp towel with her fingers, as if uncertain how to answer. "I was afraid to tell my dad what happened, because he was such a fan of the school, and so proud I'd gotten into it. And when he got the notice about the probation, he got really pissed, asked me if I'd started taking drugs or something."

Though Nilda had never met Toni's father, his reaction didn't surprise her. From everything that Toni had said about him over the years, it seemed that he cared about little more than status and appearances.

"I remember sitting there in his home office, trying to get out the words about what happened. But I just couldn't. Eventually, he got so impatient that he called in his assistant." Toni switched to her dad voice: "'Jane, my daughter is going to tell you about some problems she's having at school, and you two are going to work out a solution.' Then he took off. But not before giving me his final warning. He said, 'Toni, if this solution doesn't keep you at Fairmoore, it's public school for you.'"

Toni kept fidgeting with the towel. "I remember thinking, *Fine*. I had no intention of ever going back to Fairmoore."

Nilda thought of all the times she'd envied Toni—for her wealth and privilege, for her achievements at college and beyond, for her kind and dedicated husband, for their thoughtful parenting of two sweet, sharp-minded daughters. Now that envy felt small-minded. "So was this Jane of any help?"

Toni smiled. "Jane was kind of awesome. She got every detail out of me, maybe because I could tell she was really listening, and really seemed to care. And I'll never forget what she said to me when I'd finished: 'This guy's gonna pay.' Well, as you know, he didn't."

In fact, he got rewarded with the headmaster post. This thought upped Nilda's rage from a simmer to a low boil. She wanted to knock him off her easel, kick him across the floor.

"Jane got my dad to sign a letter to Fairmoore's headmaster that detailed everything and asked that Tenneman be held accountable. But it was radio silence, for weeks. After we sent a second letter, we got this nasty response that basically accused me of lying and threatened legal action if we kept up with our *harassment*."

"Are you kidding me?"

"I wish I were. At this point even my dad had soured on Fairmoore. And he talked about siccing his lawyers on the school. But it didn't take long for him to have second thoughts.

He started thinking that if he made enough of a fuss, the story might hit the news, and *make trouble*."

Trouble for *him*, Nilda thought.

"And honestly, Nilda? I'd grown so tired of the whole thing. Tired of it consuming every minute of every day, every corner of my mind. Tired of feeling like *I* was the one who'd done something wrong. Back then, I still believed there was a normal I could get back to, and that's all I wanted. So I transferred to another school and finished up there, and I just tried my best to move on."

Nilda assumed that trying to move on included not talking about what had happened at Fairmoore, even to Nilda. Now the reticence Toni had shown all those years ago made a lot more sense.

"Of course, I didn't just get over what happened. And sometimes that *Doomed to repeat* squawk will just start playing in my head, driving me crazy. And making me feel guilty."

"*Guilty?*"

Toni's mouth quivered. "I couldn't have been the only girl he did this to, and if I'd pressed the case, maybe I could have stopped him, for good."

"Hey." Nilda scooted closer and waited for Toni to meet her gaze. "*None* of this is on you. None of the responsibility, none of the blame."

Toni kept quiet.

"Okay?" Nilda said.

Toni nodded. Then she took one of the dry paper towels, wiped her eyes. "Over the years I've googled him and the school, looking for news about other girls, other accusations. When I don't find anything, it's never a comfort. I imagine other girls getting silenced, just like me."

Almost certainly, she was right, Nilda thought. "I wish I could do something for you. Other than just listen."

Toni smiled. "Thanks, but any *doing* has to be on me. And I haven't completely ruled that out."

"Really?"

"Yeah. The #MeToo stuff has kind of inspired me. But I haven't figured out how I might reapproach the situation. Or maybe I just lack the courage."

"No way," Nilda said. "You *never* lack the courage, for anything."

"I'm not so sure about that."

"*I* am. Maybe you just need a partner in crime, to help you figure something out."

"You?"

"Yep, me. And my first move will be to destroy that painting." She thought of the soot-stained barrel in the corner of this shed, and of all the trash that must have met a fiery end in it over the years. Maybe it was time to bring it back into service.

Toni sat up. "Oh, Nilda, don't—please. Make some money off him, and that awful school. With my blessing."

Now the prospect of lifting a brush to the painting—much less making any money off it—made Nilda feel dirty. Some type of destruction, if not by fire, was in order. Something that would have to go beyond the painting. She and Toni would have to figure out just what form it would take.

In many old houses, we discover relics of past lives—in cellars, attics, or closets, or every now and then within walls or other presumed hiding places. Especially in the latter case, curiosity leads us to withdraw, inspect, and ponder what we've found, our interest overcoming any deference to the hider, and their apparent wish for secrecy. Too often we assume that when one departs a place—or this life—such wishes expire.

—From "The Abundant Mysteries of Old Houses" by Mikka Swann

6

Climbing the stairs with the laundry basket, Nilda heard Sidney singing something familiar, at the top of her lungs: a Tom Petty song. Where did that one come from?

A year or so ago, Clay had gotten Sidney interested in old-school rock, eventually building her a playlist of songs from her now-favorite bands: Fleetwood Mac, the Talking Heads, the Pretenders, and Guns N' Roses. Nilda didn't remember Tom Petty being in the rotation, but what did it matter? It was nice to hear Sidney sing.

Nilda approached her room, called out a *knock-knock*, then bumped the basket through the half-open door.

On the bed: two small, battered dollhouses and a scattering of Sidney's smaller toys. The houses had silted the bedspread with dust, and Sidney, her singing down to a hum, was figure-eighting Finster through the grime.

Nilda put down the laundry basket and knelt at Sidney's side. "Where'd you get these?"

Sidney kept playing, as if Nilda wasn't there.

"Where did these houses come from?"

Sidney paused Finster. "The closet."

That didn't make sense. When they first moved in, the closet held nothing but a few hangers. Or was that all her mind had taken in? Throughout the move, and for all the months since her mother's death, her brain had been in a fog.

Nilda headed for the closet and opened the door, getting a lungful of dust. Coughing, she pulled the chain for the ceiling bulb, lighting Sidney's hangered clothes and her dust-covered shoes. But what consumed her attention was the square-shaped hole, low in the right wall. The panel that must have covered it had toppled to the floor.

She got the panel out of the way, shoved the clothes aside, and stepped into the closet. Squatting, she peered into what amounted to a miniature crawl space, big enough to hold a couple of suitcases. Now it contained nothing more than crum-blings of plaster, and a just-disturbed layer of dust.

Why the closet-within-a-closet?

Then Nilda remembered that this room had been the central creative space of a man who'd scattered seemingly nonsensical nooks and other oddities throughout this house. If he decided that he needed a storage space for some of his models—which the houses on the bed almost certainly were—was that any stranger? But why did this spot need to be hidden away?

Nilda grabbed two dusty pairs of sneakers and threw them into the laundry basket, along with the clothes from Sidney's hamper. It was going to be Sidney's responsibility to clean up the closet, and hear Nilda out.

She knelt again at Sidney's side and put a hand on her shoul-der. "Honey?"

She waited until Sidney returned her gaze.

"If you find anything else like that hole in the closet, I want you to get me, okay? I want you to get me before you go poking around in it."

As soon as she spoke these words, Nilda knew they were pointless. It wasn't Sidney's nature to let rules like this interfere with her curiosity, her drive to discover things for herself—things like what, exactly, might be hidden in the walls of this house. And, really, what was the worst thing Sidney might find? More of Nathaniel Farleigh's models?

Maybe it was just the unknowns of this place, and of this new life in general, that made Nilda wary. For both of them.

"Okay?"

"Okay."

Nilda followed Sidney's gaze back to the houses, which despite the grime and wear had clearly been constructed by someone with a command of details, down to the shingling, corbels, turned porch banisters, and tiny windows. The house on the left, the less battered of the two, drew her eye especially. She took in the twin-gabled roof and bay windows, the turret on the left and wrap-around porch on the right.

"This is our house," she said. "I'm almost sure."

Sidney didn't seem surprised. Probably, she'd already figured that out for herself.

Sidney looked to the other model, which had been partly stripped of its shingles and riddled with small, blackened spots. Burns? "That's the bad kid's house."

"What do you mean?"

Sidney shrugged. "I don't know. Alex told me."

The bad kid. Maybe Sidney needed a foil for her imaginary friend, a problem child to play him against.

Nilda took a closer look at the bad kid's house, with its simpler lines and narrow front porch, slit windows on either side of the door. Like Graham's. But was it his house? The porch on the model was free of the gingerbread detailing on his place, the only flourishes being fan-shaped brackets under the eaves. And weren't his upstairs windows different? More "normal"? The ones on the model were erratically sized and shaped: square, rectangular, round, oval, fan-like. Scattered over the upper floor, they reminded Nilda of spider's eyes.

Feeling a surge of nausea, Nilda closed her eyes. Another migraine? She hoped not. The new pills had been working so well.

She took a deep breath, and the nausea passed. But the

sight of that hole in the closet stayed with her. Why had these models been banished there? Farleigh had become displeased with them, perhaps. Or they reminded him of something he preferred to forget.

"Are you okay, Mommy?"

Nilda opened her eyes and smiled at Sidney. "Yeah. Just lost in my thoughts."

But she wasn't okay. Or, rather, she wasn't okay with Sidney playing with these old houses, not just because they were dusty and somewhat fragile. It was more that she didn't want her daughter messing with things that had been hidden away for a reason. This seemed a violation, though one surely without consequences. Still, Nilda couldn't fight her feelings of unease when she looked at the houses, especially the more battered of the two.

"Listen, Sidney. These houses aren't toys, and they aren't ours. They're part of history, and they belong in a museum." Make it quick, Nilda thought, like ripping off a Band-Aid. "And that's just what's going to happen."

She lifted their house from the bed, started carrying it to the laundry basket.

"*No!* The house belongs here! It *needs* to be here!"

Nilda wasn't in the mood for this, not today. "It's not your call, Sidney, sorry."

By the time she got the other house into the laundry basket, Sidney was on her butt, wailing. Nilda got up close to her, laid a hand on her shoulder. Sidney swatted it away.

Nilda waited for her to calm down, then tried another tack: "It's not like you won't see them again. I'll take you to visit them, wherever they go."

But the museum line was a lie, one Nilda hoped Sidney would soon forget. She just wanted to get the models out of Sidney's reach, and for now, some other hiding place—perhaps in her own closet—would have to do.

"I need them *here*! So does Alex!"

Goddamned Alex. "Didn't you hear me? These aren't play-things. They're delicate, nothing to be touched."

This time, Sidney seemed to be taking in her words. "Then let me *see* them."

Nilda didn't understand. Then Sidney pointed upward, to a shelf holding a doll she never played with. "Put them up there. I promise I won't touch them."

Just give her this, Nilda thought. She was too tired to keep up this fight. And the height of the shelf might encourage Sidney to keep her promise.

Once Nilda installed the houses there, Sidney didn't look any happier. Nilda tried something that almost always cheered her up. "Daddy's calling tonight."

No spark in Sidney. "When will he come here?"

"I don't know. We'll have to see."

This wasn't the first time Sidney had asked this question, and Nilda had never been able to answer it definitively, even when Clay posed the question himself. For now, and maybe for all time, she needed this to be a Clay-free space, a space that was hers—and Sidney's—alone. A place that he couldn't picture with any certainty and that lacked any associations with him, associations sure to haunt Nilda. That meant that she and Clay would have to figure out a point between here and Boston where the three of them could meet up, and where he and Sidney could spend some time together. Even though, technically, he didn't have any custody or visitation rights, he should be a presence in their daughter's life.

Now it felt like a mistake to have mentioned Clay at all. Cutting her losses, Nilda stripped the dusty spread from the bed and rushed herself, and the now-overflowing laundry basket, out of Sidney's room.

A dark field here? No, over here. Better, more balanced. As Nilda scrubbed the Conté crayon in the chosen spot, she looked to the upper left of the drawing, trying to figure out her next move.

In the back of her brain: a buzz of gratitude and relief to be working on her own stuff, making even baby steps. For months, it seemed, her noncommissioned work had gotten sidelined by personal chaos, and grief.

"Nilda?"

She started, dropping the crayon. Turning, she found Helen at the kitchen's entrance—her shoulders squared, her expression level, as if she'd materialized for a task more serious than polishing cupboards or floors. In her right hand: vintage Tupperware.

"I didn't mean to frighten you."

"It's okay." Nilda had asked Helen to let herself in with her own key, guessing she might be occupied in her studio, or with Sidney, whenever Helen chose to arrive.

Until this moment Nilda had been oblivious to the state of the kitchen: unwashed pots and pans in the sink, dirty plates and utensils on the table. The ideas for the new drawing had come to her so suddenly, she'd felt the need to get them down before they could vanish. Helen's presence turned Nilda's attention back to the post-supper mess.

When she reached for a plate, Helen raised a hand to stop her. "I'll take care of this. You keep doing what you were doing."

But the spell with her work was broken, for now. Though Nilda picked up the crayon and poised it over her drawing pad, her attention was drawn to Helen, who took a plate from the cupboard and arranged the contents of the Tupperware on it.

She placed the plate in the middle of the table, revealing mini pastry rounds topped with chunky, red-pink jam.

"Strawberry-rhubarb tarts," Helen said. "One of Mrs. Austerlane's favorites."

"Awww, you didn't have to do this."

"It's a summer tradition," Helen said, as she began clearing the dirty dishes. *Nothing special,* her tone suggested.

Though she was full from supper, Nilda couldn't resist. She grabbed one of the pastries and bit into it: a butter-tender crust topped with a tartness like no other—earthy and inseparable from summer nights on her grandma Rhea's back porch. Seated in rickety lawn chairs, Nilda and her mom and grandma would eat dessert and watch fireflies hover over the yard, pulsing light. Nilda's favorite dessert: her grandma's rhubarb pie.

Since then, she hadn't tasted anything like that dessert, or seen a single firefly. Both seemed to have vanished from the earth.

"These are *delicious*, Helen."

Helen didn't say anything, just busied herself at the sink.

While Helen worked, Nilda studied her back, or rather the fabric of her belted cotton dress: tiny pink and blue flowers on a pale-yellow field. Nilda hadn't seen, or thought of, this fabric since she was a kid. Then, Jo had made her a dress with it, a dress Nilda had loved so much she'd worn it out before she could outgrow it.

Nilda swallowed against the tightness in her throat, relieved that Helen's back was to her. After all, Helen hadn't signed on for dealing with a stranger's tears. But maybe she could answer some of the questions that had started cycling through Nilda's mind since she'd moved into this house. The latest: why were those model houses hidden in the closet wall? But even if Helen had found these models, or others, herself, she probably wasn't in a position to answer this question. And Nilda was tired of thinking of those little houses, which had been troubling her since she'd first seen them, this morning.

Nilda grabbed another pastry and moved closer to the sink, so she wouldn't be talking to Helen's back.

"A new neighbor moved in next door," she said. "Or rather, the son of the old neighbors—the Emmerlys. Did you know them?"

Helen's expression remained level, unreadable. "Depends on what you mean by *know*. We exchanged *hellos* now and then, little more."

Nilda finished the tart and started whisking her crumbed hands over the floor. Then she thought the better of this. "The son, Graham, made it sound like his parents were big-time friends with Eula Joy and her husband." Nilda couldn't even remember the husband's name. "He mentioned something about twilight daiquiris in the back yard."

Helen paused mid-scrub, her mouth pressed in a line. She seemed uncertain of how to respond. "Maybe the daiquiris were before my time. By the time I started, things between the Austerlanes and the Emmerlys were frosty at best. Why? I have no idea. But a year or so into my tenure, things took a turn for the worse."

"What happened?"

Helen rinsed the last dish, set it in the drainer. "One of Mrs. Austerlane's Yorkies went after the Emmerlys' chickens, or so the Emmerlys claimed. It didn't come to blood, fortunately. But it *did* come to words—and that fence between the properties: Mrs. Austerlane's idea."

Helen dried her hands, then took a sponge to the table. "Something she said at the time stuck with me: 'If we can't get rid of the neighbors, at least we can erase them from view.' Couldn't say I disagreed."

Helen's take on things puzzled Nilda. Were the twilight daiquiris an outright lie? Or had Graham been describing happier days, not wanting to trouble his new neighbor? This prompted Nilda's next question, one that gave her even more pause. But there was no better time to ask it. After all, she and Sidney would be visiting Graham the following evening.

"Do you remember anything about Graham? I mean, what he was like or anything?"

Helen kept wiping the table, her face again unreadable. Was she thinking through an answer, or choosing to stay silent?

Nilda's phone buzzed, and she pulled it from her pocket, seeing "Clay" on the screen. It was his time to talk to Sidney.

"Excuse me," she said to Helen, before stepping from the kitchen.

As Nilda headed up the stairs, she and Clay made the kind of small talk that had become more common between them, an evasion of uncomfortable topics, or a break from them. While

Clay described some new carpentry gig he'd gotten, she was too distracted to listen. All she could do was voice the occasional "Hmmm" or "Right," so he didn't think she was completely checked out.

"Hold on a sec," Nilda said to Clay, as she neared Sidney's room.

"It's Daddy!" she called. This sent Sidney racing into the hall, reaching for the phone.

"Let me hand you off to her," she said.

"Hey, Nilda?" She heard a plea in his voice. "I miss you."

What did you call trying not to think about someone, and getting better or worse at it, depending on the day? Was that *missing* them? She wasn't sure.

She handed off the phone and headed back downstairs, to give Sidney and Clay a little privacy.

When Nilda arrived in the kitchen, she found no sign of Helen other than the last of the tarts. No doubt, she was off in some corner of the house, pursuing whatever task she'd set for herself.

Nilda started off to find her, and once again raise her questions about Graham. Then she stopped. Helen was busy. And Nilda needed to check herself, not allow herself to get too interested in someone she barely knew.

Comfrey, feverfew, goldenseal, St. John's wort...and count-less other "medicinal" herbs. We often hear of their pow-ers to heal wounds, or to ease headaches, depression, or a roiling gut. Though there is sometimes truth to these claims, or a grain of it, it is wise to remind would-be users of the potential results of overuse or misuse: liver damage, dangerous drug interactions, and, in the worst case, death. Buyer, or taker, beware.

—From the introduction to *Herbs: Friends and Foes* by Gert Pauling (from the library of Graham Emmerly)

7

N ilda took her first sip of the cocktail, swished it, and swallowed; Graham watching her from his makeshift bar, waiting for her verdict.

"I'm definitely tasting gin, super-piney gin. And citrus, and...something flowery, but what?"

He raised an eyebrow, as if to urge her on.

She took another, bigger sip, tried again to tease things out. Then she laughed. "I have no freakin' idea. All I can say is, this is really strange—and quite good."

Nilda detected a lower tone beneath the gin and citrus, some-thing earthy, edged with a green she could place in color but not quite in taste. A mossy green. Though sunk into a velveteen club chair, she might as well have been crouched in the woods.

"You're onto something with *super-piney*." Graham hoisted the cocktail shaker and poured the rest of the concoction into his glass. "I believe you've picked up on the pine sap."

"*Pine sap?*"

"Yes." He lowered himself into the club chair across from hers, swirled and sipped his drink. "That little blue bottle on the bar?"

Nilda searched it out and found it.

"It's a syrup I made of hardened sap, boiled with anise. I added just a touch of that to the other stuff: gin, lime juice, and a splash of elderflower liqueur."

Now that he mentioned the anise, Nilda thought she detected a note of licorice. "Did you forage the sap too?"

A centerpiece of dinner had been butter-seared morels, which Graham had harvested in the woods behind their properties. The morels had been as delicious as this cocktail was strange, and to Nilda's surprise, Sidney had downed a goodly serving of them, along with all the pizza bites Nilda had brought as insurance. Now Sidney was stretched out on Graham's living room couch, dozing. Beside her: a plate once occupied by two of Nilda's toll house cookies, and a wedge of flan that Graham had made with eggs from his chickens.

"You could say that, I guess. When I was collecting the morels, I noticed some sap leaks and went for it."

Nilda supposed that the foraging, the attention to sap leaks, and the bar-as-chemistry-set were all connected to Graham's interest in science—evident from the books that filled an entire wall of this study. After supper, while Graham retrieved some goods for the bar, Nilda scanned the collection, her eyes first landing on a beat-up biology textbook, its spine bearing the label "Property of Greenbridge Middle School." She'd imagined some attachment to the class in which he'd used the book: an early inspiration perhaps?

Next she'd noticed a trove of well-worn chemistry textbooks, guides to native plants and herbs, a set of texts on "toxic agents," and a book whose title made her pull it from the shelves. *The Dose Makes the Poison.*

Paging through the book, she saw nothing surprising: discussions of "good" versus "bad" chemicals, of the various harms delivered by the latter. Here and there, passages had been highlighted or underlined, but the only marking that felt personal was the handwriting on the blank first page: *Graham Arthur Emmerly.*

Now, curiosity overcoming politeness, Nilda said, "You got

an interesting little library in here." She nodded to the shelves behind her. "What's with the books on poisons?"

Graham leaned back in his chair, giving no sign that her nosiness offended him. "When I got to the end of my undergrad years, I decided I needed something more than my chemistry degree, something that would give me a leg up in the job market. So I got a master's in toxicology."

"Sounds like a practical decision."

"Oh, it was *practical* all right. Set me up for a fifteen-year run in the pharmaceutical industry, and more income than I ever thought possible. But the jobs offered fewer and fewer satisfactions. Then, practically none at all."

Following Graham's lead, Nilda sank back in her chair, feeling she could fall asleep in it. "What's satisfaction, for a chemist?"

For some time, he stared into his drink, seeming to consider her question. As he did, Nilda took in his features, the Roman nose, the slight hitch to his smile, only intensifying the sculptural beauty of his face. It called to mind some painting of Narcissus. She couldn't remember whose.

He looked up, met her gaze. "What was it you said about your art, over dinner? How when it's going well, you lose awareness of everything else, and maybe even yourself?"

"That's pretty much it," Nilda said. Since she'd taken on all the commissioned work, that feeling had become more rare, but no less powerful.

"When I'm pursuing something in the lab—a question or theory I'm truly curious about, truly invested in—that's precisely the feeling I get. And, to me, *that's* satisfaction."

Did he think his new gig at the community college would offer such satisfaction? That seemed unlikely to Nilda, but what did she know? Maybe teaching was just a kind of break for him, until he figured out something else.

"Another satisfaction?" He raised his glass, smiling. "Mixing a good drink."

"Here, here," she said, toasting him back.

The cocktail was warming her from the middle, just as most every mixed drink did. But this warmth was settling lower, with a tingling edge that had nothing to do with alcohol.

Don't even think about it.

She looked away from him, toward the fireplace. It brought to mind something she'd noticed the moment she entered this room.

"Nathaniel Farleigh built this place, right?"

"For his eldest son, Henry. Why?"

How to put this, without insulting Graham? "Things just look a little…plainer here. I mean, the fireplaces in my house, they have all these funky details, these wild-looking carvings. But this one is, uh—"

Graham finished her sentence: "Nothing special."

Though the pillars of his fireplace were fluted, the mantel graced with dentil molding, they were standard-issue Victorian.

"Most likely, this wasn't original to the house."

"What do you mean?"

Graham set his now-empty glass on the table beside him. "Nathaniel Farleigh built this place to be just as ornate as his own. But it was *too* ornate, to Henry's thinking."

Nilda tried to get her mind around what she'd just heard. "So he just tore down whatever he didn't like?"

"That's what Farleigh's journals suggest."

Nilda finished her own drink and set the glass aside. "That seems a bit extreme."

"To you, to me, yes. But try to put yourself in Henry's shoes. Imagine you're working alongside Nathaniel at his architecture firm, seeing his designs getting stranger and stranger. Seeing clients getting more and more put off by them, until some major ones walk out the door.

"While all this is going on, your father builds you what he sees as this magnificent gift of a home, with all these unusual embellishments. But to you, these embellishments are just reminders of what you think is causing your father's downfall at work: madness. And you can't bear to be surrounded by those reminders, hour by hour, day by day."

Nilda remembered what Graham had told her when they'd first met: that Nathaniel claimed his house—*her* house—was getting under his skin. Maybe that was a factor for Henry too. But she wondered whether Nathaniel was just misunderstood, as an architect and as someone experiencing a mental or emotional crisis. A crisis for which he'd been blamed, it seemed, and ultimately punished.

"Maybe Nathaniel just got bored with doing the same old thing. And Henry didn't like his new stuff."

"Quite possibly." Graham traced a finger along the rim of his glass. "The irony is that Nathaniel's last commission was for a lunatic asylum. And it included some features that earned a lot of praise over time."

"What kind of features?"

Graham kept tracing the rim of his glass. "Some rooms included these little windows, near the level of the floor. They were intended to get patients to lie down and contemplate life and possibilities beyond the asylum walls, without the *distracting comforts* of a bed—Nathaniel's words. They were said to be quite soothing, for some patients."

This didn't sound very appealing to Nilda. "I have a couple of those windows."

"So do I." Graham smiled. "I guess they're one thing Henry couldn't get rid of."

He went silent for a moment, looking lost in thought. "You're so lucky to live among all those…idiosyncrasies."

Lucky wasn't the word Nilda would have used. Especially when it came to the carvings of those faces, of the sleeping or the dead. "It's certainly interesting. My house isn't exactly a showplace, otherwise."

Seeing the puzzled look on Graham's face, Nilda tried to explain. "Things are a little rough around the edges, not just on the outside. But there aren't any big issues. Nothing structural, I'm sure."

In truth, she *wasn't* sure.

Graham gave his glass a few turns. "What if you didn't have to pay for rehabbing it?"

That sounded like a pipe dream to Nilda. "How would that be possible?"

Graham sat forward in his chair. "Your house could be on the National Register of Historic Places. I'm almost certain. It was the home of what they call a significant person, Nathaniel Farleigh, and it shows off some of his more unusual work. If it *is* eligible, you could get grants for a rehab."

Nilda sat up too, feeling she'd become fused to the chair, too close to falling asleep in it. "Good to know."

Good to know, yes. But she had no interest in going down this road, not now anyway. Too many other things needed her attention: Sidney, the issues with Clay, and most daunting, what to do about the Tenneman commission, and about Tenneman himself. Then there was all the noncommissioned work she wanted to get back to.

"I'd be happy to help you research the—" Graham paused and looked beyond her.

Turning, Nilda saw Sidney in the doorway to the study, rubbing her eyes. "I wanna play with Chickie."

Her voice was in the register of what Nilda and Clay called the *Walking Dead* croak: a warning that Sidney was ninety-nine percent asleep but ready to unleash the still-alert one percent with force, and no mercy.

"We already had our Chickie time, sweet pea."

Before dinner Graham had captured one of the reddish-brown hens from his coop—maybe the one who'd invaded their yard, maybe a look-alike—and held her still so Sidney could pet her.

"I *have* to see her. *Now!*" With this, Sidney broke down in a wail.

Nilda cast Graham an apologetic glance and started up from her chair. Then she fell back. When he extended a hand to her, she waved it away, and got to her feet on the second try. She wasn't used to mixed drinks and guessed she'd pay for Graham's concoction tomorrow morning.

Nilda approached Sidney slowly, trying to use her calmest voice. "Come on, doll. Time to go home."

Sidney didn't stop crying, and when Nilda reached out to stroke her hair, Sidney swatted her hand away.

Nilda looked to Graham and mouthed, *Sorry*. In response he smiled and held a finger in the air, as if to say, *Wait*. Then he turned to a little stand by the bar and took something from a drawer, something so small he could enclose it in his hand.

As Graham approached Sidney, he held that fisted hand outward, an expectant look on his face, as if even he might be surprised by whatever he was about to reveal. He knelt before her and opened his hand, stopping Sidney's tears.

On his palm rested an ice-blue crystal, or maybe a conglomeration of crystals, shining planes extending in all directions. To Nilda it looked like a miniature sculpture.

Graham caught Sidney's gaze and spoke to her in a low, intent voice. "This is a Chickie messenger crystal. Whenever you miss her, do this."

He drew the crystal close and whispered into it. "Hi, Chickie."

Sidney giggled.

"She'll hear you, I promise. And she'll cluck back."

He handed the crystal to Sidney, and for a long moment she stared at it, entranced.

Nilda took Sidney's free hand. "What do you say to Graham?"

"Thank you."

"You're most welcome, Sidney."

The warmth in his eyes, as he watched Sidney, made Nilda wonder whether he wanted kids. Or maybe he already had one, or more than one, somewhere. She knew so little about him. But seeing how he reacted to Sidney, she wanted to learn more.

Watch yourself. Don't get carried away.

As she and Sidney headed for Graham's back door, Nilda

glanced at the window on the far side of the study. It looked out on a break in the hedges and beyond that, the bay window of her dining room, the new home of *Revenge in Glass*. Now she saw nothing but darkness on her side of the break. No sign of Helen tonight.

Until about a week ago, heavy curtains—velvet, she noticed now—had covered this window in Graham's study. But as far as Nilda could tell, they had remained open ever since. She couldn't help but take this as a promising sign.

As soon as Graham opened the door for her and Sidney, Sidney dashed for the chicken coop, and Nilda let her go, too tired to put up a fight.

She turned to Graham and thanked him, for dinner and the gift to Sidney.

"Where'd you get it, by the way?"

"I made it, years ago. An old trick with copper sulfate, nothing magical."

"Well, it's magical to Sidney."

"That's just what I'd hoped."

He met her gaze and held it, then took her hand, kissed the back of it.

"I'd like to see you again," he said. "Very soon."

"I'd like that too."

Still looking into her eyes, he lowered her hand but held on to it. Gave it a squeeze before letting go.

A moment later, he was back in his house, and Nilda was standing on his little back porch, feeling that familiar rush of joy, anticipation, desire.

You have a daughter. Remember?

"Sidney!"

To her surprise Sidney answered her call without hesitation, bolting from the dark as if she was nowhere close to tired. But as soon as Sidney reached the porch, she extended her hands up to Nilda, her sign that she wanted to be carried home.

Nilda obliged and began to step them down from the porch.

"Look, Mommy!"

Nilda stopped and looked in the direction Sidney was pointing: to the eaves just over the door.

"Just like the bad kid's house."

Squinting through the glare of the porch light, Nilda caught a detail she hadn't noticed before: two fan-shaped brackets under the eaves, like the ones on the more-battered model house.

"Yes," Nilda said, wishing that Sidney had never found the model, and that her imaginary friend would disappear.

I'm a scientist, and a skeptic. But when multiple people report the same types of unexplained phenomena (such as the seemingly actorless mayhem often attributed to poltergeists), it feels short-sighted to dismiss these experiences out of hand. What is lacking, and what I wish we had, is a reliable scientific methodology for evaluating such phenomena, one that would offer evidence-based explanations for what, at present, seem to be pure mysteries.

—Caroline Warthmueller, "Considering the Unexplained"

Belief creates the actual fact.

—William James

8

"Just wait. You'll see."

Her mother's last words—in reality and in the dream Nilda had just awoken from. The same dream she'd had last week, and just before leaving Boston.

In reality her mother had whispered the words, from a bed in the corner of her living room. In the dreams the words came as a command, from a Jo standing in the entrance to her studio, flushed and sweating from working glass. Clutching the knob of the half-closed door, she gave Nilda her half-annoyed, half-apologetic look, the same look Nilda got when she was a kid and didn't yet understand that her mother's studio time was nothing to be disturbed lightly.

In the dreams Nilda tried to look past Jo, get a glimpse of whatever she was working on. But all she could see was the glow of the furnace, a pulsing neon orange in the darkness.

Jo repeated her command, gave Nilda a faint smile, and pulled the door closed.

Now, stretched out on her bed in the early light, Nilda knew she'd been crying, from the ache in her throat, the sand of dried tears on her temples.

She thought of the migraine pills in her bedside drawer, sure she had them to thank for this dream, and all the others she'd had recently. In fact, "vivid dreams"—and, more rarely, hallucinations—were one of the possible side effects.

Before Nilda had started taking the pills, dreams of any kind had been rare. But now, on nights she didn't suffer from insomnia, sleep could plunge her into another reality, one more intense than this one, in color and feeling. Though she woke no more restored than she felt post-insomnia, she was occasionally left with the gift of having seen her mother.

The only way that can happen now.

The gift was bittersweet, of course. Even as her mother appeared in Nilda's dreams, Nilda knew her presence was fleeting. And Jo herself seemed to understand that she was going, going, seconds from gone—her smiles apologies.

Nilda didn't believe in heavenly reunions, as much as she sometimes wanted to.

She doubted the existence of ghosts too, though she'd long been fascinated by them. And she wanted to believe that in at least some cases, people who claimed to have seen or heard something otherworldly had experienced more than a hallucination, a trick of light, or the sounds of a settling house. But how many such experiences were just a heightened form of desire? Or a case of the mind longing so strongly for matter that it nearly willed it into existence? So far, Nilda had desired and longed to no effect, at least where her mother was concerned.

Nilda's interest in ghosts had intensified since Jo's death. Most nights, after Sidney was asleep, Nilda tuned in to one or more of the growing raft of paranormal reality shows. Most often, they featured hoodied bearers of night-vision cameras and "electronic voice phenomenon" recorders, who traipsed through old houses, abandoned hospitals, or other sites said to be haunted, asking spirits to show themselves. Nilda waited for whatever might come, though she knew she'd be disappointed.

The EVPs? However much the show-hosts amplified them, however confidently they detected certain phrases (*Leave now!...*

Look under the porch!... I murdered him!), Nilda heard nothing more than voice-like warbles or blasts of static. The kinds of sounds Clay called "trash in the signal."

The "evidence" from the cameras? Though Nilda found the replays of slamming doors, of floating, steam-like shadows, more convincing than the EVPs, she could never rule out worldly explanations: a breeze or vacuum effect, a trick of light, or more trash in the signal.

Nilda's favorite among these shows was *The See-er,* maybe because it starred not a tech-loaded ghost tracker but a plain-spoken thirty-something woman, someone not unlike Nilda. She had the air of someone looking into something suspicious in the home of a neighbor she didn't know well, out of duty more than enthusiasm.

Each episode, she'd walk the rooms of a different house that was said to be haunted, picking up "signals" along the way. During her rambles the house's earthly residents would be absent, and the See-er was said to know nothing about them, or about the house's history.

Later she'd sit down with the residents, tell them what she'd observed.

Those footsteps you heard on the stairs? I saw two girls, probably sisters. Looking for someone. A father, I think. They're wondering why he's been gone so long, if he'll ever return.

The rumbling from the attic? I saw a guy up there in a crisp, old-style suit, with a closely trimmed beard and angry eyes. And I'm getting an almost hostile neat-freak read on him. If you put those old chairs back where you found them and clear at least a walkway through all your junk, I'm betting he'll let up on you.

That shadow in the kitchen? She followed you here, and I think she's someone you know. She'd like you to get another dog, she thinks it's time. And I got a feeling for some words from her, something about her hiding in the "same old spot."

After these revelations historians or other researchers would join the See-er and the residents, share the facts they'd uncovered, about the property or its residents.

The house with the haunted staircase? It had once been occupied by the father of two sons and two daughters. A sea captain lost to a hurricane.

The house with the haunted attic? It had once been home to a bank president, whose photograph a historian revealed to the current residents, and the See-er. Taken at the turn of the last century, the photograph showed a man with a neatly trimmed beard, in arguably crisp attire—most notably, his high-collared shirt. Admittedly, nothing remarkable for the time. And his eyes? They might have been angry, or they might have been stunned by flash powder, in the manner of many photographed eyes of the time.

What was remarkable to the residents was the ghostly critique of their now packed-to-the-rafters attic. With side glances of embarrassment, they confessed that shortly after moving into the house, they'd made way for all these things by shoving aside some "old stuff," including two antique chairs.

The episode with the haunted kitchen was the one Nilda thought about most. After the See-er shared her findings with the house's residents, a wife and husband, the wife revealed that she'd lost her beagle and then her sister the previous year. Since then, she'd been unwilling to get another dog, "because you can't just replace something you've loved."

The woman got her tears under control just enough to explain that "the same old spot" was what she and her sister called a corner of an old shed that, when they were kids, offered perfect cover for hide-and-seek games. No one ever found them there, and they'd kept it as their secret.

This wasn't the only episode that had choked Nilda up, and that felt real in every way—from the See-er's manner and observations and revelations to the residents' reactions to what she'd found. Yet Nilda told herself, again and again, *The whole thing might be a fraud.*

Then why couldn't she stop watching *The See-er*, and even the crappier shows? Why was she endlessly intrigued by the possibility of ghosts?

Maybe she was trying to satisfy some need that religion might have fulfilled, had she been so inclined—a need to coexist, if not quite come to terms, with life's countless mysteries and inevitable losses.

But Nilda was never satisfied. Watching, reading, or listening to any account of the paranormal, she felt not only fascinated but also shut out, knowing she'd never see...*what*? An orange glow emanating from a darkened room? Even then, how could she possibly feel any less bereft?

Downstairs, the "all done" beep sounded from the auto-brew coffeemaker. Soon, Sidney would be stirring. But Nilda couldn't bring herself to climb out of bed. There was something else she needed to work out.

Just wait, you'll see.

If her mother were still alive, she might have said that very thing about Graham. And this morning, the caution of those words seemed just right to Nilda, who no longer felt like the sixteen-year-old who seemed to have possessed her last night. Maybe Graham's cocktail had amplified her sense of possibility and desire. Now sobriety and sense had returned to her and, thankfully, not at the cost of a hangover.

Just wait, you'll see.

Every time this sentence came back to Nilda, it took on new meanings, depending on whatever was preoccupying her at the moment. Her mother spoke it in a haze of morphine, at a time when her words were scarce, precious. When she did speak, her voice was earnest, though weak as the room's winter light.

Did you look in the garden? They're out there somewhere.

Nilda had leaned in to listen, hearing or not hearing a given utterance, and never asking her mom to repeat it, to expend whatever energy remained. She just waited for what might follow.

Everything I made is staring at me. No way to answer them all.

Nilda doubted she was the audience, or the only audience. At any given time, her mother might have been speaking to others she'd known, dead or otherwise absent. She might have been speaking to someone, or something, wholly imagined. Or she might have been speaking to no one at all, just giving voice to whatever thoughts, feelings, or images were streaming through her mind.

A boat and a horse and a blanket, of the finest, brightest blue.

Though Jo's words seemed random and disconnected, they offered glimpses of a reality that couldn't be argued with, a reality that excluded Nilda. Any glimpse of it might be her last.

At the end Jo called her by name.

"Nilda?"

She sat up, took her mother's hand. "I'm here, Mom."

Jo looked not to Nilda but to the facing window, where the view was the same as before: ice-glazed trees under a gray sky. Snow.

"It's never…"

Jo paused, open-mouthed. Long enough that it seemed she might be done. Then she tightened her hold on Nilda's hand, the strength of her grip a surprise.

"It's never what you're looking at. It's always at the edges."

Nilda had tried to avoid asking her mother for anything more than she was able to give. But now she couldn't help herself.

"What's *it*, Mom? Can you describe it?"

Still looking to the window, as if the answer might be there, Jo opened her mouth then closed it. Then she got out the words.

"Just wait, you'll see."

Her hand went slack in Nilda's, and moments later she was gone.

Several times since then, Nilda once again wondered what the *it* was. More and more, she made a connection to art.

Of course she would. But still: hadn't art been central to both of their lives?

Now, as Nilda stared at the bedroom's cracked and stained ceiling, one observation came back to her: *It's always at the edges.*

She thought of the latest drawings in the sketchpad on her dresser. She thought of her paintings-in-progress, including the one she'd wanted to destroy, and might still. Tenneman.

It's always at the edges.

She focused on the edges of that painting, now a void on the canvas, and in her mind.

The edges, *not* him. Not that horrible man.

Thinking of the edges, she pictured the parrot she'd subtracted from the painting. She thought of the parrot's voice, then of other voices emerging from the void. Not the parrot's, not Tenneman's.

Not Tenneman's.

She had an idea. Something worth trying, at least. But first, she'd need to run it by Toni.

In so-called intelligent hauntings, spirits are said to be aware of their surroundings, and capable of interacting with the living, in material ways—for example, by moving objects, opening or closing doors, or speaking. Although they are often invisible, they might appear as a shadow, mist, or full-body apparition.

The spirit may have a strong attachment to a particular place, and might not even be aware that it has departed it bodily. Or it might be driven to complete a mission—or to right some wrong—connected with the site of the haunting.

—From "Intelligent vs. Residual Hauntings" by Leslie Hatson

9

She opened the closet door, called his name. Then she stepped in, knocked on the covered hole. Even though he was too big to be in it.

Nothing.

It had been days since he'd come into her room. Maybe he was gone. *Really* gone. Just like her grandma.

"Alex?"

Still nothing.

She stepped out of the closet but left the door open, just in case. Then she sat on the bed and waited, thinking of all the ways he had appeared.

First he was just a voice. *Hey!*

A voice so quiet, it seemed to come from inside her head.

Later he was a *bump* that opened the closet door, letting out a shadow that zipped along the walls and across the ceiling, leaving a smell of grass and leaves and dirt.

She held on to Fuzzy then, but she wasn't afraid. She just wanted to see what the shadow would do next. It zipped back into the closet, vanished.

One day, when she was faced away from the closet, playing

by the windows, the outdoor smell came back. Even though the windows were closed.

Turning, she saw a boy standing in front of the closet. He was older than her. Tall, skinny, with curly red hair. He wore a yellow T-shirt, jeans, and muddy white sneakers.

"Who are you?" she asked.

Alex.

Again, the sound seemed to come from inside her head.

"Why are you here?"

I live here. Just like you.

He walked toward her, his footsteps creaking the floor. Then he sat down by her and nodded toward the window.

You look out there a lot.

She didn't know what to say.

You're interested in the woods.

She nodded. "I'm not allowed to go there. Unless I'm with my mom."

Close your eyes. I'll describe them.

She did, and he started in.

The path begins by this big old rock, covered by all this soft green stuff: moss. Step to the right of it and keep moving, and in a minute you'll see the biggest tree in the whole woods. Probably 'cause it's the oldest. It's twisty and kind of weird looking with this dark hole in the middle, and every now and then you'll see birds in there. Once, when it was getting dark, I even saw an owl...

It was like her mom reading her a story, the words making a movie in her mind. Until they stopped. When she opened her eyes, he was gone. No mud tracks on the floor.

She worried he'd never appear again, but he did. Sometimes just as the outdoor smell or shadow, or a weight at the foot of her bed. Other times as the boy, as real as she was. Whichever way he showed up, he was never imaginary: the word her mom used to describe him once, when she was on the phone with Toni and didn't think anyone else could hear.

He described more of the woods, getting as far as a creek with fish in it.

Not big ones, but cool ones. Some of them are super bright and shiny.

Later he brought this little box he called a Walkman. *Because you can walk around and listen to music on it. Here. Let me show you.*

As they sat side by side on the bed, he helped her put on the earphones that were connected to the box, then he pressed a button, filling her head with music. Songs about a tree on a hill, about free falling, about a heart of glass: like something her grandma would make for her.

The first time she listened to the music, Alex watched her, smiling and nodding his head along with hers, as if he could hear it too.

Later he leaned close so they could listen to music head to head, one earphone on her, the other on him. As she started singing, he did too, and when they held the same note together, it was like they had a special power, almost strong enough to lift them from the bed.

Why had he come to her? She didn't know. But it was like he understood her. Understood that she was too alone in this house, and sad. Because she missed her grandma and her dad. Because she didn't have any friends close by, other than her mom, Fuzzy, and Angus, who every now and then trotted into the room and circled, circled, then sat down, sometimes next to Alex. Alex would stroke Angus's fur like it was something he did all the time. Like a dog could just appear out of nowhere the way Alex had, and it was nothing to be afraid of. It was even good.

Maybe Alex stopped showing up because he thought he'd made her loneliness go away. If so, he was wrong. She looked to the closet, called his name again.

Still nothing.

She looked to the two houses on the shelf, seeing no sign there either. But sometimes, especially at night, the houses seemed to glow, and it felt like they were watching her. Sometimes this calmed her, like her nightlight did. Other times, it scared her. But she wouldn't put the houses back in the closet, because they seemed like a message from Alex, a message he was waiting for her to figure out.

He was the one who'd showed her where to find the houses. Pointing to the beat-up one, he said, *The bad kid's house.*

"Who's the bad kid?"

He didn't say anything else, and it was like he hadn't heard her. He just stared at the beat-up house, like he saw the kid staring back from inside it.

Now her half-closed door bumped open. It was only Angus.

She expected him to jump up on her bed the way he usually did whenever she was in it. Instead, he trotted past her, up to the sideways window. It was close enough to the floor that he could see out of it, and he stood in front of it, tail swishing, letting out little woofs.

She got out of bed and squished up next to him, close enough that she could see out the window too. The part of the yard she could see looked the same as always. No sign of Chickie, or any other interesting thing.

A flash drew her eye left, to the woods: a flash of yellow, moving through the trees. In a gap she saw Alex running, his hair bright even from here. Then he vanished.

Probably down the path he'd told her about.

Was he running from something? To something? Did he need her?

If her mom saw her going into the woods, she'd get in trouble. But her mom wouldn't see her.

Since they'd moved here, her mom noticed her less and less. Maybe because the house was so big, and because she had that separate space to work in. But even when they were together, even when her mom held her in her lap or combed her hair, it seemed like part of her—sometimes, most of her—was in another place, somewhere Sidney would never be able to get to. Losing Grandma Jo had changed her, but that couldn't explain the whole thing, and Sidney wondered whether her mom—all of her—would ever come back.

She ran from her room, into the hall, and called out as loudly as she could.

"*Mom?*"

No answer. The house was silent.

She ran down the stairs and out the back door, Angus right behind her.

"Love potion": a formulation celebrated in songs, poems, certain advertisements. But what is it about the word potion that suggests something sinister, aimed at a measure of control over the beloved?

—From "The Complicated Language of Love" by Callie
Danforth Rose

You never knew how much I learned from you, dear, beautiful, deeply flawed Chloe. How your every word and move and mood, even the smell of your skin, guided my adjustments to your formula.

After you left did you ever long to return to certain moments of intensity, with your photography or with me, or under circumstances beyond my imagining? Part of me wishes you knew that my efforts lay behind this intensity, and so much more. Part of me wishes you knew that I've found a far more worthy beneficiary.

—From the journals of Graham Emmerly, June 25th, 2019

10

Nilda looked to the photograph, then back to the canvas, sketching, getting down a suggestion of Toni.

Toni at sixteen or seventeen, the start of her junior year at the Fairmoore School.

"Before everything went to hell," she'd explained to Nilda yesterday, before handing over the photo. In it Toni wore the Fairmoore uniform and stood in front of some tree on the campus, its deep green leaves signaling late summer, Toni's smile signaling nothing more than that she was being photographed. No shades of the trouble to come.

Giving Nilda the photo had been an act of trust, and of faith. Faith that she could turn the idea she'd shared with Toni into something that had a shot at bringing Tenneman down.

"But I gotta be honest with you," she'd said to Toni. "Half the time—maybe more—my ideas don't work out."

All too often, the excitement that drove her to start a painting dwindled down to nothing, or turned into frustration, then defeat.

Toni had said this was okay. She'd said, "It's worth a shot."

Yet even if Nilda got to a finished painting, it was possible that Toni would hate it, maybe even be offended by it. If so, Nilda would have to ditch it and move on.

She sipped her coffee and stared down another challenge, the thing at the center of the painting: Tenneman—no longer the subject of a portrait, but something just to be gotten through, somehow. To make the work she was doing around him—her most important work—possible, she'd taped a square of paper over his face.

Nilda's phone buzzed on her worktable, "Clay" appearing on the screen. He was returning her call, finally.

She grabbed the phone and answered it.

"I'm sorr—"

"It's okay," she said, cutting him off. She'd heard *Sorry* from him so many times, it only triggered anger. "I was wondering if you're still gonna be on that Halifax job in August."

With his band on break from touring, he was back to doing carpentry work, lately at a new subdivision in Halifax, a development that was about ten minutes from Fairmoore. Three hours closer than she was.

"I think so. Why?"

"I might need you to do me a little favor at that festival there. On August third, to be precise."

In the past ten years, the Sky Tent Music and Arts Festival had grown from a small-scale venue for local artists and musicians to a regional attraction, one that was quickly outgrowing the Halifax Fairgrounds, which happened to be across the road from the Fairmoore School. Too close for comfort? Maybe. But in this case, discomfort was part of the mission.

"What do you have in mind?"

"I might need you to install a painting for me there. If I can get it done in time."

She'd need to register for the festival ASAP—and pay the entry fee, even if the painting came to naught.

"I'll make it happen."

"Thanks."

Nilda paused for a sip of coffee and looked toward the boxes along the far wall of the studio: her mother's glass-blowing tools. As much as she'd wanted them here, she hadn't been able to take them out of their boxes, not ready to be ambushed by memories, longing.

Now she had more pressing things to do.

"I'll let you know when I'm shipping the painting to you. *If* I get it done."

A shadow passed the side window, too quickly for Nilda to see who it was. Looking to the front window, she saw Graham, on his way to the studio door. Did he and Clay have some kind of ESP about each other?

If he knocked, he'd have to wait. But he didn't. After a moment he passed the front window then the side one, apparently heading back home.

Clay had been saying something she hadn't caught a word of. "Can you repeat that? I think the line cut out."

"I said, instead of you shipping the painting, why don't I come get it? That would save you a trip. And give me a chance to see Sidney."

It felt like they'd just had this conversation about Sidney. Nilda was getting tired of repeating herself.

"I'm not sure I'll be ready for you to come here." *Ever*, is what she wanted to add.

"But we're talking weeks away, right? Maybe that would be enough time?"

"Maybe. I don't know. Can we talk about this closer to time?"

In Clay's silence Nilda detected an impatience he knew better than to put into words. One of the small advantages of being the cheated on, as opposed to the cheater, was that she now got more leeway from him, practically and emotionally, and she wasn't ashamed to take full advantage of it. In earlier days, before things fell apart with them, he'd never been the king of selflessness or tact.

As soon as they signed off, Nilda headed to the entrance of the studio and opened the door. She saw no sign that Graham had been here, as she'd expected, mostly. Then, looking right, she spotted a Mason jar nestled in the grass. In it, a goldish liquid with hints of green. On the lid, a folded note labeled *Nilda*. She reached for the note and opened it.

Dear Nilda,

I humbly submit to you this herbal tonic, formulated to get (or keep) the creative juices flowing: ginkgo biloba, rosemary, peppermint, rosehips, skullcap, filtered water, and a dash of honey, for taste.

I used to be quite skeptical about these kinds of things, but I've come to swear by this particular potion. Of course, I won't be offended if you dump it down the drain.

Very much looking forward to tomorrow eve.

Warmly,

Graham

Had he seen her in the studio and decided not to disturb her? Or did he just want to leave the tonic where he believed she'd have the most use for it? Either way, she was glad that he hadn't knocked. And she was grateful that, so far, he seemed mindful of not intruding on her and Sidney's space. They barely knew each other, and she wasn't ready to invite him into her home, for more than a cup of coffee or some other brief, neighborly business. Anything more extended, more intimate, would be confusing for Sidney, and maybe for Nilda too.

When they set up tomorrow's date, she'd tried to get these feelings across to Graham, and he seemed to understand why dinner—and whatever might follow—would need to be at his place. Toni had agreed to take Sidney and Angus for the evening, leaving Nilda both grateful and nervous. As much as she tried to steer it in some other direction, her mind kept bending toward *whatever might follow.*

Nilda tucked the note in her pocket and retrieved the jar, held it up to the light. The cloudiness of the brew didn't appeal to her, nor did the whole idea of creativity tonics, which set off all her BS alarms.

Just dump it in the grass.

Then she remembered that cocktail Graham had made, and its strange appeal. The memory sparked her curiosity, and she twisted the lid from the jar, sniffed the brew, and took a sip.

Herbal tea, nothing more. She tasted the mint, the rosemary, the honey, and an earthy, leafy funk that must have been the sum of the other ingredients. Then something else: a tartness that prickled her tongue. The rosehips? No, that wasn't quite it—or all of it. Fermentation was at work, it seemed—just a hint of it. Enough to get her buzzed? She doubted it.

Taking another sip, she looked to the house. She needed to check on Sidney, get her out of her room for a change. But if she could spend just five more minutes on the painting, just get a little more of Toni down, she'd feel her studio time hadn't been a complete loss today.

Still holding the jar, she headed back into the studio and took her five minutes, then ten, then twenty, then thirty and counting. When she called it a day, an hour had passed like it was nothing.

By then the tonic was gone.

In contrast to intelligent hauntings are residual hauntings, in which the spirit has no awareness of the living world or ability to interact with it. Instead, residual hauntings are a kind of playback of a traumatic or otherwise significant event that has been "recorded" by or imprinted into a particular location. These playbacks may occur indefinitely.

—From "Intelligent vs. Residual Hauntings" by Leslie Hatson

11

As soon as she found the path in the woods, Sidney started running, passing first the big, twisted tree, then the line of stacked-up stones: "Some old kind of wall," Alex had said.

Next came the tree with the lightning burn, blackened and split in two. Then the swampy space that "smelled like farts." Everything just as Alex had described it. But he was nowhere to be seen: not ahead on the path, not in the trees on either side of it. He was too far ahead to catch up with. Or he'd vanished into nothing, like before.

Ahead she saw a split in the path. Go left or right? She couldn't remember what Alex had said, and maybe it didn't matter now. Maybe she should just go home.

But Angus didn't want to go home. He picked up speed and ran ahead, making a left at the split.

"Angus!"

He kept going until he was out of sight.

"*Angus!*"

Out of breath, she slowed to a walk, muck sucking at her shoes, like the ground was trying to swallow her.

She hated this place. Hated, hated, hated it. It had taken first her mom and then Alex, and now maybe Angus too.

Unsure what else to do, she trudged ahead in the mud, going left at the split in the path, then up a slight hill and down it. The longer she walked the farther away she got from this place, in her mind. She pictured her old room in Boston, so small it felt cozy with toys, so close to the playground that some mornings, she woke to the creak of swings. She wanted to go back there, back to her dad, back to things as they used to be.

A sound stopped her. Barking. Angus was up ahead, somewhere to the left.

Out of the mud, she picked up speed until she found him standing on a small hill, his back to her. Ears up, tail up, he was staring off at something.

Climbing the hill, she heard another sound. Voices. One boy's, then another's.

Don't do it. Don't be a dick.

Alex.

What do you think I'm going to do?

As she neared Angus, she heard a lower sound. His growl.

And when she got to him, she saw what had stopped him: down the slope in front of them, about as far away as she'd come from the path, was the creek Alex had told her about. And there was Alex on the closest shore, his back to her and Angus.

Standing in the creek, not far from Alex: another boy, who looked to be his age. About the same height and weight but with dark, shoulder-length hair. He was holding something over the water—a bottle—and giving Alex a look she remembered from last winter on the playground. The happy, twisted look of the girl who'd ripped the bunny-eared hat from Sidney's head, then threw it into some dirty slush.

Still looking at Alex, the dark-haired boy tilted the bottle, started spilling stuff into the creek.

Alex ran for him. As he charged into the water, the boy raised the bottle over his head, still smiling, like it was a game of keep-away. Alex leapt for the bottle and grabbed it, shoving the boy at the same time, taking him down with a splash.

Still clutching the bottle, Alex dashed from the creek and up the hill, running right past her and Angus, as if he didn't see them, as if he didn't hear Angus barking—a sound that was ringing in her ears. Then he vanished down the path.

Looking back to the creek, she saw nothing but water flowing along. No dark-haired boy.

Since entering the woods, she hadn't been afraid. At least not the kind of afraid that made her need the nightlight. But now something felt weird. Why had Alex ignored her? How could the boy in the creek just disappear?

And what was in that bottle?

Go home. Just go home.

But she started moving down toward the creek, Angus trailing her.

When she got to the edge of the creek, she looked left and right, seeing nothing but water, grass, rocks, trees. Across the creek more trees. No boy anywhere.

At her feet the water was still and clear, and flashing with color: yellow, green. Tiny fish, as bright as Finster. The fish Alex had told her about.

If that boy had put something bad in the creek, maybe it wasn't enough to hurt the fish. Or maybe it was nothing bad at all and he'd just been teasing Alex.

Still, as Angus started lapping the water, she grabbed his collar and pulled him back. She didn't let go until they were back on the path and heading home.

On the way she couldn't stop thinking of the dark-haired boy. Maybe he was the bad kid Alex had mentioned. The kid who lived in a house like the one from her closet.

She'd ask Alex, if she ever saw him again. The way he'd ignored her made her feel like she wouldn't.

Now her shoes were as muddy as his. She'd have to hose them off in the yard, leave no sign of the woods for her mother to find.

Check your impulse to blame your children for everything that's broken or disturbed, physically or metaphorically, in your household. Though sometimes, the odds may seem to favor their guilt, the odds aren't the same as the truth.

—Tips from *The Mindful Parent* by Hollis MacGrath

12

The smell of the auto-brew coffee. And toast. Sidney was up.

Nilda looked to her nightstand, got a jolt from the time on her phone: 9:38. She couldn't remember the last time she'd slept so late, or so deeply.

She wasn't hungover, not from alcohol. She'd had only two of Graham's lemon-thyme cocktails and didn't feel even the shade of a headache. But could you be hungover from sex?

Her thigh and butt muscles ached, as if she'd been to the gym. Yet she didn't feel post-gym fatigue, or really fatigue at all. It was more like she'd been wrung out then left to soak in something buoyant and warm. Was this what it was like to float on the Dead Sea?

Time to get up. But she couldn't. Instead, she let clips of last night play through her mind.

The two of them sitting side by side on the couch, thigh to thigh, warmth to warmth. Him holding her phone, scrolling through the paintings she'd posted to her website, remarking on color and composition in ways suggesting that he understood art, or how to talk about it. But she hadn't been listening, not really. She was studying the lines of his face, so much like those in that painting of Narcissus, down to the Roman nose, the full lower lip, the rounding of his chin. She wanted to trace the lines with her finger.

Instead, she took back the phone and put it aside, and got everything that followed started, with a hunger she didn't conceal, and with a roughness that was new to her, though it felt like second nature. At different points she clutched his hair or ass or shoved him this way or that to get just what she wanted, the way she wanted it. Until she came, with a force that felt earned.

Why the roughness? The intensity?

Maybe she was working out some of her anger with Clay, though for Graham's sake, she hoped not. Or maybe the migraine meds were a factor. If they could cause vivid dreams and hallucinations, why not extra-strength orgasms? Weren't all those things connected, really?

Probably, she was overthinking this. Maybe she should just be grateful.

Then she thought of Graham, and the possibility that he was waking not to a post-coital buzz but with some variety of regret for having her over. Though he'd seemed game during the sex, perhaps her eagerness—neediness?—had put him off, maybe even disgusted him.

If so, so be it. And if last night was their last date, that was probably all for the best. She hadn't moved all this distance to get entangled in another relationship.

Downstairs, Angus's barking started up and wouldn't stop. Nilda hauled herself out of bed and followed the sound to the front door, where Angus sat, now in his bark-growl rotation. She nudged him aside and opened the door—to no one. Looking down, she saw a vase of zinnias and snapdragons, with a folded note labeled in Graham's hand: "Nilda." Next to the flowers, another jar of the goldish-green liquid.

She reached for the note and opened it:

Although we're fairly new to each other, I feel like we're forming a special connection, far beyond the physical. I'm looking forward to seeing how things unfold, and I'm hoping you might be too. Let's get together again soon, if you'd want that as much as I do.

By the way, I'm so pleased that you liked the tonic, and I'll be honored to supply it for as long as you so desire. Keep up the inspiring work with the paintings.

With affection,

G

P.S. The vase is an antique I picked up on my travels, nothing too valuable. The green reminds me of your eyes.

Once again, that rush of joy, anticipation, desire.

She hadn't put him off. Maybe worrying that she had had kept her from confronting a truth that would only leave her vulnerable. This note invited her to face that truth: She felt a connection too—not love. But something that could lead to it, maybe.

Why?

Graham had something she couldn't quite place. Some attunement to her that existed from the moment he first stepped into her yard. It seemed this had only grown deeper.

Nilda tucked the note into the flowers and carried them and the tonic into the house. She decided to put the flowers in the dining room, where the vase was least likely to get knocked over. At the dining room entrance, she froze.

Sitting atilt on *Revenge in Glass* was one of the wooden houses, the more battered of the two. The sight shot heat through her: rage. Trying to steady her trembling hands, she set the flowers and tonic on the dining room table. Then she called out to Sidney.

No answer first, then a faint reply. "Yeah?"

"Get in here. *Now!*"

After a moment Sidney appeared in the doorway, her sleeping T-shirt smeared with jam.

"What's this about?" Nilda pointed to the sculpture, her whole arm shaking.

Sidney shook her head. "I don't know, Mommy."

"Oh, I think you do. Didn't I tell you Grandma's sculpture

isn't a plaything? Didn't I tell you to never touch that—that house?"

Sidney's eyes shone with tears. "I didn't do it!"

Another surge of fury. "Well, who did then? Huh?"

"I said, I don't know!"

The only other possibility was Helen, but she hadn't come to clean for a few days. And her doing something like this, it didn't make any sense.

Sidney broke down, only fueling Nilda's anger. She grabbed the house from the sculpture, then stomped past Sidney, into the hallway.

"Where are you taking it, Mommy?"

Nilda didn't know. Her instinct was to smash it to pieces, but even in her current state, she knew that was extreme.

The box in her closet, the one half full of her mother's shoes. That would be obscure enough.

As she started up the stairs, she sensed that Sidney was following her. She whirled around and tried for a calmer voice. "Go finish your breakfast."

Still crying, Sidney didn't move.

"I said, *go*."

Nilda waited until Sidney was on her way to the kitchen, then she turned and climbed the stairs. All the way, she never looked at the house, fearing she'd once again be sickened by the spider-eye windows scattered across the second floor.

Graham's house had them, she'd discovered last night. From the outside they were obscured by tree boughs. But inside, they were clearly visible in the upstairs hallway, and in Graham's bedroom: the site of three nonaligned cameo windows and two side-by side, bed-level portholes, like spying eyes. In all her time in that room, she'd tried to keep them out of her sight.

Lullabies soothe infants and children: Research has shown this. Yet they're also for the singers, reducing their stress and, sometimes, giving them an opportunity to vent darker thoughts and fears, things they might not feel comfortable expressing with their own words.

—From "The Timeless Lure of the Lullaby" by Nelle DeCorda

13

Nilda stepped through the back door and into the hallway, unsure of the time. After putting Sidney to bed, she'd planned to work in the studio just briefly. But once again, time had gotten away from her, tonight because she'd been immersed in the non-Tenneman parts of the painting: the parts she hoped would bring him down.

Now it seemed hours past sunset, and silence had settled throughout the house. Darkness too. The only light came from somewhere upstairs.

She carried the empty tonic jar into the kitchen and set it on the counter, next to the four other empties. Then she stopped, listened.

From somewhere, singing. A woman's voice. And a familiar tune Nilda couldn't quite place.

She crept back into the hallway, followed the singing to the foot of the stairs. There, she recognized Helen's voice, and the tune. "Night Knitter." It couldn't be.

But it was. As Nilda climbed the stairs, Helen finished the song then started it again. As she listened, Nilda remembered her mother singing that same song in darkness, on the edge of Nilda's childhood bed. The memory brought a thickness to her throat.

Night knitter, night knitter, I'll never know why
You've made it your duty to cover the sky

With a blanket so thick and so dark in its hue
That only the moon and the stars can break through

At the top of the stairs, Nilda collected herself and looked right, to the end of the hall and the source of the light: the spare room that she'd found no use for and rarely entered. She crept toward it, waiting out the final lines of the song.

Enough light to satisfy possums and owls
Who go on the hunt with their hoots and their howls
While I remain safe in your needle-made night
Hoping for dreams that will only delight

But bad dreams will come, and you know this is true
Knit me right, knit me right, knit me right through

When she reached the room, she found Helen turned away from her, polishing a dark, Victorian-looking dresser that was the main reason Nilda kept the door to this room closed. Behind each of the dresser's metal pulls were carved winged structures that reminded her of death's heads.

"Helen?"

Helen bolted upright, covered her heart.

"Sorry," Nilda said.

Helen waved a hand, as if to dismiss the apology. "That's what I get for being lost in my thoughts."

What were those thoughts? Nilda wondered.

"That song you were singing, I—"

Again, Helen put a hand to her heart. "You heard me from downstairs, didn't you? I hope I haven't disturbed Sidney."

If there was one song that wouldn't disturb Sidney, it was "Night Knitter." At times singing it was the only way Nilda could get her to sleep.

"I'm sure you didn't. I just wondered how you know that song."

Helen went back to her polishing. "I have no idea. It's been with me for as long as I can remember. Why do you ask?"

Nilda was embarrassed by the explanation on her mind. But she sensed that Helen would hear it out, without judgment. "I thought my mother made it up. She was the only person I ever heard sing it, and I never came across it anywhere else."

Helen paused at her work, seeming to consider Nilda's words. Then her lips quivered, and she glanced away, as if to compose herself. When she looked back to Nilda, she tried to smile, though her eyes were shining with tears.

"When she sang it, it was her song, your song. That's all that matters, right?"

"Right."

Nilda wondered whether, for Helen, the song conjured memories of her son. Did she used to sing it to him?

"I should let you get back to your work."

"Wait," Helen said. "I have something for you."

She laid her polishing rag on the dresser and headed toward the bed in the corner of the room. Its popcorn chenille bedspread looked straight out of the fifties, and probably was. The first time she saw it, Nilda pictured it piled with snoozing Yorkies.

From the nightstand Helen grabbed a book with a worn brown cover, then handed it to Nilda. "Since you mentioned Nathaniel Farleigh, I thought you might be interested."

Engraved on the cover in faded gold: *The Collected Journals of Nathaniel Farleigh*. The journals that Graham seemed familiar with.

"Where'd you get this?"

"I found it in that closet you asked me to clear out."

Nilda remembered now. It was the closet in the downstairs hallway, which had been full of junk that must have been overlooked by the property manager's cleanup crew.

She paged through the book, finding chronologically ordered journal entries, interspersed with drawings of architectural features, some of which she recognized from her house, or from Graham's, others that were unfamiliar: modern-looking roof deck–like structures, minarets, octagonal chambers.

Nilda flipped to the inside cover and found a dedication, in blue-inked cursive. She read it aloud to Helen.

> *Robert,*
> *On the occasion of your birthday, some insights into your friend.*
> *EJ*

Robert had been Eula Joy's husband: the only thing Nilda knew about him. Her mind lingered on the lack of "Love" or even "Warm regards" at the end of Eula Joy's message to him. Though Nilda knew from her mother that Eula Joy hadn't been the most affectionate person, she wondered whether the impersonal sign-off had to do with something more than this. Something connected to the couple's marriage, or Robert.

"*Your friend,*" Nilda said. "Do you have any idea what she meant by that?"

"Mr. Austerlane was a big fan of Nathaniel Farleigh's work. *My friend* was his nickname for him."

"He talked about him that often?"

Helen nodded. "Much more than Mrs. Austerlane cared for. She'd complain to me about it, sometimes."

One of the hazards of Helen's position, Nilda supposed. It must have been tiring to listen to such griping with patience, or the appearance of it.

"What kind of things would she say?"

Helen crossed her arms and seemed to be thinking things through. "Oh, she'd get tired of him going on about how they were living in the mind of a genius, that kind of thing. But I think what got to her most was when he'd roam around the house asking questions about this and that—why things were done a certain way."

"Questions to Nathaniel Farleigh."

"Yes." Seeming to notice the concern in Nilda, Helen said, "He never expected answers, of course. I think it was just his way of expressing curiosity, and admiration."

Helen went quiet for a moment. "I'll always remember what Mrs. Austerlane said about his one-sided conversations. 'That's what happens when social sorts move to the middle of nowhere.' Well, the middle of nowhere suited her just fine. Suits me just fine too."

Did it suit Nilda? She wasn't sure yet. But so far, she hadn't started talking to herself, any more than she had in Boston.

She thought of something else. "Nathaniel Farleigh used to make wooden models of stuff, kind of like dollhouses. Did you ever find any of them hidden away?"

Helen raised an eyebrow. "You have, I take it."

"Yes, unfortunately." The *unfortunately* came on impulse.

"You sound like Mrs. Austerlane."

"What do you mean?"

"Over the years she and Mr. Austerlane turned up quite a few of those houses. I did too. Of course, Mr. A. was a big fan of them, wanted to display them prominently. But they gave Mrs. A. the creeps, so into the attic they went."

Nilda didn't remember seeing any of Nathaniel Farleigh's models during the few trips she'd made to the attic. Maybe Eula Joy tossed them out after Mr. A. died. Maybe she would have tossed the ones from Sidney's room too, if they'd turned up during her day.

All this talk of the models got Nilda craving a glass of wine. She thanked Helen for the book and dropped it off in her room, telling herself she'd read it later. But would she? Right now, she wasn't sure she wanted more insights into the workings of Nathaniel Farleigh's mind.

Downstairs, Nilda headed for the wine cabinet in the dining room, opened a fresh bottle of cabernet, and poured herself a glass. The only light came through the bay window, from Graham's study across the way. It lit Jo's sculpture, cast the glass's red glow across the floor. As Nilda turned to leave, Graham appeared at his window, as if sensing her presence. Though he couldn't have. She remained in darkness.

Nilda sipped her wine and watched him staring ahead, his own drink in hand, seemingly lost in his thoughts.

This sparked a memory of something he'd told her the other night: Like Farleigh, he kept a journal, had for years. "It's an opportunity to reflect, of course, but there's also a practical aspect. It helps me think through work stuff, life stuff. And at difficult times it can allow for catharsis, unburdening."

What burdens had he wanted to shed over the years? Perhaps, in time, she'd find out.

For now, she took in the picture of Graham as she knew him at this point in time: still mostly a mystery, as much as he stood in the light.

Tonight, for the second time, or perhaps the third, I invited you to sit with me by the fire. For the second time, or perhaps the third, you stepped no closer, simply stood there in your overcoat, the firelight playing across your face and its look of revulsion.

Once again, you told me that you will never take your ease by those faces I carved into the mantelpiece. You told me it's a wonder that I can.

That didn't hurt me, Henry. Nor did what came next, because I'd long expected it. When you laid the agreement of separation out on the smoking table, I signed it without hesitation, and with my best wishes. What hurt me is how quickly you left once the signing was done, as if we were, are, nothing more than a doomed business partnership.

Son, I hold out hope that someday, we might return to happier relations. I hold out hope that someday, you might finally join me by the fire, and perhaps let me explain what I've tried to carve into the mantelpiece, what those faces represent: a place between sleeping and waking, between this world and the next, where all float free of earthly entanglements, and earthly rules. On certain unpredictable occasions, I am granted admission to it, never for enough time.

—From The Collected Journals of Nathaniel Farleigh

Confessions of (or a very bad Valentine from) a Besotted Chemist: With you, dear Nilda, I sense the possibility of what, for me, is that rarest of things: a covalent bond, an opportunity for true equilibrium.

—From the journals of Graham Emmerly

14

They'd woke to predawn birdsong and had been talking ever since. For an hour? More? Now the room was full of light, and a stillness unbroken by any breeze from the open windows. The day seemed on its way to being as hot as the forecast predicted.

Face to face with Graham, Nilda traced a finger along his cheek. "So I have Chloe to thank for your magic potion."

"I suppose." He smiled, and for some time just stared into her eyes. "But I make it just for you now, and me."

They'd been speaking of exes, only sketching them for each other, sparing details and darker shadings. That's what it felt like to Nilda anyway. The most significant thing she'd revealed about Clay was that he was Sidney's father, a revelation that felt essential, if things were to go any further with Graham.

So far, the only thing Nilda had learned about Chloe, Graham's previous girlfriend, was that she was a photographer, and that she seemed to have been as charmed by his cocktail-making abilities as Nilda was. So charmed that he was inspired to brew a creativity "booster" for her.

Nilda freed her legs from the sheets, already feeling too warm. "How'd you know what to put into it?"

"A simple search of the internet. No real chemistry skills were required. And no magic either."

Nilda thought of the sharpness she'd tasted in the tonic, the suggestion of fermentation. "Not even a shot of booze?"

"Not even a shot of booze. But I can add one, if you'd like."

Nilda rolled onto her back, stared at the decorative medallion at the center of the ceiling. Like the one in her own bedroom, it had been sculpted with shapes from nature: vines and lily pads.

"No, no," she said. "I guess I'm just wondering why the

tonic seems to work. Even though that feels like such—" She cut herself off.

"Such bullshit?"

"Yeah."

Graham scooched closer, enough that she could feel the heat from him. "You've probably heard of the placebo effect."

"Yup."

"Then you know that a sugar pill isn't just a sugar pill, not always. Sometimes, it can create a new reality for us, a better one. Just because we believe it can."

"It's a complete mind fuck, in other words." She smiled, not wanting him to take what she'd said as an insult.

"Yeah. But the mind fuck is *real*, or it can be."

She rolled over to face him and saw how troubled he looked. Worried that she'd hurt his feelings, she smiled and said, "Okay."

"*Okay?* You don't have to believe me."

She kissed his nose. "I believe you."

He still looked troubled.

"What?" she asked.

"I hope what I've said hasn't ruined the tonic for you."

Nilda hadn't even considered this, but it seemed possible now. Still, she didn't want to make him feel any worse. "Not a chance. Keep it coming."

Maybe it was the talk about the tonic, or the rising heat in the room—she was thirsty. She took the glass of water from the nightstand and finished it off. Then she lay down close to Graham, her back to his front. Straight ahead of her were the two round windows, the spying eyes. She stared right back at them, out of willfulness more than anything else.

He pulled her still closer, wrapped an arm around her waist. "You seem to be okay with that view now."

"What do you mean?"

"Your first night here, you wouldn't even face in that direction. Said you were too creeped out by those windows."

Nilda didn't remember saying this, but by the time they got to his room that night, she'd had a couple of cocktails.

"I guess I'm getting used to Nathaniel Farleigh's embellishments. Call it exposure therapy."

That was only part of the truth. Over the past few nights, Nilda had started reading Farleigh's journals, learning more about the "health-inducing measures" that he'd built into her house and had put to use himself: the floor-level windows he'd lie down next to to calm his nerves, the "skylit leaning chamber, in which one feels both swaddled like a babe and free to contemplate the stars." Based on his descriptions, she guessed this chamber was the narrow turret in the corner of one upstairs room, a room too small and off-kilter to accommodate a bed but too big to make sense as a closet. At the height of the turret was a skylight—suitable for contemplating the stars, she supposed.

With all these features, Farleigh seemed to have had the best of intentions—that's what the journal entries suggested. Nilda didn't have to like them, or feel comfortable with them, to appreciate what he'd been trying to do.

As for the windows she was looking at now, who knew what Farleigh's intentions had been? That he'd meant them to be spying eyes, or to serve any other malicious purpose, seemed less certain to her now.

Graham stretched then turned back to Nilda, began stroking her arm. "Have you thought any more about my offer?"

Nilda didn't know what he was talking about. Then she remembered. A few afternoons before, they were sitting on her patio, watching Sidney chase one of Graham's chickens around the yard. The greater truth, though, was that Nilda was watching Graham: noticing how he broke from their conversation to cheer Sidney on, or just to track her progress with a smile. *He likes kids,* she'd thought, sending her mind in directions that made her a less-than-perfect listener.

When he'd offered to contact the National Register of Historic Places and see if her home might be eligible for a listing, and for rehab grants, her mind had skimmed over his words. But she'd taken in enough of them to come to a conclusion that she hadn't shared with Graham then: She wouldn't be ready to embark on a rehab project anytime soon, even with grants. She had enough on her plate.

She shared that conclusion now.

"I understand," he said. "But just know the offer stands, and know that I'm here to help you, in any way I can." He kissed her shoulder, then stroked her hair. "I think we could make quite the team, Nilda Ricci."

Could they? Although her feelings for Graham were intensifying, she worried that things were moving too quickly, and that she was on a kind of high that was disguising an uncomfortable possibility: that it might be a long time before she was ready to be a "team" with any man. Maybe never.

"*Nil*-da." He repeated her name as if it were a word from an unfamiliar language, which was kind of true. "What's the story with your name?"

Nilda considered how to answer. "There isn't much of one, honestly. It was one of my grandmothers' names."

Yet there was more to the story, details that Nilda had shared only with Toni, because they felt like something private. "Nilda" *was* one of her grandmother's names; it had belonged to her father's mother. But it was Jo who'd chosen it, because it was said to mean "ready for battle" in Italian.

"I wanted to give you a good luck charm," Jo had explained to Nilda years ago, when Nilda was old enough to understand what good luck charms were.

Later Nilda wondered whether the choice of the name had come out of her mother's own experiences—one of them, perhaps, whatever had gone wrong with the man who'd inspired *Revenge in Glass*.

Nilda pulled away from Graham and climbed out of bed. "I need to get going."

"So soon?" He grabbed his phone and checked the time. "It's only seven-o-three. Stay for breakfast, or at least a cup of coffee."

"I can't, sorry."

Nilda felt an urgency to get to Toni's. Once again, she'd taken Sidney and Angus for the evening, and Nilda wanted to relieve her as soon as possible. The only things that stood in the way were a quick shower and a stop at Le Sel for some thank-you pastries.

Downstairs, at the front door, Graham asked her to hold on a second. Then he vanished into the kitchen, returning a moment later with another jar of tonic.

"In case you're still interested," he said.

"Of course I am."

She took the jar, kissed him, and left.

Occupants of purportedly haunted spaces often describe phenomena external to them: voices, footsteps on the stairs, flickering lights, moved or shattered possessions. Less remarked upon, but no less common, are internal phenomena—that is, emotional disturbances, or changes in mood or personality, that may or may not be noticed by affected individuals. Although several explanations have been offered for these phenomena—from variations in electromagnetic fields, to spiritual possession, to factors that have nothing to do with the paranormal—it is difficult to identify any definitive or unifying cause, based on the available evidence.

—From "Psychological Ramifications of Hauntings" by Tamsin Watley

15

That night, when Nilda returned to the house from her studio, she expected to step into silence, near darkness. It was long after sunset, long after she'd put Sidney to bed.

Instead, light streamed from every room downstairs, and the TV blared from the living room.

"Sidney?"

No answer.

As she headed toward the sound, she glanced into the kitchen, found it empty. The living room, too, was empty, though the TV was tuned in to Sidney's favorite network: a 24/7 cartoon parade. Nilda turned it off and stood there, thinking. It wasn't like Sidney to just leave the TV running and turn on every light for no reason. But maybe she'd entered yet another new phase. There seemed to be no end to those lately.

What about Helen? No. This wasn't like her either. And she wasn't due back until tomorrow evening.

Nilda turned off the TV and headed for the dining room.

Light from it spilled into the hallway, made something flash on the floor. Broken glass?

Closer up, she saw that it was the ice-blue crystal that Graham had given to Sidney. She dropped it into the pocket of her work shirt and went to shut off the dining room light. The sight there froze her. On top of her mother's sculpture was that beat-up house, the miniature of Graham's. The one she'd hidden in her closet.

She bolted across the room and grabbed it, stared into that cluster of windows, the spider's eyes. They seemed to be staring back, mocking her. As if the house possessed a consciousness, an awareness that it was defiling the sculpture.

"You goddamned, god*damned*—"

Rage surged through her, stealing her words. She looked away to collect herself, her eyes settling on just the answer, just what she needed: the fireplace poker. She carried the house to the marble hearth, set it down. Then she grabbed the poker by the handle and the shaft, brought down the first blow, then another and another and another, collapsing the roof, sending shingles flying.

"Mommy?"

She turned and found Sidney in the doorway.

"What are you doing, Mommy?"

What did Sidney *think* she was doing? Couldn't she see for herself?

"What am *I* doing? What were *you* doing, going into my closet? I told you *my* room is *my* space. You don't go sneaking around in it."

Sidney started crying. Again with the damned tears.

"And what were you doing leaving this—" She nodded to what was left of the house. "—this *thing* on Grandma's sculpture?"

Sidney shook her head, looking stunned, confused. She was getting pretty good at this act of hers.

"Answer me, Sidney."

"I didn't *do* it!"

"Well, who did then? *Alex*?"

Sidney stared at Nilda, still looking confused. Then her face crumpled. "Alex went away. I want to go away too."

Nilda lowered the poker and took a step toward Sidney.

Sidney stepped back. "I hate this place! And I hate *you*!"

Sidney ran off, and Nilda stood there, frozen, listening to the pounding of feet up the stairs. Her rage had dissolved, replaced by…she wasn't sure what. The shattered house at her feet seemed like wreckage she'd stumbled upon and had nothing to do with.

As she set the poker back in the stand, she took in the faces carved into the mantelpiece and down both pillars. The faces of the sleeping or the dead: some slack-jawed, none spared from such things as wrinkles, warts, or jowls. They seemed to represent ordinary people, not gods or ideals. People who'd walked this earth, once.

A face on the left pillar stopped her, one she hadn't noticed before. The rounded cheeks, the slight upturn at the corners of the mouth, she knew them, knew the face: It was a young version of her mother's—or, rather, of a woman who looked just like her.

It called to mind those times when Nilda was a girl and found her mother napping. She'd whisper in her ear.

Wake up, Mom! Wake up!

Then she'd blow at her hair, ruffling it, or trace a finger along her ear.

Though her mother wouldn't open her eyes, Nilda knew she was awake when a smile began to play across her lips. Eyes still closed, she'd pat the spot next to her, on the bed or couch, and Nilda would crawl up beside her, let Jo fold her into her arms.

"Wake up."

Nilda whispered the words now, without thinking. In them she heard a warning: she was the mother now, and it was time to start acting like one.

She stepped into Sidney's room, lit with the glow of the nightlight. Curled up on top of her covers, Sidney had her back to the door.

"Sidney?"

No movement, no sound.

Nilda set Graham's crystal on the nightstand and sat on the edge of the bed, unsure of how to begin. With hesitation she reached for Sidney's shoulder. Sidney flinched, scooted away.

Not so long ago, it seemed Sidney had clung to her, whenever she'd had a chance—something that had annoyed Nilda more often than she'd cared to admit, something she'd considered another of Sidney's phases. Now she hated herself for feeling that way.

"I'm sorry for what I said." Nilda tried to keep her voice low, soothing. "I'm sorry I got so angry. That was wrong."

Sidney kept silent, but she seemed to be listening. She was staring ahead, Fuzzy clutched tight to her chest.

"I'm going to do better, okay?"

This was a pledge to herself, as much as to Sidney, who hadn't asked for a distracted, self-obsessed mother. So what if she'd snooped in Nilda's closet? So what if she'd put the house on the sculpture, which, despite Nilda's fears, had suffered no harm? Chances were, Sidney was acting out for a reason: to remind Nilda that she needed more attention—the kind driven by care, not anger.

Sidney whispered something.

"Sorry, honey, I didn't hear you."

Sidney repeated herself, in a flat voice. "Leave me alone."

The command of a teenager, it seemed to Nilda; nothing she'd heard from Sidney before.

"Okay, honey. Sleep tight." Her voice broke on the last word. Not wanting Sidney to hear her crying, she rushed from her room and into the hall, feeling lost in the darkness.

Who was she? Most certainly, she wasn't a mother, not really. Not the mother Sidney deserved.

She wandered toward her bedroom, though she wasn't tired, and felt like she was in for another sleepless night. Just as she reached her bedroom, she looked left, to the door of that odd little room, the room with the turret. The sight of it stopped her tears.

She wiped them away and headed for the room, laid a hand on the doorknob, and paused. She felt she was on the edge of surrendering, but to what? The only clear thing was that right now, the thing she desired most was an escape, or the hope of one.

She turned the knob and stepped into what felt like a ship's cabin, with its tight quarters and pitched ceiling. The only light came from the height of the turret: a bright beam of the full moon.

She crept forward and entered the turret, a space so narrow she could extend her arms only so far before touching its edges. Then she backed into a still-narrower space, which was angled backward, slide-like, but just slightly. Leaning back, she let it take her weight, and found herself gazing upward, at a triangular window in the turret's roof, nearly full with the round of the moon.

At first, she felt only the strangeness of her position, and her embarrassment in believing it might make a difference. Yet she stayed where she was and kept her eyes on the moon. Until she lost the sense of where she was, or why. The moon was all. The moon was all. She, in the end, was nothing.

I move like a cell through blood-murk, until something—a certain voice, a bit of music, an old desire—pulls me back into the living world, for seconds, minutes, or hours. I arrive with no doubt of my purpose, or as bewildered and uneasy as anyone who might encounter me.

—From *Autobiography of a Spirit* (Hitchfield Public Library, shelved under Fiction)

16

Since Nilda's move here, *The See-er* had slipped from appointment television to habit television. She still watched it unfailingly, but now with only half her brain, the other half roaming over multiple worries or anxieties, or into that region of random thoughts, which vanished almost as quickly as they'd materialized, into the fog of the forgotten.

Tonight was no exception. After she sprawled out on the living room couch, clutching a glass of shiraz, her TV brain gathered only so many details about this episode's haunted site, a seventies-era split-level rigged with recording devices and night-vision cameras: a blacker-than-black humanoid shadow drifted down an upstairs hallway; a toilet flushed and a faucet ran when no one seemed to be near them; feelings of doom overcame the See-er when she entered the basement rec room.

The longer she watched *The See-er*, and the more wine she sipped in the darkness, the more Nilda's non-TV brain took over. She considered today's small, disappointing victories: Sidney was at least speaking to her, if minimally and with little enthusiasm. And she'd agreed to bake cookies with Nilda, once one of Sidney's favorite activities. Yet as she helped measure the ingredients and mix the batter, Sidney seemed to just be going through the motions, and when the first batch of cookies came out of the oven, she sampled one as if it were nothing more exciting than the broccoli-and-cheese mash Nilda sometimes made to get Sidney to eat more vegetables.

The bigger source of anxiety—this evening, at least—was the Tenneman painting, or rather, Toni's possible reaction to it. Nilda would get that reaction tomorrow morning, when Toni was to come by and have a look at the piece as it stood: complete enough for Toni to take in all the major elements but not so far along that Nilda couldn't make small to middling changes.

As she drained the last of her wine, Nilda considered a more troubling possibility, one she needed to be prepared for: Toni might have bigger issues with the painting, ones beyond fixing.

If that were to happen, Nilda couldn't imagine starting from scratch, taking some new approach. Because over the hours and days she'd spent on the painting, she'd gotten pulled into her vision for it, so deep that she couldn't conceive of any other direction for the piece. The doubts and misgivings that had troubled her early on seemed to have vanished. But now, on the eve of Toni's judgment, she felt encircled by them.

She also felt a measure of sadness, the sadness she always experienced when nearing the end of a painting that had deeply engaged her, that took her out of herself in the best of ways. In this new life and this new home, that escape from herself felt more necessary than ever. Why? She wasn't sure.

Maybe because she was screwing up so much with Sidney.

Maybe because…

Mind fog swallowed the thought. In its place came the glow of the moon. The glow of the moon in that window.

There, she'd lost all awareness of herself. And when she left the turret, she felt calm.

Then go back. Go back whenever you need to.

No.

Why not? What's the harm?

Seduction was the harm. Seduction by something she couldn't understand, and wasn't sure she wanted to.

Distress from the TV interrupted her thoughts. In one of the split-level's bedrooms, the See-er was doubled over, complaining of pains delivered by some invisible man. "He keeps kicking and prodding me, like he needs to make himself known… He… I need to get out of here. I need to get out of this house."

Nilda needed a refill. As the show cut to a commercial, she reached for the floor, home of the shiraz bottle, and topped off her glass.

She rose to find a pale face, just inside the doorway.

Helen's, lit by the TV's glow.

Out of relief Nilda clapped a hand to her chest, her adrenaline just now waning.

"I'm sorry," Helen said. "I should have called out a warning."

"No, no, no, it's fine. Really." But these words were all politeness. Nilda's heart was still hammering.

Helen looked to the wine Nilda had sloshed onto the floor. "Let me get something to clean that up."

"No need. Watch this."

Nilda grabbed a couple of napkins from the end table and mopped up the mess. Before she could decide where to put the wine-soaked napkins, Helen took them. Then she said, "That grout's about as clean as I can get it. Is there anything else you can think of for now?"

"No, I think that does it. Thanks."

It hadn't been Nilda's idea to scrub the grout in the upstairs bathroom, which had seemed beyond rescue. But she had no doubt that it now looked much better—just as everything Helen touched did. *Better* didn't quite capture the difference though. Whenever Nilda stepped into a room that Helen had mopped, dusted, scrubbed, or neatened, it seemed something more than clean; it felt just a bit less alien to Nilda than it had before. Sometimes even inviting.

The See-er's theme tune cut in, followed by a snippet of the last scene:

He keeps kicking and prodding me, like he needs to make himself known… He… I need to get out of here. I need to get out of this house.

As if to see what all the fuss was about, Helen turned her attention to the TV, where *The See-er* recap wound down. Now the show turned to the split-level's residents, who were sitting side by side at their dining room table, across from the See-er. She was ready to share her findings with them.

This was just the kind of thing that Helen—sensible, practical Helen—would surely regard as BS, and watching her watch the scene, Nilda felt a wave of embarrassment. But Helen looked more interested than judgmental.

Nilda straightened up on the couch, making room for her. "Have a seat."

Helen glanced Nilda's way, looking uncertain. Then, after a moment's hesitation, she sat on the edge of the couch.

Together, they learned that the residents were a married couple: Liz and Dave. And Liz and Dave had reached out to the See-er because they'd encountered all the things she had: the blacker-than-black humanoid shadow, the mysterious flushings and faucet turn-ons, the sense of doom in the basement, the kicking and prodding in the guest bedroom.

Or maybe only Liz had encountered these things. Because as she ran through the roster of incidents, expressing her fears and worries, Dave sat silent, thick arms folded over his chest, his gaze directed to some spot at the center of the table.

The See-er's verdict: A "shadow person" with male energy had slipped through a portal that "negative energy" had opened in the basement. "He's feeding on that bad energy and magnifying it. Exponentially."

This hit an eight or nine on Nilda's skepticism meter, a few points higher than usual.

Now came the part of the show that often hit a ten or more, shattering her willingness to suspend disbelief: the See-er's suggested intervention. But always Nilda kept watching—out of curiosity, and out of the sense that the See-er truly believed in her remedies, and that she suggested them with the best of intentions.

And maybe all this made more of a difference than Nilda understood. Maybe the See-er's belief that something could be done gave people like Liz and Dave a sense of hope. And maybe her remedies exerted another type of placebo effect: If you believe that you've banished something dark or evil, maybe you stop seeing, hearing, or feeling whatever had been upsetting you—whether supernatural or imagined.

As the See-er suggested tonight's remedy—a "banishing ritual" involving black salt and tourmaline crystals—Nilda studied Helen's expression: level and unrevealing. Nilda was afraid to ask what she thought, but she did anyway.

Helen didn't answer, just watched the credits roll. Then she turned to Nilda.

"I'd skip the salt and the crystals and get rid of the husband. He's the biggest problem in that house."

"What makes you say that?"

Helen rose from the couch and checked her watch. "Just a feeling. But a strong one."

Nilda had seen Dave as a keep-to-himself kind of guy who looked less than enthusiastic about being on a television show, which she guessed had been Liz's idea. She didn't read anything darker into him and wondered why Helen had, with so much certainty. Knowing that Helen was a private person, she didn't press the matter further.

Yet after Helen left, Nilda couldn't stop thinking about what she'd said, and about what might be behind it. Maybe Dave reminded Helen of someone she'd known, someone who had hurt her. Or maybe, and this felt like more of a stretch, Helen was extraordinarily perceptive—perhaps beyond the level of the See-er.

What about her own husband, Russ? To Nilda he was nothing more than headlights at the top of her drive, so blinding that Nilda could never see his face when he dropped off Helen or picked her up. But as Helen left or approached the car, it was always with a smile or wave, suggesting no trouble at home.

No, if there was a dark history with any man, Nilda guessed it wasn't with Russ.

As she drank the last of her wine, her phone buzzed on the end table. Retrieving it, she saw a message from Graham:

Night-night, love. Thinking about you and looking forward
to Friday.

She was too. And she was grateful to be reminded of something good in her life.

In the bloody, baroque-era painting *Judith and Holofernes*, by Artemisia Gentileschi (1593-1653), Judith stands in for Gentileschi, and Holofernes represents Gentileschi's rapist, Agostino Tassi. As she plunges a knife into the throat of Holofernes, Judith is a study in cool determination, and perhaps satisfaction. Holofernes, regarding the viewer in horror, is a study in agony.

This painting delivered the only justice that Gentileschi was to achieve, a circumstance that was all too common at the time and, unfortunately, is not a thing of the past.

—*Art and Revenge*, master's thesis by Nilda Ricci, 2008

17

As soon as Toni saw Nilda's face, her smile faded. "What's wrong?"

Nilda was standing in the entrance to her studio, afraid to let Toni in, though that was the reason she'd invited her here.

Her mind spun and spun then landed on an answer, something maybe only Toni would understand. "I don't really want to be here when you look at it, okay? I'm just too wound up, and I don't want to weird you out and—"

Toni laid a hand on her arm. "I get it. Just give me five minutes. Or do you want me to come get you when I'm done?"

"No, no. Have at it, and I'll see you in five."

The painting occupied the same easel it always had, so Toni would know where to find it. Same as always, it faced away from the door, partly because that allowed Nilda to work under the best lighting conditions, partly because she didn't want anyone seeing the painting until now. She'd told Toni as much the few other times she'd stopped by while Nilda was working on it.

Nilda let Toni by then stepped into her yard, purposeless for now. She didn't want to return to the house, where Sidney was playing with Toni's girls, something that always made Sidney happy, a joy Nilda's presence would surely dim. So she headed down the drive, toward the road she rarely walked, so distant from town it must have been considered unworthy of sidewalks. Aside from her house and Graham's, there were a handful of homes in either direction, for at least a few miles.

Walking the road's shoulder, past Queen Anne's lace and chicory, past the gray remains of a sag-roofed barn, she pictured what had come to guide her work on the painting and had sustained her during the hours she'd spent on it: Judith with her knife in Holofernes's throat, her fury turned to cool expedience. Her face and force, and his murder, lit against blackness.

For Tenneman there was no knife. Yet there was light, and he was one of two figures picked out by it. Nilda imagined the light coming from a bare bulb, outside the painting's upper frame, the kind of light suitable for an inquisition.

On either side of Tenneman, and extending back into the shadows, an army of teenaged, uniformed Tonis stared forward, their accusations floating above them in painted cursive: "Predator," "Violator," "Monster," and "No one listened," "No one listened," "No one listened."

In the lower left of the painting, Tenneman's toy parrot, now blindfolded, issued the same warning Toni had heard at the time of her assault: "Doomed to repeat," "Doomed to repeat," "Doomed to repeat." To the right of Tenneman was the other lit figure: another Toni. But instead of staring forward, she was speaking into Tenneman's ear, with an expression of cool expedience. Her message: "Doomed."

His reaction showed in his eyes—Holoferenes's eyes, aglow with the same terror.

Although Nilda had once dreaded taking on the Tenneman portion of the painting, rendering that look of fear turned out to be one of the most satisfying parts of the job. As she daubed brights about his pupils and irises, she'd pictured her mother shaping *Revenge in Glass,* the heat from the furnace merging with the heat of her anger. Nilda hoped that as Jo worked, she'd experienced some of the same type of satisfaction, however fleeting.

But did Jo ever think she'd rouse fear in the man who'd inspired her sculpture? Nilda doubted she'd ever inspire fear in the real Tenneman. More likely, she'd inspire quite the opposite. Her only hope was that the painting would set off alarms among viewers, enough alarms to make a difference.

As she reached the blind curve in the road, Nilda looked at her phone. Six minutes had passed. She turned and jogged back to her studio.

Toni was just outside the door, waiting. When she saw Nilda, she smiled, but Nilda wasn't reassured. This was Toni's *It's gonna be okay* smile, which she tended to use after one of her girls had taken a fall, or before she needed to tell them something they wouldn't want to hear.

This isn't about you, Nilda reminded herself. It was about Toni, who wasn't responsible for protecting Nilda, or for lessening the blow of any criticisms she might have of her painting.

When Nilda reached Toni, Toni took her by the hand and led her to the improvised "lounge" Nilda had set up at the front of the studio: two facing folding chairs and between them a banged-up coffee table she'd brought over from the house. After they sat down, Toni spoke right up.

"I'm just gonna let my feelings roll, okay?"

"Sure."

"When I first saw him, it was a blow. Just because it was him. It brought that time in his office right back. So did that stupid parrot."

Nilda fought the urge to apologize. She needed to shut up and listen.

"Then I started taking in all the other stuff, all the images of me, all the words, and I felt a little disoriented at first, like I was having a—what do you call it? An out-of-body experience. And that ended up being a good thing, because it gave me some distance, and I started seeing the painting from another perspective—an outsider's perspective, kind of. I felt like all those me's weren't just me, like they stood for all the other women who've had to deal with this stuff, not just from Tenneman."

That was just what Nilda had intended.

"And the *Doomed* part, it just felt so good to see that, Nilda. It really did."

Thank goodness, Nilda thought.

Toni went silent, and Nilda took this as an invitation to speak. "So you think the painting's okay."

"It's more than okay. It makes a powerful statement, and I think it belongs in the festival. If you can get it past the gate-keepers there."

Nilda had already taken some steps to deal with the gate-keepers, and to cover herself. On the registration form for exhibitors, she'd described the painting simply as a portrait, and in response to a request for an image of it, she'd included a photo of a non-incriminating study she'd made during her early work on the commission. Her name on the form? An invention. Her address? A PO box she'd opened in town. Her phone number? The number of a burner phone. The payment? Cash. If everything went to plan, the festival runners would soon be sending their approval of her application to a new Gmail account she'd created, the address beginning with "RIG," a nod to her mother's own work of retribution: *Revenge in Glass.*

Nilda ran through these precautions with Toni. Then she said, "How do you feel about having media there?"

The look on Toni's face suggested she wasn't pleased about the prospect. "I know we should probably do that. But are reporters gonna take the word of a painting? They'll probably want charges against Tenneman before they run with a story, or even a picture of the painting. Not that I'm unwilling to file charges. But there's only so much time before the festival, right?"

"A month and change."

"That would be cutting it close."

As much as she'd wanted to have some reporters on the scene, Nilda knew Toni was right. She also knew that social media might be their best, and maybe only, bet. "We could get some mileage with Twitter."

"Yep."

Just how much mileage, Nilda wasn't sure. She wasn't optimistic.

"There's a Fairmoore alum hashtag we could use, for one thing."

"Great."

Toni sat forward, as if getting ready to leave. "From now on let's figure out stuff together, okay? I don't want all this to be on you."

Just hearing this offer made Nilda feel less overwhelmed. "Maybe we could talk tomorrow night?" She knew Toni was pressed for time today.

"Sounds good."

Toni started to rise from the chair. Then she stopped. The troubled look had returned, and Nilda wondered whether she was already having second thoughts about this whole thing. "I wasn't sure if I should say this, but I'm, uh…I'm worried about you."

Nilda felt a jolt of surprise. "Really? Why?"

Toni seemed to be considering how to respond. "You've been looking so tired and pale. Like you've come down with something."

Other than her migraines, which hadn't been as bad lately, Nilda didn't really feel sick. Maybe the long hours she'd been spending on the painting had worn her down more than she'd thought, but she didn't want to bring this up with Toni and make her feel guilty.

"I think it's probably just my insomnia."

But was it? She pictured the model house she'd smashed to pieces, and its spider eyes. She thought of the leaning chamber and the faces on the mantelpiece, and her spells of dark moods. Maybe all of this was getting to her, in ways she hadn't imagined. But as she considered how she might put these things into words, they all seemed so out-there. She didn't want to give Toni even more cause for concern.

"Well," Toni said, rising to her feet, "I'm going to be keeping an eye on you, friend. And you better rest up before your big date, save up some energy."

A reference to sex, Nilda was sure. Though this was something they rarely talked about, as close as they were, the subject had come up days before, when Toni asked how things were going with Graham. Nilda had said only that their sex was "intense," in a good way, and she and Toni had spent much more time discussing Nilda's concerns about the relationship getting too serious too quickly. Toni's response: "Hate to tell you this, doll. But sometimes *serious* is beyond our control."

Now Toni made her way to the door, then stopped. "That's Friday, right?"

"Yep."

That evening Toni was going to take Sidney and Angus for another overnight, while Nilda stayed at Graham's. And Nilda and Sidney would be seeing him tomorrow, for a backyard picnic he'd suggested. Sidney's excitement about this surprised Nilda and gave her some hope. Lately when any activity included Nilda, Sidney had been lukewarm about it, at best.

Toni picked up the glass of tonic that Nilda had left on the ledge by the door. "I don't remember you being a tea drinker."

"It's not really tea. It's this herbal drink Graham thought I'd like."

"Do you?"

If she were being honest, Nilda would have told Toni that since she'd started drinking the concoction, she'd been painting with more energy and feeling than she'd experienced in a long time. She would have said that although she might just be willing that connection into existence, she didn't really care. Damn the means; it was all about the ends.

Yet she knew that any skepticism from Toni might shatter the connection for good. So she decided to keep things simple. "It's okay. Wanna try it?"

Toni sniffed the drink and made what the two of them had come to call her "cilantro face."

"What?" Nilda asked.

"Herbal stuff, it's just never been my thing. And this smells extra herbal-ly."

Nilda had stopped noticing the smell, or the taste, of the tonic. Lately it went down as easily as her coffee.

Toni put the glass back and smiled. "But if you like it, that's all that matters, right?"

After a wave she was gone.

With their height and their wealth of colorful tubular flowers, foxgloves have become a mainstay of gardens, in our growing zone and beyond. It is crucial that they be grown in rich, well-draining soil with a pH no higher than 6.

Foxgloves are worthy of honor and care, not just because of their beauty. As a doctor, I am grateful for their gift of digitalis, a life-sustaining treatment for certain heart patients. But it should be borne in mind that this substance can also act as a deadly poison. Thus, it is best to plant foxgloves at the very back of borders, away from pets and small children.

—From the "Discerning Gardener" column by Dr. Clifford Emmerly, the *Hitchfield Spectator*, April 5th, 1978

18

Left, right, and straight ahead: flowers. Daylilies, stargazers, foxgloves, zinnias, cone flowers, bee balm, tea roses, and orange-red poppies.

Orange-red poppies everywhere.

Everywhere, too, the scent of the lilies and roses. It weighted the air all around Nilda and Graham, who were stretched out on a blanket between two of the flower beds, the remains of lunch before them. At their feet Fuzzy slouched by a sandwich crust that Sidney had left for her, along with a cup of lemonade. Past Fuzzy, Sidney chased the chickens back and forth, now and then tossing her beach ball in their direction, giggling as they flapped their wings and pepped up their struts to escape.

Thank goodness for the chickens, Nilda thought. Thank goodness for the beach ball. Thank goodness for the lemonade that Graham had made, with Sidney's help. Each of these things seemed to have boosted Sidney's spirits one notch higher, and it had been a long time since Nilda had seen her so happy. Did it matter that she had nothing to do with this?

A breeze delivered a dose of the lilies' perfume: almost too much. Just as this garden was almost too much—an Eden on overdrive. It seemed that in the last couple of weeks, some switch had been thrown in the earth, doubling or tripling the blooms and their scents.

It occurred to her what that switch might be.

"Did you make one of your magic potions for your flowers? I mean, this is all so… incredible."

Graham finished another strawberry, left the stem in his empty cup. "I've used nothing more magic than compost. But I've also been putting in long hours out here. Trying to make as much hay as I can before school starts up in August."

Nilda had been so preoccupied with her own work that she hadn't been paying much attention to whatever he'd been up to on his side of the fence.

He reached for one of the cookies she'd made and took a bite. "Sometimes, when I can't sleep, I come out here and weed or prune or just keep myself occupied until I feel ready to climb back into bed."

A revelation of something else they had in common: insomnia. But it had been a long time since Nilda had used those waking hours to sketch or paint, which tended to make her more wound up, less likely to be able to get back to sleep.

She took another look at the closest flower bed. "It's hard to imagine there's anything left for you to do out here. I'm not seeing a whole lotta weeds."

He smiled. "There's always more work to be done. And more projects."

"Like what?"

"Like the hotel." A reference to the nickname that he and Sidney had coined for the coop: the chicken hotel. "It's probably time to tear it down, start from scratch."

Nilda followed his gaze to the coop, which was as gray and weathered as the barn down the road, its wood rough with dry rot. To the right of the coop was an equally weathered stump. A chopping block? She couldn't imagine Graham using it, but perhaps his parents had.

"My dad would give me an earful about the state of it. If he could."

Nilda knew little about Graham's father. Only that he'd been a doctor and that he'd aged into frailty, dying around the same time as Eula Joy.

"Do you miss him?"

Later she'd wish she hadn't asked the question so casually.

At the time she seemed to have dropped from Graham's awareness. He kept his eyes on the coop as he spoke. "To the world my father was a prince among men. *Old Emmerly's still making house calls, can you believe it? Rain, sleet, or the devil himself won't keep him away.* Yeah, people around here held him in pretty high regard."

Remembering what she'd learned from Helen, Nilda wondered whether Eula Joy was one of the exceptions.

"But to me, he was a controlling perfectionist, a stone-cold bastard. I could never live up to his standards, no matter how hard I tried." Graham looked her in the eye. "So, no, I don't miss him. And honestly? It's a relief that he's gone."

Nilda didn't know what to say, or whether she should say anything at all. As if sensing her confusion, Graham scooted closer, took her hand. "I feel like we've gotten to the point where we can be honest with each other, even about difficult things. I hope you feel that way too."

She nodded but found it hard to meet his gaze. Maybe because she hadn't gotten to the point where she could reveal difficult things to him, at least not the most uncomfortable ones.

She tried to change the subject. "So tell me your plans for the hotel. Are you going to do anything special?"

This seemed to cheer him. "Yes, indeed. I was thinking of taking a page from Farleigh's playbook. Maybe build something with minarets."

"Seriously?"

"Seriously."

Nilda thought of the model houses and her time in the leaning chamber. Given his interest in Nathaniel Farleigh, Graham would want to hear about these things, more than anyone she knew. Yet she wasn't finished thinking them through for herself. And if she were to share them with anyone, Toni would come first.

"I can't wait to see what you come up with," she said.

Wanting to get off the subject of Nathaniel Farleigh, she thought of something that had occurred to her during lunch, something she hadn't wanted to bring up when Sidney was in earshot.

"Question for you. Do all poppies contain opium?"

Graham didn't quite smile, didn't quite scowl. It was a *Where did that come from?* kind of look.

"Some of them do, some of them don't."

"What about the ones here?"

"These are *Papaver somniferum.* And, yes, their seed pods contain opium. But I assure you they're nothing remarkable. You'll find them in gardens all over the world."

"And that's not at all illegal."

He downed the last strawberry and tossed the stem in his cup. "With poppies it's all about intent, and action. If I grew them to extract opium, that would be illegal. But I grow them for their beauty, nothing more. Like most every other gardener."

She remembered his stories of harvesting sap in the forest, of foraging for mushrooms. It wasn't hard to imagine him bending over a poppy plant and slicing into one of the pods.

"You've never even considered extracting opium? Just for curiosity's sake?"

"No, I haven't." He gave her a cold, appraising look, as if she'd accused him of something far worse. "Just who do you think I am, Nilda Ricci?"

She felt a shock of guilt, confusion. "I…I'm sorry, I didn't mean—"

He gave her a *fooled-you* smile, which didn't amuse her at all. Still, she held her tongue.

"It was a good question," he said. "And I never want you to feel you can't ask me about...about anything."

The beach ball landed on the blanket, just missing the cookies.

Graham grabbed it and got to his feet, and soon he was off with Sidney, tossing the ball back and forth with her, and chasing the chickens. Watching them, Nilda returned to his question. *Just who do you think I am?*

If he'd truly wanted an answer, she wasn't sure what she would have said. And how would he have answered the same question about her? Would he have been at just as much of a loss for words?

Those mutual voids of information, they weren't always a negative. Surely, they kept a good share of romantic relationships from falling apart, or at least delayed their end. She didn't want to know who Graham fucked in his dreams, or how he might have fantasized about killing his father. And if he'd extracted opium and used it, she wasn't sure she'd want to know that either. Not if it was just a fleeting product of his curiosity, or distant enough in his past.

Certainly, there were things he wouldn't want to know about her, and one of them had been coming to mind more and more: Clay. She missed him. More than she'd been able to admit to Clay, or to herself. And though she couldn't help this feeling, she could help what she did about it: keeping her distance from him, and more important, reminding herself that he wasn't going to magically turn into someone who deserved her trust.

It was time to get home, make progress on the piles of laundry she'd left in the utility room. She rose from the blanket and called to Sidney, who ran for the lemonade she'd left for Fuzzy and drank it down.

"Can I have more, Mommy?"

"I'm not sure there's any left."

Graham was with them now, helping Nilda gather things up from the blanket. "There's just enough for you," he said to Sidney. "Let's go get it."

In the kitchen Graham poured Sidney the last of the lemonade. Then he patted Nilda's shoulder.

"Let me get you that book."

"What book?"

"The one with the ant remedy."

"Oh yeah."

On their last date, she'd mentioned the armies of ants who seemed to have taken up an endless march across her kitchen floor. "I have just what you need," he'd said: a compendium of DIY household "solutions," including natural ant repellants.

As Graham headed for his study, Nilda washed the empty lemonade pitcher, taking a closer look at something she'd noticed in passing before: a chipped ceramic plaque, not much bigger than a coaster, to the right of the sink. *Bless This House*, it said, the message bordered by roses.

So unlike Graham, who seemed not at all religious or into kitsch of any sort. Perhaps it was a trace of his mother? Something he couldn't bring himself to take down? Graham hadn't spoken much of his mom, saying only that she'd died a few years before. Now Nilda imagined that this reticence had come from grief, not from the sort of ill will he bore for his father. She understood the long reach of grief all too well and knew that certain belongings of loved ones weren't so easy to toss.

"I have to go to the bathroom, Mommy."

Nilda placed the pitcher in the drying rack and started washing the cutting board. "You know where it is, right?" She nodded behind her, toward the hall, and heard Sidney push away from the table.

A moment later, Graham's voice echoed through the hall. *"Stop!"*

Nilda dropped the cutting board into the sink and rushed to the hall. There, Sidney was stepping away from the bathroom door, looking more confused than frightened. She kept her eyes on Graham, who was standing in the entrance to the study. Nilda had never seen him so wild-eyed, so alarmed.

Then she realized why: Sidney had been about to open the door to the cellar, just a few steps away from the bathroom door. An easy mistake, and one Nilda could have made herself.

In a calmer voice, Graham pointed out the error. Then he approached the cellar door, turned the key in the lock.

He knelt before Sidney and lifted his chin, pointed to a spot just beneath it.

"See this scar?"

"Yeah."

"I got it when I was about your age. From falling down the cellar stairs."

Sidney studied the scar, the way she studied bugs or caterpillars or any small thing that had captured her curiosity.

"I don't want anything like that to happen to you," he said. "Because I care about you. Do you understand?"

Sidney looked to Nilda, as if for an answer.

She didn't have one, too distracted by Graham's words. *Because I care about you.*

Was he implying that Nilda didn't? That her lack of oversight could have led to a trip to the emergency room, or worse? She knew her daughter far better than Graham ever would, knew how observant she was. If Sidney had opened the cellar door, it was unlikely she would have stepped blindly ahead, down into darkness.

Unlikely but possible, no? The sort of possibility a responsible mother would never take a chance on.

Part of Nilda wanted to apologize, to Graham or Sidney or both of them. Part of her wanted to tell him to fuck off. Neither response would make the situation better, or relieve her guilt.

"Time to go home," she said.

Angus met them at the back door, tail wagging. With a squeal Sidney ran down the hall ahead of him, Fuzzy in a football hold, Angus on her heels. After both of them vanished into the living room, Nilda took Graham's book of household remedies into the kitchen, set it on the hutch for future reference.

Laundry had to come first. As she started for the utility room, she noticed a high, distant hum. She stepped back into the hallway and followed the sound to the dining room, where the pedestal fan was running at its highest speed. She hadn't turned it on today, she was sure—the morning had been unusually cool.

She shut off the fan and started back for the hall. Then she caught a glimmering, to her left: shards of green glass, scattered across the floor in front of her mother's sculpture. The shards were so tiny—some of them glinting like sand—that it was hard to tell what had broken, even when she got up close. Then a curved bit gave her the answer: part of the handle of the vase Graham had given her, after their first real date.

It didn't make any sense that the vase had smashed here. Once the flowers in it had faded, she'd washed it and put it back on the credenza, which was across the room from the sculpture.

Could Helen have broken it? If she had, she would have cleaned up the mess and copped to the accident, no doubt with apologies. But this didn't look like an accident. The vase seemed not to have toppled from a surface but to have exploded spontaneously. Trying to get her mind around how this might have happened, Nilda pictured Helen tossing the vase to the ceiling, then jumping back to behold the results.

She laughed at this absurdity, then dismissed it.

Another possibility came to mind, perhaps just as absurd: she'd gained entry into that world that was as clear to the See-er as these shards of glass were to Nilda. As much as she'd doubted that world's existence, she'd longed for it, hoping for a connection to her mother. Now that longing had turned into unease, from the sense that more of her life might be slipping beyond her control.

Once again, she reached for rational explanations. The running fan? Some defect in the switch. The shattered vase? Some…some *what?*

As she lay in bed that night, she couldn't take her mind off those scattered shards, and behind them, the red waves of her mother's sculpture. They looked like a force of destruction, frozen in time.

Was the shattering a message from her? A warning?

Although that seemed a stretch, she couldn't fight the thought. And as she drifted closer to sleep, her mother's last words returned to her. *Just wait, you'll see.*

This house makes me feel like a big kid, Jim. Seems every week I'm noticing something new about the architectural features or finding something that the guy who built it left behind. Yesterday it was blueprints for a wacky looking treehouse with a snail shell kind of structure. It's the kind of thing I'd want to climb up into and explore, even at my age.

—From a letter from Robert Austerlane to his brother,
July 12, 1968

19

H e rises from his chair by the fire, points to the one next to it. A wing chair of gold brocade, worn at the seat and the arms.

"Have a seat," he says.

And she does, not asking him what he's doing alive and in her house—his house. She's close enough to waking to know he isn't actually there; nor, really, is she.

As he sits back down, she considers his resemblance to the photograph she'd found on Wikipedia. He has the same long chin and high forehead, and the same eyes, which remind her of Mark Twain's: on alert for bullshit, and topped with bushy, up-winged brows.

The clothes match those from the photograph, except that they're in color: the tweed of his vest, jacket, and trousers brown, the silk of his tie a shiny black. The only anomaly, his shoes: purple Converse, just like the ones her mother used to wear.

He studies her with those Twain-like eyes and says, "It's been a gift to have you here."

From somewhere, the weighted tick of a pendulum clock.

"Mrs. Austerlane lived for her dogs and cigarettes, mostly. And all of this"—He gestures toward the room—"was mere background to her. As for Mr. Austerlane, God rest his soul, his endless questions about this house called to mind the eagerness of a schoolboy, not the sophisticated interest of someone like you. Someone with an artist's eye for details."

He sits forward, his watch chain swaying into the firelight. "I detect fellow feeling between us, Nilda. Perhaps some common understanding."

She wants to disagree, wants to say—and believe—that their feelings, and their minds, are in no way aligned, a connection that now seems dangerous. All she can say is this: "But I destroyed that model of yours. It—" It *what?* She can't find the right words. "It overcame me."

He smiles, gold flashing from a crown. "As a man who's torn apart as many things as I've built, I'm in no position to criticize you, my dear. What was it that Bakunin said? About the urge to destroy being a creative urge? I'd hazard to say you know that urge as well as I do. I'd hazard to say it drove your work on Tenneman, to brilliant effect, I might add."

He sits back, no longer smiling. "If that painting makes one thing clear, it's that you have a keen sense for scoundrels. You know one when you see one, even if you don't want to believe what you're seeing. Or can't bear to."

Unsure of what to say, she holds her silence.

"My advice is to always trust your senses."

Feeling pinned by his stare, she looks to the mantelpiece, to the carved faces animated by the flickering blaze. There, on the left pillar, is her mother—sleeping, smiling. A comfort.

"I hope that my mantel work pleases you. Same with the leaning chamber."

She keeps her eyes on her mother, says nothing.

"I meant it—and everything I've done—as a balm for the soul. May it be that for you, whenever you should need it."

She sleeps. I commit this belief to paper, close as I can get to a prayer: She'll come around. I'll do everything I can to make it so.

—From the journals of Graham Emmerly, July 19th, 2019

20

She woke to full light, his side of the bed empty, cold. Maybe this absence was his most honest response to what she'd said, speaking more truth than his words: *I'm glad you felt you could tell me this.*

Before he'd said them, before she'd fallen back to sleep and into that strange dream, they'd lain together in the predawn dark, talking. About books they loved or didn't, bands they loved or didn't, places they'd hoped to travel to, someday. Nothing profound, really. Not at first.

At some point he started musing about the Badlands, and their buttes and spires of layered rock, something he'd always wanted to see. "I'd love to see them with you, Nilda. I'd love to see *all* these places with you."

She squeezed his hand, hoping she could leave things at that. After a moment he went on.

"I'm feeling like we could have a future together. And I'm hoping you might be feeling the same thing."

Future. The word landed on her like a weight. So did his sense of hope. She struggled to sort through her feelings and figure out a response. Did she have feelings for him? Yes. Yet they seemed more of the loins than the heart.

She pulled her hand from his and rolled over to face him. Then she told him the truth, or most of it, trying to spare the more hurtful details.

She told him she wasn't sure she'd ever want another long-term romantic relationship, with him or anyone else.

She told him she'd understand if he'd like to break things off and look for someone more open to commitment.

Then she watched him stare at the ceiling, his face revealing nothing of his thoughts, and calling to mind a carved bust— Narcissus in profile. In time he glanced her way and smiled.

"I'm glad you felt you could tell me this," he said. "And I don't want to break things off. For now, let's just take things from day to day. As long as that's okay with you."

She scooched in closer and kissed him on the cheek. "It's more than okay."

Now, in the Graham-less bed, she felt a surge of regret. Maybe she should have given things more time before delivering a reality check. Maybe, in a month or two, she'd feel different about their relationship and its potential.

Not likely. Soon enough, she was sure, she'd feel relief for having said what she'd said. Relief to no longer be shadowed by the sense that Graham was constructing a different reality from hers where their relationship was concerned. A process she'd abetted by just letting things roll along.

Nilda rose from the bed and threw on her T-shirt, stepped into her underwear. Then she headed downstairs, toward the aroma of coffee and frying eggs.

She found him at his stove, spatula in hand. "Sunny side up, right?"

"Right."

She headed for the toaster and dropped two slices of bread into it. "Just shy of burned, right?"

"Yep."

As she grabbed the butter dish from the fridge, he started whistling a tune she couldn't place, an old, upbeat number. It was almost as if they'd never had that uncomfortable conversation. Or maybe he was just putting up a cheery front.

Setting the butter on the table, she noticed something on one of the chairs: a box with six jars of gold-brown liquid, darker than the tonic he'd made for her.

"What's this?" she asked.

He glanced her way, then slid their eggs onto two waiting plates. "More tonic, for your new work."

She'd told him that she was putting the finishing touches on her "portrait," the Tenneman painting, and ready to start on something new—what, exactly, she wasn't sure.

"Why's it darker?"

"I concentrated the formula, to give it a bit more oomph. But the ingredients are all the same."

She didn't remember seeing the jars last night, when she'd gone to the kitchen for a drink of water. But it had been dark, and perhaps she'd overlooked them. Or maybe he'd pulled all this together this morning, as his side of the bed went cold.

This raised a question, and she saved it until they'd sat down to breakfast.

"Do you do all your chemistry stuff in the kitchen?"

She was thinking not just of the tonic but of the Chickie messenger crystal and the various "hobbyist" experiments he'd mentioned in passing, with descriptions that were always Greek to her.

"Some of it. But for more technical work, I use a very rudimentary lab I set up in the cellar."

She took another bite of the eggs, then gave them a rest. Never a big breakfast eater, she seemed to have less and less of an appetite for it.

"I'd love to see it sometime." She'd always been interested in how and where things got made, starting with the tours of factories she'd watched as a kid, on *Sesame Street*.

He started buttering the second slice of his nearly burned toast. "I doubt you'd find it very interesting. And the floor's a bit puddled now—sump pump problems. But once those are fixed, you can definitely have a look."

Not exactly a warm invitation. If he didn't want her nosing around his workspace, she respected that. She'd always felt the same way about her studio space, and she kept a lot of her drawings and paintings, whether in-process or completed, out of others' view. Some pieces were just for herself, ways of figuring things out or letting off some creative steam. Maybe chemists needed the same kind of leeway.

She tried to change the subject. "Wherever you make the tonic, I'm grateful for it."

He reached across the table and took her hand. "Anything for my favorite artist."

Nilda didn't try the new tonic until long after dinner, long after she'd put Sidney to bed. As she flipped through her most recent sketches, looking for something that might inspire a painting, she sipped the dark liquid, which did indeed taste like a distillation of the old tonic, the fermentation-like bite even more acute. If Graham had told her this was some earthy cocktail he'd invented, she would have believed him. Except for the fact that although half the jar was gone—no, well over half—she didn't feel the least bit buzzed.

But something was different. The white of her sketchpad looked brighter, and against it, the lines and shapes she'd drawn in pencil and Conté crayon seemed to vibrate. Everything around her looked brighter too, the walls of the studio, the canvases stacked in a corner, the diner mugs by the coffee pot.

For relief she closed her eyes, lowered her face into her hands. With the darkness came memories: a flashing gold crown, a watch chain swaying into the firelight.

She remembered little else about the dream of Nathaniel Farleigh. He'd said something about the Tenneman painting—just what, she couldn't recall. And then there was the quote from Bakunin, about the urge to destroy being a creative urge: a recycled bit of reading from graduate school. Surely, nothing more. Yet the image of Farleigh persisted, even as she tried to push it from her mind.

A challenge, she decided. *Take it.*

She pulled a fresh canvas onto an easel and readied her paints. Then she started working, not giving up until she'd reached exhaustion, near dawn.

The eastern screech owl will prey upon almost anything that moves, within certain limits of size. Though they may flee from approaching humans, this is not always the case, and they have been known to attack individuals who get too close to their nests.

—From *Field Guide to Owls of the Northeast* by Carlane Pritchard

21

MAY 1992

The back yard, after dark

In her left hand: a gin and tonic. In her right: a newly lit Salem. Within reach, on the side table: her ashtray, cigarette pack, and lighter, and also Robert's binoculars, from their long-ago excursions to Fenway Park, which these days, might as well have been on another continent.

From her lap Bea and Rex watched the woods with an intentness perhaps exceeding her own. As if expecting the trees to launch treats their way, they were sitting up straight, ears perked forward like radar dishes.

A whinny sounded, answered by a trilling. Same as last night, and the night before. Again came the whinny, then the trilling. Possibly the calls of a mated pair, according to her Audubon guide.

As quietly as she could, she dropped her cigarette into the ashtray, traded her gin and tonic for the binoculars, and searched the trees for the owls. No easy feat as they were gray, and the only illumination came from the failing porchlight behind her. No sign of them in the beeches, where they'd landed two nights running. The spruces were likewise empty.

Looking to the oak, she spotted something in the knot hole: a tufted V of beak and ears, a pair of blinking eyes. Of course he—she?—had picked that spot: a storybook cave-let, perfect for setting up housekeeping. The owl whinnied. Then came the trilling, from higher in the oak. As she scanned the upper branches, Bea growled, then Rex followed: an answering call and response.

Knowing they saved their growls for humans, she trained her binoculars lower and saw a figure flitting through the more distant trees, running the path on the rise. The Creeper. Who else could it be?

"Monster," she said, not loudly, but enough to scare off the owls. She found the knot hole empty, and scanning the higher branches and the beeches, she saw no sign of either bird. The Creeper, too, had vanished into the woods.

Damn him.

She traded the binoculars for her G&T, sipped it as she rubbed Bea's ears.

Though he'd been home just a couple of months, it seemed like an eternity. Over that time she and Robert had spotted him in the woods at all hours, when they let out the dogs or were up to some other business in the yard. They'd notice him roaming up or down the path, or just slinking through the trees. Whenever he was close enough, they'd see a bag of something swinging from his hand.

What was he up to? At first, she hadn't a clue. Then she did, and the knowledge brought no relief. To the contrary.

This was enough to make her gulp the last of her G&T. She set down the glass and turned back to her cigarette, petting the dogs as she smoked. All the while, she kept an eye out for the Creeper's return.

Though he and his parents lived just next door, the specifics of his expulsion from Hawling Prep had come to her and Robert through the rumor mill, the two of them having avoided the Emmerlys since the chicken debacle. But even before it she'd barely tolerated Clifford Emmerly. With his impressive array of flower beds and vegetable plots, he seemed to regard himself as a country squire, entitled to dispense gardening advice—and criticism—to anyone who would listen.

Robert did, sometimes.

Eula Joy, never. Every time Clifford had approached her with "just a suggestion," she'd cut him off with the truth ("I'm afraid you're wasting your time"), until he gave up entirely. And in the days before the fence removed their yard from Clifford's sight, she'd come to see each of its weedy patches, unpruned shrubs, and blooms of leaf rot as forms of protest-by-neglect—no doubt, the most maddening form of dissent where he was concerned.

As for Dora Emmerly, from the beginning she'd been about as friendly as Eula Joy, which was to say that a wave from a distance (pre–chicken debacle) was as sociable as they'd gotten. That had suited Eula Joy just fine.

What of their son? In earlier years, on the rare occasions she'd encountered him, he'd come across as a quiet child, existing in the shadow of his know-it-all father. Yet something in him seemed to have changed of late, not for the good. Or perhaps some preexisting darkness had been cut loose—by the freedoms he'd found at boarding school maybe, or by puberty's leading edge: dangerously sharp for some.

As she and Robert had learned, there'd been more than one cause for the boy's expulsion from Hawling, but apparently the last straw had been the most dramatic one. God knows how, or where, he'd managed to make a set of cherry bombs, which on a single tear he'd lobbed into three of Hawling's lavoratories—one of them reserved for faculty—before creating an explosive finale in his dormitory's study. By some miracle no one had been hurt, and for that reason, as well as Clifford's status as a major Hawling donor, the boy had been spared a worse punishment.

Her first encounter with him, post-Hawling, had come a month or so before, after she'd let Rex out for a pee, then stepped back inside to finish her lunch. Minutes later, Rex's barking sent her back into the yard. There, she found him yapping at an arm's-length gap in the fence, where the last slats needed to be installed. As she crept closer, she heard the boy's voice over the barking.

"Here, doggie, here."

Then his hand emerged from the gap, holding something out to Rex. This sent her running for the pup. She snatched him up and held him close, then looked into the gap.

There was the boy, squatting in one of Clifford's hosta patches, fixing her with a glare. No, not quite a glare. It reminded her of the look on the face of the troll from *The Three Billy Goats Gruff*, a book that had been a childhood gift, one she wished she'd never received. Its illustrations had been woodcuts, giving the troll's eyes a flat, dead look as he stared upward from his crouch beneath the bridge, waiting to devour the crossing goats. His mouth's black gap made her think of a panting that was nothing like a dog's.

Once she was able to compose herself, she said, "He doesn't trust strangers," hoping her scowl expressed the deeper truth: *And he certainly doesn't trust you.*

He'd withdrawn his hand and whatever had been in it—a cracker? a piece of cheese? Thoughts of the morsel, and his trollish look, brought a revelation. So did the sight of the chickens behind him, strutting free from their coop.

"You lured Bea into your yard, didn't you?"

Bea, Rex, and every other Yorkie she'd ever owned went mad for squirrels, and for the mice that ventured indoors with the first chill of fall. Yet over all the years she and Robert had lived by the Emmerlys, the dogs never chased the chickens— not into the Emmerlys' yard anyway. Whenever the birds were loose from their coop, the pups might bolt in their direction, getting as far as the yard's edge. But they always stopped there, just as she'd trained them to do.

So when Clifford came knocking one afternoon, Bea tucked under one arm, she'd been perplexed.

After claiming that Bea had "invaded" his yard, he said, "She might have taken down a prized hen."

"Well, she didn't, did she?" This probably wasn't the most diplomatic response, and it precipitated a battle of words that culminated in Clifford's threat to "take out any future offenders."

His final words: "I have a shotgun, and I'll use it if I must."

The next day, she called the fence company, and within a week they got to work, at her and Robert's expense, a cost she saw as necessary. Her only regret at the time: that the fence hadn't gone up years before.

Yet a new regret arose as she confronted the boy through the gap in it: that she hadn't caught on to him sooner. When had Bea's "invasion" occurred? Just a week or so after his return from Hawling. Clearly, he'd wanted to make trouble, despite the risk to her dogs. Maybe even because of it.

After she'd accused him of luring Bea, he kept silent, still fixing her with that look. Then he got up and started back to his house.

Did he hear her call him a devil? At the time she wasn't so sure. Soon after, she had little doubt.

Certain mornings since their encounter—four to date— she'd discovered dead animals at the edge of the woods, just in front of her bird-watching chair: two squirrels laid face to face like bedmates, a chipmunk, a rabbit, another squirrel. No signs that they'd been mauled, or dropped at random by a coyote, hawk, or other natural predator. No, there was nothing random about this at all. And now, whenever she caught the boy roaming through the woods, plastic bag swinging from his clutch, she couldn't help but imagine what that bag contained: poison, or its aftermath.

She'd wanted to confront Clifford and Dora about their son's gruesome leavings, but Robert kept discouraging her. Each time, he brought up the hawk explanation, though she could tell he didn't really believe it.

"You can't go around making accusations, Eula, not when you don't have solid proof. And you really shouldn't call him *the Creeper.*"

Yet that's who he'd become to her, and there was no way to push that name, that notion of him, from her mind. As for

getting proof of his crimes, she could set up nighttime surveil-
lance, she supposed: sit by a window for hours, waiting for him
to leave one of his ghastly gifts. But that would give him too
much importance, and too much of her time, which was far
better spent on her loves.

Out of an abundance of caution, she no longer left them in
the yard unattended, even though the fence was now complete.
And just yesterday, she'd warned Helen's son away from the
monster, who come fall would almost certainly be attending
Greenbridge with him. A public school with none of the privi-
leges that wealth could buy.

She scratched Bea's head, then Rex's, and snuffed her cigarette in the ashtray. As she started up from the chair, a sound
stopped her: a whinny...then a trilling, more distant than
before. Surely, the owls were out of her sight. But maybe not
the boy's. She wasn't worried though. They were birds of prey,
more clever than him—and any other mere human—by half.
Under threat they'd attack.

As she made her way back to the house, trailed by the dogs,
the smell of night-blooming flowers assaulted her, from the
direction of the Emmerlys. This brought to mind her long-
ago roamings through Kresge's cosmetics department, where
she'd tried to dodge those perfume-peddling girls with their
ever-spritzing atomizers. Yet she never quite escaped the
miasma of those scents, bringing it home on her clothes.

The perfume of Clifford's flowers was just like that: insinu-
ating itself where it wasn't wanted. Just like his son.

Why waste chaos of the heart, or of the mind, by making order of it? Embrace it. Let it drive you toward something new and unexpected.

—From *The Collected Journals of Nathaniel Farleigh*

22

Nilda paused in her reading, took another sip of wine. Chaos. Lately she'd had more than enough of it, in both heart and mind.

Had it driven her toward something new and unexpected? Where her painting of Farleigh was concerned, she wasn't sure. But she felt freer than she had with other portrait jobs, getting looser and more abstract with her technique, and bringing in whatever elements sprang to mind from his work: carved faces, spy windows, minarets, and more. If these choices weren't exactly unexpected, they'd seemed so at first.

At more calculating moments, like this one, she felt she might get a whole series out of Farleigh. But whenever she was back in her studio, calculation slipped away, mostly. She was all about working ahead on that single portrait of him, which soon enough would be done. Then she'd have to decide whether it was a one-off or the start of something more, whether it was worth sharing or best kept to herself.

Maybe she'd end up pulling a Farleigh, hide it in some closet or cubbyhole for a future resident of this house to discover and puzzle over, or not.

Her phone buzzed on the kitchen table, "Clay" appearing on the screen. Not wanting to wake Sidney, she carried the phone out the back door, answering it as she stepped onto the patio.

"Thanks for calling me back," she said.

All around, the deep blue just before dark. As her eyes adjusted to the dimness, she found her way to the lawn chair she'd placed by the fence, alongside Sidney's kiddie pool. She lowered herself into the chair and pulled a couple of floaters from the water—a leaf and a dead beetle—and tossed them toward the fence.

"I'll be crating the painting tomorrow," she said, drying her hand on her shorts. "You should get it within a week of that."

"Sounds good."

"I also have some more details about the big day."

When she'd first asked Clay about setting up a painting at the Sky Tent festival, she'd given him next to no details, not sure she'd be able to pull off her plan: to transform a traditional portrait of the Fairmoore School's new headmaster into something intended to subvert him and, with any luck, take him down. She'd told Clay nothing of the reason for the subversion: what the headmaster had done to Toni.

Since then, she'd brought him up to speed about all of this, underscoring the greatest benefit and disadvantage of the festival's setting: the Halifax Fairgrounds, which were just across the road from Fairmoore's campus. There, the painting could have the biggest potential impact and pose the greatest possible risk: to Clay, most immediately. When he said he was willing to accept that risk, she promised she'd come up with a plan for dealing with it, as best she could. That's what this call was all about.

"You gotta pen and paper handy?"

"Give me a sec." A moment later, he was back on the line. "I'm ready."

"You need to get the painting to the exhibit area by nine a.m. on the third. Tell the set-up crew it's for exhibitor 359, and they'll tell you where it needs to go."

"What's the pick-up time?"

"You don't have to worry about that."

Silence on Clay's end. Then "I don't understand."

"I don't want the painting back. They can trash it, as far as I'm concerned." Most likely, she'd be getting calls about the abandoned painting on the burner phone. Nothing she couldn't ignore.

"Jesus. Are you sure?"

"More than sure." She'd had her fill of Tenneman and wanted to be shut of him, or at least the painted version of him. One thing she wasn't shut of: her portrait commission from Fairmoore. She'd been dreading calling her contact there and withdrawing from the commission, but she couldn't put that off any longer. Tomorrow would have to be the day.

"One other thing," she said. "I don't think you'll need to be there for the uncrating. But let's say the set-up crew wants you there, and they don't like what they see. Let's say they start asking uncomfortable questions, like, 'What's your beef with Tenneman?' Just say you're not in a position to answer them. You're just doing the artist a favor. And then hightail it out of there." She'd already told Clay that *the artist* was fictional, that she'd entered the show under an assumed name and hadn't even signed the painting. "But if you feel like you're in over your head, for any reason, you can call Toni's lawyer."

Nilda gave Clay the number for Rosie Martinez, who, with Toni's help, was already starting to build a case against Tenneman. Rosie knew all about the painting.

"All right," Clay said. The tone of his voice suggested the opposite.

"I don't think there's anything to worry about, really. I just want you to be prepared."

Nilda slapped the mosquitoes that were buzzing around her ankles, delivering stinging bites. She needed to change the kiddie pool water, which seemed to have turned into a bug hatchery.

As she straightened up, she noticed that a familiar tune was playing on Clay's end. She couldn't quite place it.

Now his voice cut into it. "What's your social-media plan?"

Nilda's reluctance to telegraph bits of herself, bits of her work, into the potentially hostile but mostly indifferent void of the internet had become a running joke between the two of them. Clay saw this telegraphing as necessary for any artist who cared about building an audience. She saw it as something she'd never be able to put more than a half-hearted, half-assed effort into, and thus a waste of her time. For the push against Tenneman, she'd have to adjust her attitude.

"Toni and I are gonna send out some alerts, around the time the exhibit opens."

"Great. I'll pitch in as soon as I can. And I'll use the band's handle too." This was no small favor. Between his personal handle and the one for the band, Clay had thousands of followers on Twitter. Same with Instagram.

"That would be fantastic, Clay—thanks. Thanks for everything you're doing to help."

"It's no problem. If I can play any role in taking that asshole down, I'm happy to do it."

In the silence that fell between them, the familiar song seemed to take up more space. Or had Clay turned up the volume?

Left on Main, right on Elm, straight ahead till you see the river
Then keep on driving, keep on driving, right to the water's edge…

"The Bridles," Nilda said. The name of the band, not the song.

"Yep."

A decade ago, the Bridles had come and gone with little notoriety, leaving a single album behind. But to Nilda they were inseparable from her and Clay's beginnings. She remembered him leading her up those creaking wooden stairs, up to his third-floor apartment, for the first time. A moment later, as if this were the sole reason for the climb, he put the band's album on his turntable, dropped the needle.

A turntable, she'd thought then. *And vinyl. Rows and rows of it.* Records seemed to have overrun Clay's tiny, slant-walled living room.

The first song on the album—the song about the water's edge—pushed thoughts of the records, thoughts of the room, aside. It started with that ghostly female voice—solo at first, then threaded through a banjo-mandolin call and response.

Catherine, Nilda had thought, when she'd first heard that voice. *From* Wuthering Heights.

The song took a weightier turn, with drums and guitars, the singer's voice rising above this. Then it went solo again, before fading out.

The whole time, Nilda was entranced, as if she were hearing the pleas of a ghost. The whole time, she was equally aware of Clay, of how close he stood as they watched the record spin.

I knew you needed to hear this.

She felt these words before he said them.

When he reached for her hand, she took his and held it tight, and neither one of them let go during the next song and maybe the one after that. This time of holding hands, and just listening to the music, had become more memorable to her than the kiss that followed, or maybe any first kiss in her life. From time to time in the years that followed, when either she or Clay came across a "need-to-hear" song or record, they'd listen to it together, holding hands. But none of these moments equaled the first, maybe just because it was the first. Eventually, they gave up on trying to recreate it.

She guessed it was no accident that she was hearing this old Bridles' album now. Clay must have dropped the needle just before calling her, and he must have been sitting next to a speaker.

"Feeling a bit nostalgic?" The words sounded harsher than she'd intended.

"Yes."

The first song, whatever it was, ended. The next one began.

"We had some good times, Nilda."

She couldn't deny this, and she didn't. "Yes. We had some very good times."

Those times would exist for as long as she did, in a compartment within herself that she struggled to keep closed, and sometimes didn't want to. Whenever it opened, the memories played back with a background hum of sadness from what she'd lost: not just the way she and Clay used to be but also trust—in him, and maybe in her own judgment where men were concerned, a loss that was possibly all to the good.

"Nilda?"

"I'm still here."

"I miss you."

"I miss you too." She did, maybe more than ever, but it wasn't the whole truth. "I mean, I—"

A twig snapped, startling her. Looking over her shoulder, she saw nothing in motion, just Sidney's kickball in the middle distance, beyond it the woods. The next thought froze her: the sound could have come from Graham's side of the fence. She listened for footsteps, but all she could detect were faint clucks from the chickens, and the scent of Graham's flowers. Even here, it weighted the air.

"You mean *what?*" Clay said.

Probably, some creature had snapped the twig. Perhaps one of the raccoons that, according to Graham, regularly trundled from the woods to his trash barrels and posed a growing threat to the chickens. Still, she rose from her chair and started for the opposite side of the yard.

"I miss what we were," she said, "when things were good. But there's no going back there, Clay."

The Bridles filled the silence on his end, but they sounded fainter now. Perhaps he'd turned down the volume. As she waited for him to speak, headlights flooded the drive, grew brighter. Helen. Nilda had forgotten she was working this evening.

"Sorry," she said. "I have to go."

She signed off and headed toward Helen, feeling more fatigued than she'd realized. That wouldn't necessarily spare her from another sleepless night, or from more weird dreams, and whatever troubling fragments they might leave behind.

A child with a vivid imagination is never really alone. That doesn't mean she's never disquieted by her company.

—From "The Active-Minded Child" by Emily Straw

23

Sidney felt a weight on the bed. Turning, she saw no one in the nightlight's glow. "Alex?"

Night knitter, night knitter, I'll never know why
You've made it your duty to cover the sky

Her grandma's voice, whisper-singing the way she used to. This had always helped Sidney fall asleep. Now it made her more alert.

With a blanket so thick and so dark in its hue
That only the moon and the stars can break through

She reached for the weighted spot and felt warmer air, nothing else. So she turned all her attention to the song, taking in every word.

Enough light to satisfy possums and owls
Who go on the hunt with their hoots and their howls
While I remain safe in your needle-made night
Hoping for dreams that will only delight

But bad dreams will come, and you know this is true
Knit me right, knit me right, knit me right through

The end of the song.

"Grandma?"

No answer. Sidney reached for the spot where she'd felt the warmth. Now it was gone.

She whispered some of the words to herself: "But bad dreams will come, and you know this is true." This part had never bothered her before, but now it felt like a scary promise. Was something bad coming? Something only her grandma knew about?

She closed her eyes and pictured her grandma sitting on the edge of the bed, smiling at her. Together, they repeated the end of the song, now a wish: "Knit me right through, knit me right through, knit me right through..."

There are no facts, only interpretations.

—Friedrich Nietzsche

24

B y 10:00 a.m. it was eighty degrees and climbing, the house awhir with fans that recirculated the humid air. Already, sweat had soaked through Nilda's T-shirt. Lifting it to the fan in the kitchen window, she finished her third glass of water. As she set the glass in the sink, she glanced at the shelf to its right. Hadn't she left the tonic there last night?

Looking about, she found no sign of it on the counters, on the table, or on the hutch across the room. She dug through the draining rack, setting aside the mugs, plates, and bowls that Helen must have washed after Nilda turned in last night. Lifting a saucepan, she found the tonic jar: spotless, sparkling, empty.

"What the hell?"

It had been Nilda's last jar.

As she thought things through, her temper cooled. Helen would have seen not a wondrous tonic but a half-full jar of brown liquid, not far from a sink full of dirty dishes. No doubt, to Helen, it had been just part of another mess that Nilda had left behind, and God only knew there'd been plenty of them.

Just be thankful for everything she does around here, Nilda thought.

And it wasn't as if her tonic supply would run out, unless she wanted it to.

One excuse for a re-up was sitting on the hutch: the book of household remedies she'd promised to return to Graham. The cure it had suggested for her ant invasion—a mash-up of orange rinds and black pepper—seemed to have done the trick.

Third knock, no answer, though his car was in the drive. As Nilda turned to leave, she heard footsteps behind the door. Then Graham appeared, looking distracted, as if she'd interrupted something.

"I'm sorry," she said. "I should have called first."

"Not at all. It's always a pleasure."

Handing him the book, with thanks, she once again turned to leave.

"Come in for a minute, please."

"I shouldn't really, I—"

"Please. I just made some lemonade. How can you pass up a glass?"

He stepped aside, and she took the invitation. As he led her down the hall, toward the kitchen, an aroma grew more and more intense: like that of Christmas greenery, but with tones of mint, florals, underlying earthiness. The kitchen table proved to be the source, its surface covered with various sprigs of green, some of which she recognized: rosemary, basil, peppermint. There were also clumps of dark purple berries, and clusters of tiny flowers, yellow and white.

"What's all this about?" she asked.

"Tinctures. I've decided to make a bunch of new ones."

"For cocktails?" Nilda took a seat by a pile of pine sprigs.

"Some of them, maybe. But most of them will be medicinal."

He pointed to one of the berry clumps. "Elderberries. They can reduce inflammation. Same with rosemary, which is also great for the circulation. And possibly the eyes."

Though Nilda understood that herbs could be medicine—at least some of them—her enthusiasm for plants-as-remedies would never equal Graham's, as much as she'd taken to his tonic.

"Are you going to use all the tinctures?"

Graham laughed. "Certainly not. I'm just playing around, seeing what I can come up with. But maybe I'll try to sell a few of them, if they're up to snuff."

He took two glasses from the cabinet and filled them with the sweating pitcher on the counter. "You'd be welcome to try any of them, of course."

"Thanks," Nilda said, almost sure she'd take a pass when the time came.

Graham pulled a bowl from the fridge, dropped something from it into one glass, then the other.

"What was that?" she asked.

"Herb-infused lemon slices."

What kind of herbs? Not wanting to seem rude, she kept this question to herself.

"I can take yours out," he said.

"No, it's fine."

He handed her a lemonade. Then he turned a chair around to face her, sat down.

"Cheers," he said, clinking her glass.

"Cheers."

As before, the lemonade was perfect: cold, not too sweet, and intense with flavor, suggesting the presence of zest. She also tasted a greenness—no doubt, the herbal infusion. It added a layer of complexity. A welcome one, she concluded.

"What do you think?" he asked, looking uncertain.

"It's delicious."

He smiled, it seemed with the satisfaction of a job well done.

Graham Emmerly, alchemist of nature.

The look on his face. His long, unruly hair. The smells of herbs and earth that suffused the humid air. They brought to mind someone—some*thing*?—Nilda hadn't thought of for years: the Green Man, nature personified. A professor of hers had been obsessed with him, showing multiple slides of his representation in medieval stonework: sometimes as a face surrounded by foliage; other times as a face overtaken by it, or made of it.

He's all about the cycle of life, the professor had said. Birth then decay then death, echoing the change of seasons. One of the images of the Green Man that Nilda remembered best melded death and birth: a gravestone etching of a skull sprouting flowers. Yet this image unsettled her no more than the others; or, rather, all of them troubled her equally. Nature, they suggested, wasn't benign, but an indifferent, devouring force.

"Something on your mind?"

Nilda didn't want to bring up the Green Man, though she imagined that Graham would take great interest in him. But another subject surfaced, something she'd decided to keep to herself, until now.

"Were you gardening last night?"

"Why do you ask?"

"I thought I might have heard you out there around eight-thirty, nine."

Actually, she wasn't at all sure it was Graham she'd heard. But since last night, she'd been troubled by the possibility that he'd caught her side of the conversation with Clay, or at least some of it. Hopefully, not the "I miss you" part.

"Couldn't have been me. I wrapped my yard work up before dinner."

"Maybe it was the raccoons then."

"Most likely."

Graham finished his lemonade and made room on the table for his glass. Then he scooted closer and took her free hand. "If you ever think I'm out there, come on over, if you're so inclined. I'll always be happy to see you."

Nilda smiled. Then she set her half-finished glass on the table's edge, rose from her chair. She'd been here longer than she'd intended, and the tonic refill could wait.

"I should get home. Sidney will be wondering where I am."

Would she?

Graham didn't try to convince her to stay, just followed her into the hall. There, the front door seemed farther away than ever, or maybe she was just willing that to be so. The closer she got to it, the more aware she was of him, and of an unexpected bloom of desire.

She stopped at the door, sensed him drawing nearer. Then he pressed himself against her back, closed his arms around her waist.

"I really should—"

Nilda let the words drift off. Despite the heat, despite her better judgment, she wanted him. She turned and pulled him into a kiss. A moment later, they were climbing the stairs.

এ

Nilda woke with a start and sat up in bed.

She looked around for her phone and found it on the floor. The time on the screen sent a jolt through her: 11:23.

"Shit." She was as pissed at Graham as she was at herself, though she knew that wasn't fair. He hadn't exactly forced her up the stairs and into his bed, and it wasn't on him to wake her from a post-sex nap.

As she pulled on her clothes, a scene from a dream returned to her. She'd found herself standing in one of Farleigh's oddities: the narrow, doorless nook in her living room. And she'd been trapped by some force that froze her in place, helpless as water seeped up from the floor and rose to her ankles, then her shins, then her knees. Whatever happened next, she couldn't remember.

Now she noticed that she'd roused Graham. He was propped up on one arm, watching her dress.

"What's wrong?" he said.

The dream must have shown on her face. "Nothing. I just need to get home."

He patted her side of the bed: an invitation.

"I can't."

"Give me just a minute. *Please.*"

To make it clear this was all the time she could spare, she sat down on the farthest corner of the bed from him.

"I just wanna make sure you're okay," he said. "It sounded like you were having a nightmare."

"Oh God. Was I talking in my sleep?"

"A little."

"What did I say?"

Absently, he traced a finger along her side of the bed. "At first, I couldn't make out your words. You were just tossing and turning, mumbling, but clearly distressed. Then you cried, 'Get me out of here!' Like you needed to escape from somewhere."

"I did," she said. She told him everything she could remember of the dream, and when she'd finished, he looked even more troubled. "It was just a dream, Graham. I mean, I'm not going to go all Farleigh." She smiled, trying to lighten things up. But Graham didn't seem to see any humor in the matter.

"What do you mean, *all Farleigh?*"

"You know, getting freaked out by the house, or however you put it." If Nilda was remembering Graham's words correctly, Farleigh had sensed that the walls of the house were closing in on him.

Graham climbed out of bed, sat down by Nilda, and took her hand. "Farleigh's work is powerful, Nilda. Not to be underestimated."

Sweat trickled down her back, making her crave a cool shower. "You think it's getting to me. The way it got to him."

Graham looked down at their clasped hands, seeming to consider his words. "I can't speak for you, of course. But what I can say is this. Many features of Farleigh's constructions were intended to influence the mind. He meant that to be a healthy influence, and it seems like it was, at the asylum he designed. But maybe there can be too much of a good thing, an overload that can affect you emotionally, especially if you're exposed to it day in and day out. I'm concerned that your house is on overload, Nilda."

She wanted to push back against this. But she was finding it hard to dismiss his concerns entirely. She thought of the faces on the fireplace mantel and pillars, the oddly placed windows, and worst of all, the model house that had literally sickened her. When she smashed it, she wasn't herself, and whoever—whatever—she'd become then scared her.

Then she thought of Eula Joy.

"The house didn't get to my great-aunt, as far as I know."

Graham seemed to be thinking this through. "My feeling is, not everyone is equally sensitive to architectural details, or any details, for that matter. There's a reason you're an artist, Nilda."

She'd never imagined that such a sensitivity could have this kind of downside, but it seemed plausible.

"So what am I supposed to do about this? Move?"

"No, no, no. Not at all." He moved his hand to her thigh. "You aren't Nathaniel Farleigh, in multiple ways, and in one critical one."

Graham stared into her eyes, as if he might convey the answer telepathically.

"He came to be an isolated man, out of circumstance and his own choosing. And I believe that was his undoing. But *you*, you'll never have to worry about that. I'll always be here for you, to talk you through any of this, help you with anything."

He tightened his hold on her thigh.

"No one will ever be willing to do more for you, Nilda. I can promise you that."

This didn't comfort her—quite the opposite. She pulled away from him, rose from the bed, and headed for the door.

"Nilda?"

Not wanting to see his reaction, she spoke over her shoulder before stepping into the hall. "Let's talk soon."

Not a wish or a promise, just the best thing she could think of on the fly. As she headed down the stairs and out the door, he made no move to follow her. For that she was grateful.

At home Nilda rushed to the living room, finding Sidney just where she'd left her—sprawled out on the floor and drawing with her crayons, Angus curled up at her side. The only sign that Sidney had left the room: a crumb-covered plate on the coffee table. No doubt, the remains of her favorite snack, cheese and crackers.

Next to the plate was a stack of drawings. Nilda picked it up and started paging through Sidney's work: Angus and Fuzzy lounging on grass, presumably in the back yard; one of Graham's chickens strutting past his flowers; a Finster-looking fish swimming in blue water.

"These are really great, Sidney."

Sidney kept her eyes on her work. "Thanks."

The last picture showed a dark-haired boy in a T-shirt and shorts, standing in more blue water. He was holding what looked like a bottle of soda.

"Is this Alex?"

Sidney glanced at the picture. "No. It's a boy who plays in the creek. Me and Alex saw...I mean, Alex told me about him."

"Did you go to the creek, Sidney?"

Though Sidney didn't speak, Nilda knew the answer.

"You're not supposed to go there without me, remember?"

Sidney nodded.

Not wanting to start another fight, Nilda said, "I'll take you there anytime you'd like. Maybe later today?"

Sidney paused at her drawing, then shook her head. "I don't want to see that boy again. He scares me."

Another figment of Sidney's imagination?

Again, Nilda studied the picture, trying to remember whether she'd seen any boys around who looked like this. In town, maybe. But out here, the only children she'd encountered were Toni's girls, when they came for visits. If the boy from the drawing was real, maybe he'd come from the suburb on the other side of the woods? Though that would be quite a hike, she supposed it was possible.

Taking a closer look at the picture, she realized that something was off about it. The eyes. Usually, when Sidney drew human eyes, she made two circles and put a dot of color in the middle of each: blue, brown, green, purple, or sometimes orange. This time, each circle was solid black, the crayon so thick it glossed the paper. Nilda imagined Sidney scrubbing that blackness into existence, sensed a desire to both create and annihilate. She knew that desire well.

What had it left? A soulless stare that seemed meant just for her. It reached right through her middle, delivering a sickening twist.

She put the drawings on the table, face down.

"I'm going to get some water. Want anything?"

"No, thank you."

As she headed for the kitchen, she felt unsteady on her feet, unsteady in this world. The leaning chamber rose to mind. Would it help?

Graham's words warned her away. *I'm concerned that your house is on overload…too much of a good thing.* Maybe he was right.

When she got to the kitchen, her phone was buzzing on the table. *Don't look.* But she did. Already, she'd received three texts from him:

I didn't mean to upset you. Please forgive me.

I'm so sorry, really.

Call me, please.

She left her phone on the table and skipped the water, then headed straight for her bed.

When she was little, my daughter called the lingering smell of baking "the goodie ghost." May this book fill your home with years of comforting ghosts.

—From the introduction to *The Home Baker's Companion* (in the possession of Helen Thurnwell)

25

Long after she rose, the fog of sleep stayed with Nilda. And it seemed to have crept through Sidney too. Shortly after dinner, she'd fallen asleep on the couch—so soundly that Nilda had carried her up to bed, with no interruptions for toothbrushing or a change into her nightie T.

As Nilda descended the stairs, she heard humming from the kitchen: Helen. She followed the sound and found her scrubbing the backsplash behind the sink.

"Hey," Nilda said.

Helen glanced her way with a smile. "How was your day?"

Where do I start? Nilda thought. But she didn't want to get into her feelings about the house, or Sidney's drawing, or Graham. She wanted to blot all of that from her mind. "Pretty good. I'm just a little tired."

"Why don't you turn in then. I'm not planning any work upstairs, and I'll be careful not to disturb you."

"You never disturb me."

Nilda noticed that the vintage Tupperware was back and sitting in the middle of the table. Lid sealed. "More treats?"

Helen glanced her way again. "Homemade pretzels. Help yourself."

Nilda realized that a snack was just what she needed. She'd barely touched the soggy quesadilla from dinner.

Planning to eat on the go, she grabbed a napkin and pulled the lid from the Tupperware.

What she saw made her sit down. The pretzels had been shaped into hearts, just the way her mother used to make them.

This sapped her appetite. And the knot of hunger in her stomach—now, it was just a knot. Still, she reached for one of the pretzels and took a bite, detecting first a tang of sourdough and then a buttery finish. Just like her mother's pretzels. Then again, such flavors couldn't be that unusual in pretzels.

She took another bite, her hunger returning along with a memory of her mother, from twenty or so years before: the height of her pretzel-making days. She was seated at their old kitchen table, and brushing butter across the tops of heart-shaped ropes of dough. They were lined up on that old cookie sheet, black from years of use, and so big and heavy that Nilda had once used it as a sled.

Her mother stopped and held out the brush.

Wanna give it a try?

Nilda wished she could take that brush, get pulled back into that world. But the memory vanished, along with her mother, and any interest in the pretzel. She swallowed hard to get her third bite down. Then she noticed Helen watching her, her brow knit.

"Are you all right?"

Nilda nodded, lying.

Helen will understand. Go ahead and tell her. "These pretzels, they—" She couldn't get the words out. Instead, she broke down.

Helen rushed to the table, pulled a chair right up to her, and sat down. It was perhaps the closest they'd ever been. She started to reach for Nilda's arm, then pulled back. "The last thing I'd ever want to do is make you cry. With pretzels, of all things."

"I know." Nilda grabbed another napkin and wiped her eyes, blew her nose.

How to put this, so she didn't make Helen feel any worse? "The pretzels kind of bring my mother back to me. So these are good tears, really." She tried to smile.

But Helen looked no less concerned than before, as if she'd heard the lie in the talk of *good tears*. Her eyes locked on Nilda, and when she spoke, her voice was barely above a whisper. "We never get over losing our mothers, do we? And we know that if they possibly could, they'd stay with us to our own end, and maybe beyond it. They'd see that we were taken care of for all of time. And nothing would get in their way. *Nothing.*"

Helen's words seemed to extend beyond Nilda, reflecting her own grief and desires and perhaps encompassing her son, or the loss of him.

Helen straightened up and gave Nilda's arm a quick double pat. The way Jo used to.

Cut it out.

She needed to stop connecting Helen to her mother, and looking to Helen—or to random things like pretzels, or lullabies—for something that could never be replaced: everything Jo had been to her.

She thanked Helen, said goodnight, and headed up to her room.

She's starting to remind me of Chloe, becoming more and more distanced. Because of <u>him</u>? I don't know. What I <u>do</u> know is that this new formula is close to magic. No, it <u>is</u> magic. How could she want to go without it, or me?

—From the journals of Graham Emmerly, July 21st, 2019

Still no word from her. And here, I must confess something if only to banish the possibility of acting on it: I'm starting to feel the urge again, for the first time in years. Maybe this is just a reaction to the possibility of losing her, and a love that feels <u>exceptional</u>. After all, I never felt a trace of the urge with Chloe.
Then again, maybe Chloe just left too soon.

—From the journals of Graham Emmerly, July 22nd, 2019

The moment's come, you've reached that low
You know it's time it's time it's time to let go

—Lyrics from "The Break" by the Mortal Coils (Clay's band)

26

What if Sidney and I just stayed here?
As the sauvignon-blanc buzz kicked in, as she and Toni melted into their matching recliners, watching the girls zip around the yard and through the sprinkler, Nilda asked herself this question more than once, knowing it would have to remain rhetorical.

It wasn't just that she loved the summer-camp feel of Toni's screened-in porch, or that Toni's company always restored her—whether they sat together in silence, like now, or talked through a problem in one of their lives, or in the world. It was that she always felt unburdened here. Or, rather, the space itself felt unburdened, so unlike her own house and even her yard. She had no idea how to define or describe those burdens, but if she ever figured that out, Toni would be the first to know.

Toni sat up. "I almost forgot something. Hold on a sec."

A minute later she returned with a small shipping box. "I went ahead and had these made, but if you don't like them, I'll pitch them. They were cheapo-deepo."

Nilda sat up and lifted the flaps of the box. Inside were pin-on buttons showing the hashtag they'd come up with: #TennemanOut.

"This is awesome, Toni."

To show her appreciation, Nilda pinned one to her T-shirt, then topped off their wines.

Toni eased back in her recliner and took a healthy sip from her glass. "I thought Clay could include them in the painting display. If you don't think that'd be asking too much."

"I'm sure he can handle it."

Toni smiled. "I guess he kinda owes you something."

Nilda felt a little less that way, perhaps because Clay had been so cooperative about the festival stuff. Whatever the reason, she felt closer to letting the old hurt and anger go.

Perhaps reading something into Nilda's silence, Toni gave her the eye. "Any more news flashes with him?"

Toni knew that things had always been complicated between Nilda and Clay, and that they'd remained so. Just a few nights ago, Nilda finally admitted to her that she'd had sex with him just before leaving him and Boston behind. Toni wasn't surprised.

Now Toni's question reminded Nilda of another complication, one she'd been trying to push from her thoughts.

"If there's any news, it's with Graham. Things got a little weird with him."

"Oh no. What happened?"

"You know how I tried to cool things off with him?"

"Mmm-hmm."

"I don't think it's working. I mean, he's been getting kinda…"

As she struggled to find the right word, she thought of one of his lines: *No one will ever be willing to do more for you, Nilda.*

"…pushy? clingy? Maybe a little of both?"

"I don't like the sound of pushy, Nilda."

Nilda set down her glass and grabbed another olive from the cheese plate. "I don't mean in a dangerous way. It's more like he's way more confident in the future of our relationship than I am, and he's trying to infect me with that confidence."

Toni took an olive for herself. "Do you think it's time to break things off?"

"Maybe. I'm not sure." Nilda wasn't proud of the main reason she'd been keeping things going: the sex. But hadn't there been something else—something more—at least at the beginning of their relationship? "I just wish you knew him better, so you could weigh in."

Toni and Graham had crossed paths just once, when Toni dropped Sidney off after a sleepover.

"Want me to give you my gut impression?"

Nilda did and didn't. Toni's gut impressions spared nothing. Yet as hard to hear as they could be, they usually got at a truth, or the grain of one.

"Lay it on me."

"I found him charming, but it felt like a bit much."

"What do you mean?"

Toni took her time answering, staring off toward the yard, where the girls had started a game of badminton. "You know how actors sometimes give their lines a little too much oomph? And it reminds you you're watching a movie, instead of something real?"

"Yeah."

She looked back to Nilda. "That's what I mean."

Nilda didn't remember Graham coming off that way, but at that stage of things, maybe she'd been too taken with him to notice. Possibly, he'd just been trying to win Toni over and had gone a little too far. "So you think he's not exactly genuine."

"Maybe. I don't know. It's not like I think he's a pathological liar or anything. It just kinda put me off." Toni's expression softened, as if she'd registered Nilda's concern. "This comes from, what, five minutes with the guy? You know him way better than I do."

Way better was probably overstating things. So much of Graham still seemed a mystery to Nilda, even after all these weeks. Toni's words left her even more unsure about him, and about her own judgment.

Toni reached over and squeezed Nilda's arm. "You'll figure this out. You always do."

Another overstatement, surely. All too often, especially where issues with men were concerned, Nilda didn't so much figure things out as let them drift along until a crisis forced her to act.

"Can I give you my impression of something else?"

"Sure." To prepare herself, Nilda drank the last of her wine.

"You still don't look well. I mean, you're just so pale, and I've never seen you with circles like that under your eyes."

Though she'd never been big on makeup, Nilda had started patting concealer under her eyes. That hadn't fooled Toni, apparently. "My insom—"

"It's not just insomnia, I'm sure. I think you should see a doctor."

Physically, Nilda didn't feel any worse than she had the day or the week or the month before. Just tired. Then again, maybe she was like that proverbial frog in the gradually warming pot of water, moving toward some boiling point without even realizing it.

"I will, I promise. After the festival."

"Screw the festival. This is your health."

Nilda reclined and took in the scene in the yard. Now just Mae and Livia were at the badminton net, swatting the birdie back and forth. Sidney had returned to the sprinkler, dodging the spray then dashing straight through it, joyous. In a way she never was back home.

How to put into words what was different there, and why that mattered? Nilda had to jump in and try.

"I think my house might be affecting me. Emotionally."
Now she wondered whether the effects were physical too.

Toni was familiar with the unusual features of the place and
had seen many of them for herself. Through Nilda she also
knew something of Nathaniel Farleigh, and of how he'd tried
to influence the mind through various features of his work.
Now Nilda found herself parroting Graham's theory that those
features were on overload in her house, making her feel off.
Although she'd dismissed this theory at first, she'd come around
to thinking that Graham might be onto something.

It was hard to tell how Toni was taking this new spin on
things. She seemed stunned into silence.

"Does that sound too out-there to you?"

Nilda hadn't even mentioned what had happened in the
dining room, with the fan and Graham's vase. That would be
dumping too much weirdness on Toni all at once, and Nilda still
hadn't processed what she'd seen, felt.

"Not at all," Toni said. "I've always thought your place was
a bit much, honestly. I mean those faces on the fireplaces? Pure
nightmare fuel."

Nilda wondered whether Toni had noticed the face that
looked like her mother's. Probably not. If she had, she wouldn't
have said this.

"But I seriously doubt that kind of stuff can make you sick."

"I'm not s—" Nilda stopped herself. It was clear from Toni
that she wasn't her old self, and whether the issue was physical, mental, or some combination, it deserved more attention
than she'd been giving it. "I'll call that GP you recommended. I
promise." After the festival, she told herself.

"I'll be holding you to it."

Toni still looked troubled, and Nilda feared that another gut
impression might be coming her way.

"What?" she asked.

"Are you still drinking that herbal stuff from Graham?"

Sensing where this was going, Nilda said, "It's harmless,
Toni. I mean, it's basically herbal tea."

"Herbs aren't necessarily harmless, Nilda. Maybe you're having a reaction to one of them. Maybe that could even be behind some of your feelings about the house."

As far as Nilda could remember, those feelings had started before the days of tonic. But they seemed to have grown more intense.

"If I were you, I'd stop drinking the stuff. Just to see if things improve."

No way, Nilda thought. Since she'd started on the tonic, she'd been unusually productive in the studio, and whether that was the result of a placebo effect or some alchemical magic wrought from ordinary herbs, she didn't really care.

Still, Toni had a point, and the fact that Nilda had grown dependent on the tonic, however ordinary it was, was cause for concern on its own.

"Okay. I will."

"And maybe you should have it tested? Just to be sure nothing else is going on?"

"Oh, Toni, *really?*" Although Toni always had the best of intentions, they sometimes became over-fueled by enthusiasm or worry and rocketed past common sense.

"Really. If Jack can't do the test, he'll find someone who can." Jack, Toni's husband, worked in a state lab whose mission had never been clear to Nilda. "You think I'm overreacting, don't you?"

"Just a bit," Nilda said. "Graham has his flaws, for sure. But I don't feel like he's slipping me mickies or anything. I mean, why would he even do that?"

Toni downed the last of the olives and sat back in her chair. "I'm not sure. And maybe the herbal stuff is completely innocent. But let's say it's making you just a bit weaker, just a bit more vulnerable. And maybe even causing you to think the house is getting to you."

Getting to you. Were those Graham's words, or Nilda's?

"That might make you more dependent on him, no? Pretty ideal from his point of view."

Toni had a point. Yet Nilda still couldn't believe that Graham would go so far as to drug her. And what about the ways she'd been affected by the fireplace carvings, the leaning chamber, and the models Nathaniel Farleigh had made? What about the running fan and shattered vase? Weren't those all beyond Graham's control?

"Maybe," Nilda said. "Can I think on your offer?"

In truth, Nilda didn't have any more tonic to pass on to Jack, and she no longer wanted to ask Graham for a re-up. It was probably best to stay off the stuff, for good.

"Of course." Toni lifted the bottle to Nilda's glass, but Nilda waved her off. Sometime between now and supper, she needed to drive herself and Sidney home—not before this buzz wore off.

Filling her own glass, Toni said, "If your place is really bothering you, you and Sidney would be welcome to stay with us, until you figure something else out."

Something else surely would mean another move, and Nilda really didn't want to do that, not so soon after settling in here.

"And, hey, why don't you guys stay here while we're gone? Take a little break from your place?"

In a little over a week, Toni, Jack, and the girls would be traveling to Denver for the hastily announced wedding of Jack's brother. Toni had expressed guilt about making the trip, because it overlapped with the art festival. But Nilda urged her to go, knowing that if anything bad went down at the festival, Toni's lawyer would be on call.

"We just might do that, Toni. Thanks."

"Well, if the spirit moves you while we're gone, come on over. You have a set of keys, right?"

"Yep."

Now Nilda needed to pee. As she made her way to the bathroom, she checked her phone and found a new text from Graham:

Are you okay?

She hadn't responded to his first run of texts, her guilt not having yet exceeded her desire to delay and avoid. Now her conversation with Toni had made one thing clear: she'd reached the proverbial "moment of truth" the two of them first spoke of in college. It was time to break things off with Graham, completely. But she'd have to do that in person.

To buy some time, she texted him back:

> Yes. Sorry to be incommunicado, just a lot on my mind lately. Okay if I come by tomorrow?

Seconds later, his response:

> You know where to find me.

For Helen comfort doesn't come in the form of pets, cigarettes, chocolates, or cocktails, or any other material thing,
as far as I can tell. It's all about work, work, work, God love
her.

—From a letter from Eula Joy Austerlane to her sister,
September 15th, 1993

27

SEPTEMBER 12TH, 1993

At times he'd forgotten her "shoes off" rule, tramping
dirt across floors she'd made glow.

But now she'd never scrub away this black streak in
the corner of the Austerlanes' dining room, connected forever
to the motion that had made it: him running for a ball Mr. A
had tossed him, then skidding to a stop as he caught it.

Once again, she mopped around the mark, remembering her
child in motion, his joy in catching that ball.

That day she'd meant to polish the mark away, immediately.
But Mrs. A had called to her—for what task she couldn't now
remember. By the time she returned to the dining room, out
of habit more than purpose, days had passed and her boy was
gone.

Mr. and Ms. A seemed to know that today marked a year
since her loss. They said this in indirect ways.

Mr. A, always kind, brought her a bouquet of dahlias.

Mrs. A, always well-intentioned, said something this morning, on the patio. It wasn't kind, necessarily, but it was true.

Together, they watched as the next-door boy trekked along
the woods path, then vanished into the trees.

Mrs. A blew a column of cigarette smoke after him. Then
she said, "Nothing's fair in this world, is it?"

What Helen heard: *If one death could be traded for another, your
boy would be here, and that one would be gone.*

It wasn't right to think this—even if it could be proved that the boy had left a dead squirrel or two, or even three, by Mrs. A's lawn chair. It couldn't, according to Mr. A.

Anyhow, life didn't work that way. And if it did, it would be a devil's bargain.

Still. What if the devil had come calling that night, as her child was leaving this world? Wouldn't she at least have invited him in, and listened to what he had to say?

She turned the mop on a soda spill, as if she could scrub these thoughts from her mind.

One wise thing the old prick told me: Try to prepare for the worst.

—From the journals of Graham Emmerly, July 22nd, 2019

28

Nilda rang Graham's front bell, hoping this would keep them from falling into their old routine, so much as they had one. To her mind the back door, her usual point of entry, led one of three ways: down the hall to the kitchen and small talk, to the right for drinks in the study, or up the stairs to his bedroom and sex, something that couldn't happen again. For both their sakes she wanted to keep this exchange to the front porch, and get it over with as quickly as possible.

As she waited her heart quickened, for nothing like the old reasons. She almost wished he wasn't home, though that was unlikely. She'd spotted his car in the drive.

After a moment she reached for the bell again, then stopped at the sound of approaching footsteps. It sent her heart racing.

The lock turned, then the door opened to Graham: in shorts, bare feet, and a T-shirt, his hair matted on one side and mussed on the other. This made her wonder whether she'd woken him from a nap or an extra-long night's sleep. So did the scowl he'd just banished.

"I'm sorry," she said. "I should have texted you first."

"Nonsense. You said you'd be coming." He stepped back and waved her in, smiling now, or trying to.

"I can't. There's something I've been wanting to tell you, and I just need to come out with it."

Graham stepped from the doorway, onto the porch, so they were now just an arm's length apart. Though he was no longer smiling, he didn't look alarmed. "You want to break things off."

"Yes." Chances were, he'd been expecting this. She'd made it clear her heart wasn't where his was, and she'd left him waiting for responses to his texts, longer than she should have. "I just want to focus on my work right now. And Sidney."

Graham said nothing, just fixed her with a stare.

It was clear he knew she was lying, and she tried to dig herself out of this hole. "It hasn't been that long since Sidney's dad and I split, and I just want to reduce the complications, for me and her."

A faint smile played across his lips, not the kind he'd invited her in with. This one had an edge.

"What?" she said.

"I suspected you weren't quite done with, what's his name? *Clay?* I mean, the look you got when you talked about him, it pretty much telegraphed your feel—"

"You have *no* idea what my feelings are. About him or anything else."

But maybe he did. Maybe he *had* been on the other side of the fence that night she'd spoken to Clay. Or maybe he'd just picked up on feelings she'd found hard to admit to herself. She'd never been great at hiding her emotions.

"Of course I don't. I'm sorry to have been so presumptuous."

Now Nilda felt embarrassed by her outburst, and she didn't want to leave things on a bad note. But what to say? *I hope we can still be friends?* That would be an insult to him. And for her part, it wouldn't be true. "I'm really glad we've gotten to know each other."

Graham crossed his arms, seeming to put up a barrier of his own. "That sounds pretty formal. And final."

"I didn't mean it to. It's just—" But she did mean this to be final. She didn't want to open the door to future dinners, future picnics, future anything. She wasn't even sure how much longer she'd be his neighbor. "It's just how it needs to be. For me."

She turned away and started down the porch stairs.

"Nilda?"

She looked back at him.

"I made another batch of tonic for you. If you don't take it, it'll just go down the drain."

Since finishing the Farleigh painting, she'd lost momentum with her work, and a bit of tonic might give her just enough of a push. Then she remembered the promise she'd made to Toni, and to herself.

"I can't."

He frowned. "I hope the last batch wasn't a dud."

"No, no, not at all." Aiming for kindness, she cooked up another lie: "I'm laying off anything but water these days. For this cleanse I'm doing." As soon as she spoke, she thought of her nightly dose of wine. Whenever she went for a fresh bottle, she'd have to remember to keep the dining room lights off. Although it was unlikely he'd catch her hitting up her supply, it was possible.

Again, Graham was fixing her with that stare. "All right, then. I'll be wishing you the best, Nilda."

Now he was the one who was sounding formal. But she didn't blame him, given the circumstances. She turned away and headed home, more relieved than she'd imagined.

That evening, Nilda delivered the news about Graham as she tucked Sidney in—later than usual and after the sun had set, leaving only the glow of the nightlight.

"Nothing bad happened between us. We just decided—*I* just decided—that this was for the best."

Sidney didn't look surprised, and Nilda wondered whether she'd started catching on to what Nilda already knew about herself: that she might be incapable of sustaining a lasting relationship with any man.

"Can we still see the chickens?"

Nilda wanted to say "Yes" and mean it. But that would be a mistake. "I don't think so."

She tried to think of something that might cheer Sidney.

"Let's do something fun tomorrow, take a little trip." Both of them could use a break from this house.

"Where?"

"How about that water park? It's supposed to be super-hot tomorrow." Toni's daughter Livia had raved about the place to Sidney.

Sidney's frown remained. "I'd rather stay here."

Nilda felt a rush of anger, then tried to check it. If this house wasn't a problem for Sidney, maybe that should be cause for relief. But Sidney's attachment to the place—or her reluctance to leave it—didn't seem healthy. "I don't love it that you're spending so much time in your room." For a stretch Sidney seemed to have broken the habit, but now it had returned. Was Alex back on the scene?

"But I like it here, Mommy. It's a bomb for the soul. A *good* bomb."

"Where'd you hear that?"

"Hear what?"

"Balm for the soul." Although Sidney had a knack for picking up on grownup-ish words and phrases, Nilda had no idea where this one had come from.

"The old-fashioned man."

The old-fashioned man. Nilda thought of a cartoon Sidney watched now and then, which featured various moments in history and starred such figures as Frederick Douglass, Eleanor Roosevelt, and Rachel Carson. She struggled to recall the name, then it popped into her mind. "From *History Bits*?"

"No, from there." Sidney pointed to the chair by her night-light.

Jolted, Nilda looked to the chair and to the shadow it cast up on the wall: a far larger, distorted double, like a giant's roost. Something from a fairytale.

Sidney had dreamed of this man, or concocted another imaginary friend. And *balm for the soul*? She could have heard it from some show on the utility-room radio they'd inherited from Eula Joy. Nilda often left it playing while she did laundry, threw a meal together, or went about some other chore. Half the time she tuned it out, and it probably wasn't uncommon for her to ignore bits of news or shows that Sidney grasped onto.

Nilda was eager to change the subject. "Let's figure out something for tomorrow, okay? Even if it's just a trip into town."

"For ice cream?"

"It's a deal!"

Nilda kissed Sidney's forehead and headed for the door. Usually, she trained her gaze away from the remaining model house, not wanting to be reminded of its companion, the wreckage of which still lay at the foot of the cellar stairs. She hadn't been able to bring herself to clean up the mess, fearing glimpses of the black, burned spots, the spider-eye windows, whatever it was that had set her off that day, turning her into a furious stranger.

Now she stopped to look at the remaining model. *Our house,* Sidney had called it.

Studying the twin-gabled roof, the bay windows, and the turret, Nilda thought of Nathaniel Farleigh and of how he'd appeared in her dream: in brown tweed and a black silk tie. *An old-fashioned man.* And hadn't he said that something—she couldn't remember what—was balm for the soul? Her mind felt so fogged, she couldn't be sure.

"What's wrong, Mommy?"

"Nothing, sweet pea. Everything's fine."

Nilda left the room and descended the stairs, sure of one thing: She and Sidney couldn't both have dreamed of Farleigh. Sidney wouldn't have had any reason to. Her dream, or her new imaginary friend—and his words—had to have been inspired by something she'd seen or heard, or encountered in one of her storybooks. Something ordinary.

Craving more wine, Nilda headed to the kitchen and poured the last of the Côtes du Rhône into her glass: barely more than a thimble-full. With a cabernet franc in mind, she made her way to the dining room. There, faint moonlight set *Revenge in Glass* aglow. It cast a ruby sheen on the floor.

Surely, whoever had inspired the sculpture was a far worse character than Graham, perhaps even dangerous. Still, Nilda was certain her mother would have supported her decision to break up with him. Any man who was the slightest bit manipulative would have set off alarm bells for Jo, especially given her personal history.

Nilda crept closer to the sculpture and the window beyond it, the wine cabinet just to its left. Beyond the window there was no Graham to catch her breaking her cooked-up detox vow. He'd drawn the curtains over his study window, blotting the room from her sight.

There's something eternal about the beauty of fine wooden furniture. Keep that beauty going with GrainGlo.

—From the back of a GrainGlo can, under the kitchen sink

29

S he was polishing the dresser, polishing and polishing and polishing it. As if bringing a shine to the dark, dead wood would count for some form of life.

All the while, Mrs. A's words played in the back of her mind: *No need to work your fingers to the bone.* Her way of showing kindness, and sympathy. But work is what she needed now, more than ever. It kept her going, moment by moment, day by day, in this new, unbearable world.

"Mom?"

His voice, but it couldn't be.

"Mom, I'm here."

He was closer. Behind her.

She tried to turn but couldn't. Then she felt his hand on her back. Warm.

"*Mom!*"

Jolted awake, she rolled over to find Sidney standing before her, her face a dim gray in the moonlight. She was staring straight ahead, with that flat-eyed look Nilda knew all too well. Sidney was sleepwalking: her first episode in this house.

As quietly as she could, Nilda pulled back the sheet and rose from the bed, starting to do what she'd done in Boston: guide Sidney back to her own bed, trying not to wake her. Gently, she took Sidney's arm and led her toward the door.

As they neared it, Sidney stopped and turned that flat-eyed gaze on her. "Mom?"

Nilda dropped her hand from Sidney's arm, unable to move or speak. This wasn't Sidney's voice, or even her *Walking Dead*

Croak. The change in the sound seemed physical, down to the level of the vocal cords.

Sidney spoke again: "He likes watching their eyes turn to glass."

The same voice. A *boy's* voice. But it couldn't be.

Sidney turned her gaze back to where it had been, the doorway. On this cue Nilda led her out of the room, back to her bed. Back in Boston, she'd tuck her in, wait for her breathing to fall into the rhythm of deep sleep, and leave. Now, though, she crawled into bed with Sidney, circled an arm around her waist. She didn't want to be alone with her fear, or with the questions that were playing through her mind.

The nonsense talk? Although this was new for Sidney, it wasn't uncommon for sleepwalkers, or so Nilda had read. The change in her voice? Maybe that could happen with sleepwalking too. The brain seemed capable of strange and mysterious things, perhaps especially during sleep. But could it trigger what seemed like a *physical* change? Nilda wasn't sure she wanted an answer. Pushing this question aside, she returned to Sidney's words.

He likes watching their eyes turn to glass.

Perhaps not all of it was nonsense—at least not the glass part. Sidney had watched her grandma work in her studio, not often but enough to become entranced. It wasn't hard to imagine her dreaming mind crafting some story or image from Jo's handling of glowing, shape-shifting glass.

But what was with the eyes? And who might the *he* or *their* be? Nilda had no idea. Maybe Sidney wouldn't either, if she remembered her words upon waking. That was the way of dreams.

Nilda stared off to the nightlit chair, which reminded her of Sidney's "old-fashioned man." Perhaps he was the *he*. Or perhaps it was Alex, or Sidney's "bad kid," or the boy she'd seen or imagined at the creek. Or perhaps *he* was a mix of all these figures that Sidney had concocted, a mix of things she missed or wanted or feared. In the missed or wanted category, Nilda imagined a steady, fatherlike—or grandfather-like—presence. And another child to play with in this isolated locale. In the feared category, she drew a blank.

Then she thought of this house, and Graham's suspicions that it was affecting her emotionally.

Maybe it was affecting Sidney too, in ways Nilda couldn't imagine.

No. She was overthinking all this, over-psychologizing it. She closed her eyes, blocking out the nightlit chair. Now all she sensed was Sidney's warmth, and the rise and fall of her breathing: deep and steady. Though Nilda dared not move to check, Sidney seemed fast asleep.

May your dreams be sweet. Or your sleep a dreamless respite.

As she drew closer to sleep herself, she remembered polishing that creepy dresser in the spare room. Not a real memory, but a fragment of that dream Sidney had interrupted. This was the only thing she recalled from it now, and the polishing felt like another reminder of everything Helen did around this place.

Nilda tightened her hold on Sidney, let her breathing sync with hers. Soon, everything but Sidney slipped into the darkness: every worry and fear, every surface, object, and shadow....

She pressed her face to his head, once again breathed in the smell of his skin, his hair, the smell that had been fading from those clothes she'd kept. She would hold on to it, hold on to him. Never ever let go.

I am consumptive, I am <u>consumed</u>?

Not yet, not utterly. My hands still answer to my mind and my heart. So in this haven of my study, on this daybed, I draw plans for things I'll not survive to build, even in miniature form.

What is the point, one might ask, of plans with no hope of execution? There <u>is</u> no point, perhaps, other than that all too soon, these hands will be stilled, leaving my mind, my heart—for I wager they will persist, in some form—adrift with their dreams and desires, and with no means to manifest them. Presuming that nothing is drawn or built or sculpted or painted in the afterlife, at least not in physical form, I must commit my imaginings to paper for as long as I am able.

Though these efforts sustain me, I near death with certain regrets. One being that perhaps I have devoted too much time to too many works that repulse others, a consequence of being inspired by visions that, at times, are as disturbing as they are revelatory. Yet if an artist feels he must steer clear of discomfort, in his thinking and in his work, what revelations are possible, for himself and his audience? His work risks becoming mere background, unable to touch the mind, the heart, the soul.

Among those repulsed by my work is you, dear son, and you <u>do</u> remain dear, though it seems to pain you to visit me, even as my days draw down. And here we come to another regret: the house I built for you. From this distance of years, I have come to see it as a primitive, tossed-off sort of thing relative to my later achievements. A thing unworthy of you, Henry, and of architecture's most salutary potentials. Thus, I find no fault in the news I have heard from Mother: that you are removing such features of it as you can and that you are considering a move into town.

The model I made of your house? In alliance with you, I keep it close at hand, but only to snuff my cigars on it.

—The final entry in *The Collected Journals of Nathaniel Farleigh*

30

Nilda closed the book and watched a moth flit past the kitchen window then land on the flour jar. She didn't budge to squash it, too distracted by what she'd read and not sure what to make of it.

The last journal entry explained the burns on the model house she'd smashed to pieces, which should have offered some relief. But even now, just picturing the thing troubled her. And she'd never know why she'd had such a fiercely negative, and ultimately violent, reaction to it.

As the moth crept over the jar lid, looking for a point of entry, she reached for explanations of her own. Maybe, somehow, the model version of the house had held on to the negative feelings that Nathaniel Farleigh and his son had about the real version. Maybe Nilda had sensed them, driving her to destroy the model. Maybe Sidney had picked up on these feelings too, and calling the model "the bad kid's house" was her way of expressing this.

Maybe. But most likely, this was woo-woo bullshit.

Still. Sidney's placing the model on Jo's sculpture couldn't account for Nilda's reaction to it, not all of it. Neither could the migraine pills, or Graham's tonics.

Nilda pushed the book away and grabbed one of the oatmeal cookies that Helen had left on the table.

She took her first bite but couldn't enjoy it, considering something else that troubled her: what the journal entries *didn't* say. In none of them did Farleigh speak of feeling that the walls of this house were closing in on him, as Graham had claimed. And in every entry, he sounded completely rational. The only "strangeness": his descriptions of inspirations and ideas that must have been unconventional for his time.

Graham had been lying about the house's influences, or

exaggerating them. He'd wanted to make her more vulnerable, more dependent on him. Just the MO that Toni had described.

Or perhaps not. Maybe Nilda's version of the journals was abridged, and he'd read a more complete collection. This wasn't improbable. Certain entries in Nilda's version were dated days after the previous one. Also, many other details Graham had shared about Farleigh were confirmed by Nilda's copy of the journals: Farleigh's ouster from the architecture firm he'd founded and run with his son, because his designs had become "too odd to be palatable to anyone save myself." And just as Graham had said, Farleigh called his design of a local asylum his "finest work."

Enough of this. She needed to stop giving Graham so much real estate in her mind.

She took another bite of the cookie, savoring it this time. Its salty-nutty sweetness soothed her. So did the golden-red light of the sunset, which now filled the kitchen and seemed to be reaching its peak.

Catch it before it's gone.

She headed out to the patio, where the light nearly forgave the yard of its weeds, its blighted hydrangea bushes. Their white blooms glowed in the shadows, not a mottled leaf in sight.

Even the air felt transformed. The heat and humidity had lifted, promising if not a deep or lasting sleep, at least a more comfortable one.

She froze at a sound from Graham's side: an outburst of squawking. One hen or more? As she listened, the squawks slipped to a higher register. Shrieks.

A raccoon on the hunt?

Call him. Tell him.

No. If I can hear this, he can too. Let him deal with it.

More shrieks. Then something else: a low voice. Graham's. Though she couldn't make out his words, she heard anger in them. Curses.

Go back inside. Leave this be.

But curiosity overcame her. She crept up to the fence, up

to where she remembered spying a knothole. Pushing aside a tangle of vines, she found it and peered through.

She saw nothing but what was right in front of her: lilies in the fading light. No hens, no Graham. She heard no squawks, no shrieks. Probably, he'd chased the stray—or strays—back into the coop, and she hoped no harm had been done, by a raccoon or anything else.

A *thunk* broke the silence. A second one followed.

Seconds later, a hen rushed into view, wings beating as she zigged and zagged between flower beds: an aimless yet desperate attempt to escape, or so it seemed. Where her head had been, blood spurted, black as oil in the dimming light.

Sidney. What if she's watching?

Nilda bolted into the house and up the stairs, up to Sidney's room. But she was nowhere near the window with a view of Graham's yard. Instead, she was sound asleep in her bed, Fuzzy clutched to her chest.

Thank God.

Their day in town had worn Sidney out—in a good way, it seemed. After getting ice cream, they'd browsed stores for books and toys, picked up two bubble-making paddles, and put them to use in a local park, where they happened upon a skateboarding competition and watched it to the finish. Sidney seemed to have no memory of her sleepwalking, same as usual, and Nilda wished it had been blotted from her own thoughts as well. Now and then, that voice that had come from Sidney played back through her mind.

Nilda turned to leave then stopped at what she saw on the nightstand: the ice-blue crystal from Graham, a gift that once seemed so kind, so perceptive. She grasped it and carried it down the stairs and into the kitchen, up to the trash pail. After lifting the lid, she stopped.

She didn't want the thing in this house.

She headed to the back door and after a moment's hesitation pushed it open, listened. The only sound: crickets. She stepped down to the patio then into the yard, and as she neared the edge of the woods, she detected a soft chorus of clucking on Graham's side—a sound that, on other evenings, she'd found calming: hens settling in for the night.

It hadn't been a mass slaughter, clearly. Maybe he'd killed a sick member of the flock, finally doing a job he'd been dreading.

She opened her hand and stared at the crystal, deeper blue in the fading light. Maybe she was overreacting to what she'd seen. Maybe Sidney would ask about the crystal, and she'd have to answer with silence, or lies.

Then the memory intruded, of those flapping wings, that spurting blood. She wound up her pitch and hurled the thing into the woods.

None of the search results were setting off alarms.

Farleigh Community College listed Graham as an adjunct instructor of chemistry, just as he'd claimed.

And a trade magazine piece, dated two years before, quoted a Graham Emmerly on "human-cell testing models." The writer referred to him as a toxicologist at one pharmaceutical firm and said that he'd worked in that capacity at two other companies. This was also in keeping with what Graham had told her about his background.

Nilda leaned back against the headboard and closed her eyes, watched the ghost of her laptop screen fade into darkness. Though worn out, she knew sleep would elude her, and that more internet searching wouldn't help. Anyway, how often did the internet reveal the truths that mattered, about anyone? And would she really want it to?

Give it a rest. Maybe a permanent one.

Her thoughts wandered to her studio, where she'd become adrift. The feverish spell under which she'd painted Farleigh felt like something she'd dreamed, and the prospect of getting another painting out of him—much less a series—seemed unlikely. One difference between now and then? She was no longer drinking Graham's tonic. But she didn't want to assign too much importance to it. She'd had fallow stretches before, and she'd always gotten through them.

Looking for inspiration, she thought through her most recent sketches, of interlocking shapes: boomerangs and amoeba-like blobs.

Then her mind caught on something. Something that had nothing to do with her drawings: a memory of a book she'd flipped through in Graham's study. His full name had been handwritten on an opening page: Graham Arthur Emmerly. She typed this into the search engine and got several results she'd already seen.

But at the bottom of the screen, she found something new. It sent a shock through her.

Former Dever U Student Accused of Poisoning Roommate

She clicked the link, which brought her to an article on the DeverValleyLive website.

A former Dever University student, Arthur Emmerly, pled not guilty today to charges of attempted homicide, aggravated assault, and reckless endangerment in connection with an alleged plan to poison his one-time roommate, Jason Nevins, 20.

According to prosecuting attorney Rachel Gomes, Nevins began feeling ill last March, and he experienced nausea, vomiting, and various neurological symptoms throughout the university's spring term. Gomes said that Nevins first contacted police at the start of these symptoms, alleging that someone had poisoned his drink during a social event at the dormitory. He also told police that he'd begun receiving threatening handwritten messages, which he said had been slipped under the door of the room he shared with Emmerly.

The investigation of Nevins's initial complaints

seemed to stall. But over the spring term, Gomes said, Nevins's symptoms of illness intensified, and after receiving "an especially alarming note," he contacted police again. At this point investigators recovered evidence that they said connects Emmerly, 19, to the alleged poisoning incidents. Among this evidence were traces of thallium, a toxic soft metal, discovered in certain of Emmerly's possessions. Gomes also said that handwriting evidence connects Emmerly to the notes that Nevins received.

The thallium finding is significant, Gomes noted, because a blood test that Nevins had received after "an especially acute event" showed dangerous levels of this substance.

According to Gomes, Nevins had not suspected Emmerly of the alleged poisoning, because he'd considered Emmerly "a friend and confidant, someone who seemed really upset by what was going on." Asked what the suspect's motives might have been, Gomes said, "Only Mr. Emmerly can answer that question. But Nevins believes that he was made the subject of some perverse experiment. Unfortunately, his organ function has been compromised, meaning he may never fully recover."

Emmerly, who is free on $200,000 bail, has declined to comment on the charges. But his attorney, Maxwell Jorgenson, said, "My client strongly disputes these accusations, and with good reason, as the evidence I'll present will make clear. I look forward to pressing forward with the case against these baseless charges."

With trembling hands Nilda managed to enter "Arthur Emmerly" and "poisoning" into the search field, narrowing the results. But all she turned up were other media outlets' take on the DeverValleyLive story. She couldn't find any news of what had happened after the not-guilty plea—whether the charges had led to a conviction or been dropped. Just as frustrating, the only pictures with the articles were of Jason Nevins. When she searched just for "Arthur Emmerly," she found photos of an elderly man, and of a school-age kid who looked nothing like Graham. She also found road race times, news of a city council dispute, links to a financial-planning firm, and various other entries that had no connection to Graham as she'd known him.

Yet in the poisoning articles, there *were* connections. The Arthur Emmerly in the stories, published in November 1998, would now be thirty-nine, Graham's age. And then there was the suspect's apparent interest in toxic substances. With a chill Nilda remembered the title of the book that bore Graham's name: *The Dose Makes the Poison.* Had it been more than just a college textbook?

She shut her laptop and leaned back once again, closed her eyes. But there was no forcing calmness on her jangled nerves.

This is what you get for diving into an internet rabbit hole. It was far from the first time she'd come out of a search more frustrated than enlightened. Yet she'd never been left so disturbed.

Still, if Graham were this Arthur from the articles, wouldn't he have made a bigger change to his name? Surely, he would have figured that prospective employers might do more than a cursory background check. Why leave even a single bread-crumb for them?

"Nilda?"

She sat up, startled to find Helen in the doorway. She thought she'd gone home for the evening.

"That window's working fine now. Do you need anything else before I leave?"

A few nights before, Helen had noticed Nilda struggling to open the window in the utility room, and she'd pledged to remedy it. *A vinegar solution'll unmuck things pronto. And it'll shine up the glass too. Like that grime never existed.*

"No, Helen. Thanks."

Helen stayed where she was, her eyes fixed on Nilda.

"Is something wrong?" Nilda asked.

Helen stepped closer. "I was going to ask the same thing of you. You look…overwhelmed."

That pretty much summed things up.

"I don't mean to insert myself where I don't belong. But if there's anything I can do to help you, even if it's just lending an ear, I'd be glad to."

Nilda's throat tightened. She sensed, perhaps beyond all reason, that she could tell Helen every single thing about Graham—about how she'd been drawn to him and then made wary of him, about his tonics and their effects on her, about the articles she'd found on the internet, and why they'd troubled her so—and Helen would listen with kindness, not judgment, and perhaps with a measure of understanding.

In the end there was only one thing she could bring herself to mention. "I saw something this evening, in the neighbor's yard, and it really got to me." She described what she'd seen while sparing the more gruesome details, for her own sake as much as Helen's. And she never mentioned Graham specifically, not because Helen would have no idea who he was but because speaking his name now suggested a connection with him, an intimacy that no longer existed, and that Nilda now regretted. "I know chickens are killed all the time, but it wasn't anything I'd expected to see. Ever. Especially so close to—" *Home* didn't fit what this place was to her. "—to where I live."

Helen didn't look the least bit surprised. "I'm sorry you had to witness that. Sounds to me like a botched job."

"What do you mean?"

"It takes two people to do an axe kill right, unless you have a good restraint. Your neighbor acted alone, I presume?"

"I think so." Nilda didn't remember hearing another voice. "You seem to speak from experience."

"I grew up on a farm not far from here. And, yes, I killed a few chickens there, just like everyone else in my family. But never with an axe."

Of course Helen knew how to slaughter chickens. She seemed capable of every task. "How'd you do it, then? If you don't mind me asking."

"Not at all." Yet Helen's hesitation before answering made Nilda doubt the wisdom of her curiosity. "We raised our chickens to trust us, to get used to us handling them. So whenever we approached them for the slaughter, they never ran away or made a fuss. They let us pick them up the way we always did: gently. And we'd stroke them and stroke them, in a motherly sort of way. Till they were on the edge of sleep."

Helen was cradling an invisible chicken, petting it slowly. "Then bit by bit, we'd maneuver them like so—" She put the imaginary bird in a football hold. "—and bring the stroking hand to the neck. And then—" She made a quick, twisting gesture, as if opening a jar. "—all went to black before they knew it. No blood. No needless suffering."

Nilda couldn't imagine wringing the neck of any creature, let alone one she'd bonded with. Fortunately, she'd never be in that position.

Headlight beams flashed in the window, crawled along the ceiling, then came to a stop. Helen's husband had arrived.

"I should be going."

"Of course."

"Good night, Nilda."

"Good night, Helen. And thanks for listening to me."

Nilda expressed her gratitude to Helen as often as she could, and she'd always meant it. But tonight, Helen's description of a merciful killing left Nilda even more unsettled than she'd been before. Maybe because the method seemed more cold-blooded than compassionate. Almost businesslike.

But for those chickens Helen had cradled and lulled, all must have seemed right with the world, to the very end. A deception, perhaps, yet far preferable to the alternative: those final, desperate moments of the hen Nilda had glimpsed through the fence.

I emerge in a hall I walked countless times in life, in a dress as familiar to me as my skin. My purpose? To tread forward, to once again feel the sweep of my skirt on that floor whose every creak is known to me. To once again experience motion, routine, and life as I'd lived it. To once again connect to a house so sealed in my bones I could never be fully free of it, even if I might want to. A house I swept and scrubbed and tended to as lovingly as my own.

—From *Autobiography of a Spirit* (Hitchfield Public Library, shelved under Fiction)

31

For most of her time in this house, Nilda had ignored the weeping, gunk-filled gaps between the kitchen sink and counter.

And the orphan socks, the underwear with holes or failed elastic, in her dresser drawers.

And all the crap—old running shoes and sandals, Angus-chewed Frisbees, and other nameless, forgotten things—she'd thrown into the hallway closet.

But over the last few days, she'd scraped gunk and caulked gaps; she'd tossed from the drawers and closet what should have been tossed months ago, before she'd moved it here; and she'd cast about for other things to fill her hours, trying to keep at bay her guilt over what she wasn't doing: her art.

The Tenneman and Farleigh paintings had been the last pieces she'd been able to bring to completion. Now it seemed pointless to go to the studio, or even sit at the kitchen table with her sketchpad. She was too distracted to accomplish anything that required creativity. Too distracted by what she'd seen through the fence, and learned of this Arthur Emmerly, however unlikely it was that he was Graham.

The kitchen table had become the base of operations for another new task: checking out online apartment listings. It had become clear that she needed to move out of this house, where she was never going to feel at home, where Toni's friendship and proximity could never compensate for the offness of this place and how that was affecting her, and also Sidney, it seemed.

Now she was sipping iced tea and cruising through some under-$1,500 listings in Providence, Rhode Island, which was looking like her best bet: not as expensive as Boston, yet reasonably close to her friends and connections there—and to Clay. *For Sidney's sake*, she told herself.

The overhead light flickered and dimmed, yet it held. So did the sound of the living room TV: high-pitched voices from one of Sidney's cartoon shows. So did the light from Nilda's computer screen. Probably, the house's ancient electrical system was to blame, though it hadn't acted up before.

On an ordinary afternoon, there would have been no need for the kitchen light. But around midday, clouds rolled in, darkening the sky and the house and defying the forecast of mostly sunny weather. Now a greenish light pervaded the room, making it look like a dreamed version of itself. Even the lemon wedge in her tea seemed transformed, its yellow bright but tainted, like some tempting-yet-menacing thing from a fairytale.

She remembered Graham's herb-infused lemonade, the greenness of its taste. She remembered what happened after she'd finished her glass: a round of intense sex followed by that troubling dream about this house, the details of which Graham had seemed to savor. Had the infusion been an aphrodisiac, or something more sinister?

She thought of Toni's concerns about Graham's tonics: how they might have been making Nilda just a bit weaker and more dependent on him. Maybe the lemonade was no different.

"*Mommy!*"

Nilda bolted for the living room, but Sidney met her halfway, in the hall. She was holding something out to her: a photograph.

"It's *Alex*, Mommy!"

Nilda took the photograph, saw a smiling pre-teen boy with curly red hair. He was sitting cross-legged on what looked to be the back patio, a shaggy little dog on his lap: a Yorkie. Almost certainly one of Eula Joy's. On the back of the photo, a date in black marker: *7/8/91*. Nothing else.

"Where'd you find this?"

"The toy cabinet."

That didn't make sense. Nilda had rooted around in there countless times and never come across any photographs. She headed to the living room, Sidney on her heels, then edged past the couch and a snoozing Angus, stopping at a nook beneath the built-in bookshelves: the toy cabinet. Scattered before it were stuffed animals, a Nerf ball, blocks, cars from Sidney's battered train set, and sections of the track. The contact paper that covered the floor of the cabinet had been pulled forward, the result of Sidney digging around for something, Nilda guessed.

She set the photograph aside and knelt before the cabinet, looking to where the contact paper had been pulled away. After removing the remaining toys, she pulled the paper back some more, then stopped. On the bottom side, the sticky side, she discovered another photograph—or, rather, the back of one, bearing the same black-markered date: *7/8/91*. She peeled it from the paper and turned it over, brought it into the light.

At the center of the photo, the red-haired boy, grinning again. On the left, leaning close to him, Eula Joy, for whom it had seemed a point of pride to never smile. But here she seemed to be fighting one, looking the happiest Nilda had ever seen. On the right, with her arm around the boy, Helen, grinning as widely as he was. Nilda realized she'd never seen her smile before—really smile, in a way that wasn't just a courtesy.

Loss had transformed her, Nilda supposed. The loss of her son. Was he the boy in the photograph? If so, was Sidney's Alex something more than an imaginary friend—in other words, a ghost?

Nilda sat back, dizzied. Not because of the boy in the photograph, or the possibility of his ghost. This couldn't be the Helen she knew. The Helen who'd seemed to appear out of nowhere, so intent on cleaning this house.

But it was, down to the shirtdress and the neatly pinned-up hair. And Nilda could no longer deceive herself that the Helen she knew was the daughter—or some other, younger relative—of the housekeeper who'd worked for Eula Joy: the housekeeper Eula Joy had described as "ailing" nearly ten years before. *That* Helen would be far older, and possibly even dead. Yet the Helen Nilda knew didn't look a day older than the one pictured here: her spitting image. What else could she be but a ghost?

Still, Nilda couldn't quite accept this. The Helen she knew polished floors and furniture, scrubbed grout, and cleaned windows. She brought Nilda tarts, pretzels, and cookies that were every bit as real as anything Nilda could make, or purchase at the store. And she'd listened to Nilda with understanding and kindness, and shared bits of knowledge about Eula Joy and her husband that Nilda couldn't have invented.

Could a ghost be such an active presence, physically and emotionally? That didn't seem possible.

"Mommy? Are you okay?"

Nilda looked to Sidney, who had taken up one of the stuffed animals, a chipmunk Jo had given her for her fourth birthday. "I'm fine, honey. My mind's just wandering." She pocketed the photo, relieved that Sidney hadn't asked to see it. Probably, she'd been too distracted by the toys.

"Can I get my snack?"

"Sure."

As Sidney ran to the kitchen, Nilda struggled to her feet, still lightheaded. She needed a bite too, though that wasn't why she felt so off. She reached for the couch to steady herself, then sat down by curled-up Angus. As she stroked his velvety head, she wished she could trade places with him, just briefly. She craved a break from her current reality, and at least one round of deep, trouble-free sleep.

If Helen were a ghost, why might she have reappeared here, other than out of a sense of devotion to Eula Joy, a devotion she'd described when Nilda first met her?

Nilda remembered something from Eula Joy's memo, about how Helen's son used to play in the house and yard: one of the reasons Helen had felt so connected to this place, even after he'd died. Maybe that connection had persisted past death, for mother and son alike.

No. Helen couldn't be dead. It just wasn't possible.

But Nilda felt the need to confront her, to say…what?

I found an old photo of you that put this crazy idea in my mind, and I'm sure you're going to tell me it's absurd.

There was something that made her more anxious than the prospect of a confrontation: the possibility that it would drive away Helen, living or ghostly, for good.

From the journals of Graham Emmerly:

July 25, 2019
Hen or human, the old and infirm deserve the most gentle of ends, not the one I delivered to you, dear Lucy. If only you could know that my rage had nothing to do with you and everything to do with the urge.

It's returned, and not in the "this too shall pass" way. Like before, it's making that movie play through my mind, of the delivery, the transformation, the ebbing. The only new thing is the star.

The loop repeats and repeats, and it seems it will not stop until I answer the urge or kill it. The latter being the only option, one of the tinctures must come to my aid.

Chemist, heal thyself.

July 27, 2019
Tinctures 23 and 24: utter failures. 25? It makes the movie feel a bit more distant, but still it plays. Surely, I can find a more effective formulation.

To the lab I go.

From *The Odyssey:*

Then I tried to find some way of embracing my poor mother's ghost. Thrice I sprang towards her and tried to clasp her in my arms, but each time she flitted from my embrace as if it were a dream or phantom, and being touched to the quick I said to her, "Mother, why do you not stay still when I would embrace you? If we could throw our arms around one another, we might find sad comfort in the sharing of our sorrows even in the house of Hades."

"My son," she answered, "…all people are like this when they are dead. The sinews no longer hold the flesh and bones together; these perish in the fierceness of consuming fire as soon as life has left the body, and the soul flits away as though it were a dream."

32

S he'd found only two Helen Thurnwells, and no obituaries for either one of them. The first was a management con- sultant in Iowa City, according to her LinkedIn profile; the second was a nine-year-old member of a family of five, according to the 1930 Census. No way either one could be the Helen Nilda knew.

Needing a break, Nilda looked up from her laptop. Straight ahead: the dark TV screen. On any other Thursday, at this very moment, she'd be on this same couch, a glass of red wine in hand, or within reach. Same as now. But the TV would be aglow with *The See-er* and the show's nighttime views into the rooms of other troubled houses, views that set up and unfailingly delivered on expectations that something would be revealed: a wandering shadow, a slammed door, a hurled object, or some other disturbance. Afterward the See-er herself would deliver on expectations too: that meaning could be derived from these disturbances, individually or collectively, however random they might have seemed at first.

Yet her time in this house had reminded Nilda of something she'd known all along: that meaning wasn't necessarily a given, in anything. And maybe some mysteries were ends in them- selves, impenetrable by design.

She took a big sip of wine, draining her glass, then typed *Alex Thurnwell death obituary* into the search bar.

The first entry: *Local Boy Dead after Heat Stroke*.

She clicked on the link and arrived at a page from the *Farleigh Eagle*, dated September 13, 1992. At the top of it was the same headline, and beneath it a picture of a smiling red-haired boy. The boy from the photos in the toy cabinet.

Alex.

Sidney hadn't imagined him, or not in the way Nilda had supposed. Now she struggled to remember what Sidney had said about him. Her mind a blur, she started reading the article:

A Hartwell boy died yesterday from multiple organ failure, apparently a result of heat stroke, according to the Sanford County Medical Examiner.

On Wednesday Alex Thurnwell, 12, was rushed to Sanford Memorial Hospital after losing consciousness during a soccer game. That day, temperatures reached an unseasonably high 99 degrees and remained in the nineties until dusk.

"It's an absolute tragedy," said Janeen Pascoli, who teaches math at Greenbridge Middle School, where Thurnwell was a student and where he and other boys had been playing an impromptu game of soccer after class. "I just wish I could have done more."

Pascoli said she was heading to the parking lot after school when one of the boys ran to her and asked her to call 911.

"While we waited for the ambulance, he told me that Alex took a break from the game, saying he wasn't feeling well. Then things took a really bad turn. By the time I got to him, he was just lying there, staring up at the sky. It was an awful sight to see. Not just for me but for all those other boys."

Pascoli said there was no ice on site to cool Thurnwell, and the boys didn't have any water. "All I saw was an empty bottle of Gatorade. By the time I got some water to him, he wasn't conscious enough to drink it."

Lynn Romero, director of public affairs for the Sanford County Department of Health, observed, "We put out this warning every summer, but it bears repeating: When temperatures climb into the eighties and beyond, everyone should limit or avoid strenuous exercise, and everyone should stay hydrated, regardless of their activity levels. These simple measures can and do save lives."

Picturing Alex collapsed on that field, helpless, Nilda thought of Sidney. If such a thing happened to her—

No.

She turned her thoughts to Helen. Wherever she'd been when she'd gotten the news—at home? here?—Nilda hoped that she wasn't alone, and that if Eula Joy had been her only witness then, her only companion, she'd shown as much compassion as she could. Eula Joy's near-smile in that photo, and the way she'd leaned toward Alex, suggested this was more than possible.

And those other boys, that kind teacher, that school, hopefully they'd been a source of—

That school. She realized why it sounded so familiar.

The beat-up biology textbook in Graham's study had been labeled as the Property of Greenbridge Middle School. Doing the math, she figured that Graham and Alex would have been at Greenbridge around the same time. Possibly, they'd been in the same grade.

And if Alex had spent as much time around this house as Eula Joy had claimed, maybe he and Graham had played together. Here, or in the woods. Or next door.

The bad kid's house.

Alex's words, according to Sidney. His description of the model that Nilda had destroyed, the model that looked like Graham's place.

She felt a twist to her gut.

Take a break. Take Angus for a walk. Vinegar some windows if you have to.

But there was no escaping what she was thinking, feeling. Instead, she started back through the article, stopping at the first sentence.

...died yesterday from multiple organ failure...

Hadn't Arthur Emmerly's victim experienced organ failure, or something approaching it?

Nilda pictured the sidelines of that soccer field, Alex slumped on a bench—flushed, fading, then collapsing to the ground. She saw the other boys running for him, Graham among them, or lagging just slightly behind. She saw the teacher rushing to the scene, trying to hide how worried she was, then trying to say calming things. To her Graham would look as innocent as the others. And if that empty bottle had once contained something other than Gatorade, she would never know. She would never begin to imagine such a thing.

Nilda went back to the search field and typed in various combinations of *Alex Thurnwell, Arthur Emmerly, Graham Emmerly, poisoning, suspicious death.* But she found only two other articles about Alex. Both mentioned heat stroke; neither mentioned poisoning, or Graham or Arthur Emmerly.

Maybe he'd just gotten away with it.

Or maybe she was overreacting, reaching for connections that didn't exist. Heat stroke wasn't uncommon, and she'd heard of other young athletes dying from it.

Nilda's thoughts circled back to the teacher, to how helpless she must have felt. Her words for what she'd witnessed on that field suggested the kind of mental picture, the kind of trauma, that no amount of time could dissolve. *He was just lying there, staring up at the sky. It was an awful sight to see. Not just for me but for all those other boys.*

...staring up at the sky. The words triggered a memory of that boy's voice, spoken by a sleepwalking Sidney: *He likes watching their eyes turn to glass.*

Alex's voice?

Her phone buzzed on the coffee table. She put her laptop aside and grabbed it, found a text from Clay:

Let me know if you need anything else for Saturday. If not, just wish me luck.

Saturday, the start of the festival, was the day after tomorrow, but it might as well have been ten years into the future. Nilda felt so distanced from the Tenneman painting, and from the rage that had fueled its creation, that it seemed like someone else's work. In a larger sense, she'd never been more detached from her art, and everything connected to it.

She texted back "I'm all set" and her thanks, then brought Toni's number up on her phone. She wanted to call her, tell her everything. Everything that troubled her about Helen, and all her new fears about Graham. She wanted to tell her about the model house that had driven her to destroy it, the mysteriously shattered vase, and the leaning chamber. She wanted to tell her about Sidney speaking in a voice that wasn't hers, possibly the voice of a dead boy. A dead boy Sidney had come to see as a friend. Nilda's old concern that this would all be too much— even for Toni—had vanished.

But Toni was in Denver for the wedding, and a mini family reunion. Not the time or the place for what would surely rank among the top five neediest and most emotionally draining phone calls she'd ever receive. Nilda could wait a few days, though they might prove to be the longest of her life.

She reached for the wine bottle, then stopped. Going beyond her two-glass limit wasn't going to make tonight any easier, and it would get tomorrow off to a rough start.

She took the bottle and her empty glass to the kitchen and went to find Angus, who had assumed his usual nighttime post at the foot of her bed, where he was curled up, asleep.

"Angus?" He remained sound asleep. "*Walkies!*"

Still nothing.

What, then?

She paced the room, half-expecting headlights to shine through the window, announcing Helen's arrival, something Nilda desired and dreaded with equal measure.

She kept on pacing, though it offered no comfort and made her feel more and more directionless, helpless. She wanted— needed—to get away. Away from herself.

This thought stopped her. She stepped into the hall and then to the door of the strange little room. Pushing it open, she found nothing but darkness. Then her eyes adjusted, allowing her to make out the room's odd angles, and the turret. Yet the window in the turret's roof admitted barely any light. Then she remembered the heavy cloud cover.

The moon wouldn't save her tonight.

There was another option though: one she hadn't tried. She stepped down the hall to the spare bedroom, then opened the door. In the light from the hall, the dresser glowed from its polish, its death's head–like carvings more pronounced. She entered the room and rounded the bed, stopping at the arched, floor-level window. What Farleigh—and Graham—had claimed didn't seem possible: that lying down by one of these windows, and contemplating the world beyond it, could soothe a troubled mind or soul. Yet Farleigh had written that for certain patients in the asylum he'd designed, the experience had proved "transformative."

She thought of the drawing from his journals, of a night-gowned patient lying on her side and staring out of a window identical to the one at Nilda's feet. She lowered herself to the floor and assumed the same position, feeling foolish, not soothed.

Give it some time.

The hall light reached the window, returning a faint reflection of her face resting on her hands, of her shoulders and middle. Straining to see beyond this, she found the old maple at the yard's edge, picked out by the one functioning, and increasingly dim, spotlight in the eaves. A gusting wind swayed its branches, and she fixed her eyes on them, as if they might deliver a sign.

They didn't, of course. Nothing was different.

Give up. Get up.

Not yet. Stay just a bit longer.

As she watched the tree, she became less aware of it, more aware of the reflection beneath it—hers—and her proximity to it. It reminded her of those times in her childhood when she'd snuck up on her napping mother and whispered in her ear.

Wake up, Mom! Wake up!

She whispered the words again, knowing they were pointless, hopeless. All they did was speak a truth: that right now, she wanted—needed—her mother more than anything in the world. Out of that need, she sang the old lullaby:

Night knitter, night knitter, I'll never know why
You've made it your duty to cover the sky
With a blanket so thick and so dark in its hue
That only the moon and the stars can break through

She sang every verse and started in again, all the while listening for a trace of her mother's voice in her own. Wasn't there an echo of it, in those ending, rhyming words? The way she drew them out, just slightly? The wind picked up and, blowing past the eaves, echoed the rhyming *oo*'s.

Keep singing. Keep singing, and listen.

The window, so close, brought back to her her own breath, her own voice. But when she closed her eyes, she could imagine it was her mother's breath and voice, the two of them singing in unison. As she neared the edge of sleep, it seemed her mother's voice surrounded her, and sounded throughout the house.

33

So you want a falafel roll-up with extra hummus."

"Yep."

"Wanna split some fries?"

"Absolutely."

"Okay. Meet you back here in five. Or ten."

"I'm guessing fifteen." Wandering the grounds, they'd noticed long lines at almost every food truck, including the one for Falafel Genie. And though they'd been here less than an hour, Ardley's patience with the crowds was wearing thin. Already, she'd flat-tired two strangers as she and Becca pushed their way through bottlenecks of people, many of them looking as slack-mouthed and aimless as Ardley felt.

"See you then."

As soon as Becca vanished into the crowd, Ardley entered the attraction they'd chosen as a meeting spot, mainly for its lack of a line: the art exhibit. Looking ahead, she saw a sparsely populated maze of tables displaying pottery, glassware, quilts and other textiles, and various unidentifiable tchotchkes. At the farthest end stood what looked like a giant function tent. Next to its entrance, a sign: "Fine Art."

Knowing her time was limited, and having little interest in artsy-craftsy stuff, she made her way through the maze and toward the tent. Inside, it had the look of a miniature museum, the art displayed on wall-like panels that created another kind of maze. As she moved through it, she noticed several people holding plastic tumblers of wine. It seemed that a bar had been set up somewhere, one possible reason the tent was busier than the space outside of it.

With that bar in mind, Ardley kept up her pace, hoping she'd have time to score some drinks for herself and Becca.

After their first museum visit together, Becca dubbed Ardley "the drive-byer," because she rarely cared to linger before paintings or sculptures, preferring breadth and motion to the "rabbit-holing" Becca was given to at museums. Now Ardley was living up to her nickname, striding past still lifes of flowers, fruit, and glassware; past renderings of landscapes and seascapes; past abstracts that were blurry, blocky, or blotchy, or some combination thereof. Though all the pieces in this exhibit looked accomplished, and worthy of closer attention, none of them slowed her down.

Rounding another bend in the maze, she entered a row of portraits—of everyday people, it seemed: a teenager holding out a fish on a line, the fish half as big as he was; a toddler smiling at seashells cupped in her hands; an elderly man and woman standing shoulder to shoulder, no smiles, as if they were barely tolerating the artist's intrusion.

The next painting stopped her. Or, rather, the man staring from it did. She knew that stare and, years before, had felt singled out by it—in a good way, at first.

You're a very promising young woman, Ardley.

Now that stare seemed edged with something she'd never seen in him: fear.

Good.

The girls around him—actually, they seemed to be repetitions of one girl—wore the same uniform Ardley had at Fairmoore: the pleated skirt of Cameron plaid, the matching bow tie and white oxford. Unlike Tenneman—*William Fletcher Tenneman,* according to a brass plate bolted to the frame—they looked fearless, their faces showing resolve, and the anger of the accusations that floated above their heads.

Predator. Violator. Monster. No one listened. No one listened. No one listened.

No one listened to Ardley either. For years she'd suspected she wasn't the only girl he'd assaulted, and then had her reports about it gone unheeded by Fairmoore. Now she knew she'd been right.

Was the girl in the painting the artist? Was the "Doomed" she was whispering in Tenneman's ear a truth or just a wish?

There was no signature at the bottom of the painting, just a series of hashtags: #MeToo, #FairmooreAlum, and #TennemanOut.

She could check Twitter now and maybe get some answers. But she didn't want to do that without Becca.

With a new sense of urgency, she hunted down the bar, ordered beers for Becca and herself, and hurried back to the exhibit entrance. A minute later, Becca emerged from the crowd, toting a grease-speckled paper bag. Seeing it, Ardley realized that her appetite had vanished.

"You're a goddess," Becca said, glancing at the bottles of beer. Then she noticed the look on Ardley's face. "Are you okay?"

"I'm fine," Ardley said. "But I need to show you something."

She took a fortifying sip of her beer, then led Becca back to the painting, knowing she didn't need to offer any words of explanation.

Years before, when it was clear that things were getting serious between the two of them, Ardley told Becca the whole story about Tenneman and what he'd done, about how the school had failed her. As much as she'd wished otherwise, the story had become a part of her, a part she didn't want to hide from the person she'd decided to share her life with.

Becca studied the painting, then set the bag and her beer on the ground. She put her arm around Ardley's waist, laid her head on her shoulder. "You must have felt ambushed when you saw this thing. I'm so sorry."

Ambushed was just the right word.

"It's kind of confusing, you know? I mean, I'm kind of relieved I'm not alone in this. But that sounds so terrible."

"That doesn't sound terrible at all. It makes perfect sense."

As Becca checked out the hashtags on the painting, Ardley remembered what she'd wanted to ask her. "Would you mind checking out those Twitter feeds for me? I'm not ready to look at them myself."

Becca grabbed her phone and fiddled with it for a moment. Then she looked up at Ardley. "Wanna hear the opening post for TennemanOut?"

"Sure."

"Well, the poster included the painting, and then they wrote, 'A sexual predator has no business leading the Fairmoore School.'"

Yes. Ardley had long thought that very thing. But the reality that he'd never face consequences had made this line of thinking painful, something to be submerged. Now she felt an edge of hope, and fresh anger.

Becca kept scrolling and reading other posts: mostly expressions of agreement and support. Then this tweet: *So I wasn't his only target, huh?* And this response, not from the original poster: *Sadly, no. But Fairmoore's like a stone wall around him.* Then this, from still another poster: *Enough force can break down a wall, right?*

Ardley looked back to the painting. Maybe she should be part of the wrecking crew. But how? Whatever that involved, she wasn't sure she'd be up for it, not after what she'd gone through the first time. And that hint of fear in the painted Tenneman: surely, it was a product of the artist's imagination, nothing more.

Still, she reached into the Lucite bin hanging to the right of the painting. It was full of #TennemanOut buttons. She held one of the buttons in her hand, unsure of whether to wear it or put it back. In the end she stashed it in her back pocket.

A microphoned voice echoed in the distance, followed by strumming on an electric guitar—a sign that the first band was starting up, and that they should start heading toward it. The musical lineup had been their main reason for coming here.

Becca took Ardley's hand, but not to lead her out of the tent. "You sure you're up for some music?"

Ardley wasn't at all sure. Still, she said, "Yes."

They found a spot to finish their beers, sandwiches, and fries, Ardley's appetite having returned, the beer taking the edge off the feelings that the Tenneman ambush had brought back to the surface.

Yet once they reached the performance space, Ardley couldn't give the bands her full attention, and these words kept playing through her mind: *Enough force can break down a wall.*

If anything, the feeling is getting worse, more intense.
That's not all. Today, while working on 28, Papa Nix came
to mind. (No accident, I'm sure.) I remembered I hadn't rid
myself of all of it. Yet even if I went looking for it, which I
won't, delivering it would be nearly impossible given our
lack of contact. Thank God.

—From the journals of Graham Emmerly, July 31, 2019

34

"You working out or something?"

Nilda set the rag aside and turned up the volume on the speakerphone. "I'm cleaning windows." Her latest chore of distraction.

"*Cleaning windows?* Someone plant a chip in your brain?"

"Very funny." But part of her wished this wasn't a joke. At least a chip implant might explain why the last few days—no, weeks—had felt so surreal and disturbing. "I just need a little break from my painting." Nilda was glad Clay wasn't here to see the lie in those words. She didn't need a break from something she'd given up on, at least for the time being. Now she just wanted to change the subject. "I'm really glad things went so well at the festival. Thanks for everything you did."

In the hours leading up to this call, Clay had texted her with various updates, the most important one being that his comings and goings at the festival had barely been noticed. As instructed, he'd left the crated painting at its assigned spot in the exhibit area, where he installed a dispenser for the #TennemanOut buttons. Then he departed the grounds unharassed, with no need of Toni's lawyer. Far from it.

"Well," Clay said, "the good news keeps coming. Have you checked out the feeds yet?"

He'd texted her the same question a couple of hours ago, but she hadn't responded to it. His description of the Twitter and Instagram feeds as "hopping" had filled her with anxiety and made her worry that reactions to the painting had already gotten back to Fairmoore, which was just across the road from the festival and one of its major sponsors. Maybe authorities at the school were already trying to hunt her down, vengeance in mind. If so, so be it. She'd understood this risk from the start, and worrying about it now felt selfish considering everything that Toni had gone through.

"I did, a few hours ago." At that time there were just the opening posts from Toni, Clay, and herself, and a few support-ive responses.

"A lot's happened since then. You gotta take a look."

"I will. As soon as we get off the phone." To give her arm a rest, she set aside the cleaning rag. Beyond the window the sky looked bruised, a sign of the heavy rains that had been forecast for this evening. "Are you back in Boston?"

"Yep. I'm actually on kind of a deadline."

"What for?"

"Gotta get another apartment ready for Rick, a month-to-monther." A former bandmate of Clay's, Rick was now a property manager, and a small-time landlord. "Fortunately, it just needs a paint job."

Nilda pictured an empty space, an echo of her old living room in Boston: light streaming in from the front bay window, spilling on the worn wood floors. The image filled her with longing. "Is it still available?"

Until speaking these words, Nilda hadn't realized how much she wanted to get out of this place, and how quickly.

"I'd have to ask. You know someone who's interested?"

"Yeah. Me."

Clay went silent. Then he said, "Is something wrong with your place?"

Giving him a full explanation would take more from her, emotionally and maybe physically, than she could spare right now. She aimed for a shortcut. "It just feels so unfamiliar to me here, so alien, and that's not getting any better. Being in the middle of nowhere isn't helping."

"I had a feeling country living wasn't gonna agree with you."

It was so much more than that, but Nilda didn't disagree. "It'd be nice to be back in Boston for a couple of months, think through some next steps." She guessed that two months would give her enough time to put this house on the market, nail down a new place in Providence, and get her stuff moved there.

"Rick could find you something longer term, I'm sure. Want me to ask him?"

"No. Short-term would be better for me right now."

"All right. I'll ask him about the month-to-monther."

Nilda detected a hint of disappointment in Clay's voice, and she wondered whether he'd hoped for a different response: that she wanted to return to Boston for the longer term. The part of her that was still in love with him, that missed her life back in the city, *did* want that. But she couldn't afford that choice, in more ways than one.

"I should let you go," she said.

"Yeah, I gotta make some hay. I'll let you know what I hear from Rick. In the meantime *check out the feeds.*"

"I will. I promise."

As soon as she signed off, she did just that, starting with Twitter. Just as Clay had said, the responses to the opening tweet had multiplied since her last check. Scrolling through, she stopped at this run of posts:

So I wasn't his only target, huh?

Sadly, no. But Fairmoore's like a stone wall around him.

Enough force can break down a wall, right?

Count me (another target) and my sledgehammer in. This one got several likes and retweets.

One of them from Toni.

Lightning flashed, drawing her attention back to her bedroom window. Seconds later, thunder rumbled, rattling the glass.

She watched as the sky opened up, the rain graying her view of the yard and the trees at its edge. She looked for the old maple she'd spotted last night from the floor-level window. There it was, swaying again, as if it might give her a sign.

She remembered singing to that window's glass, her mother's breath and voice returned to her. If only in her imagination.

I exist both in and apart from the world of the living, no
more free of pain or want than they are.

—From *Autobiography of a Spirit*

35

They barely talked as the storm raged around them, their
world down to the screech and thump of the wipers,
and the rain-blurred road ahead, only so much as the
headlights showed.

Russ could drive through anything, had for years. As for her?
Few things frightened Helen anymore.

From the corner of her eye, she saw him glancing her way.

"You're looking so tired these days. Maybe it's time to give
this work up, for good."

She met his eye and smiled.

"Is that a *Yes?*"

"Ask me again tomorrow."

He laughed. "Seems I've heard that line before."

She looked back to the road.

"I'll never understand what keeps you going back."

How many times had he said that? She'd lost count.

Did he remember that, once, she'd tried to give him an
answer? *I see him there.*

Then, Russ acted as if he hadn't heard her, though she knew
he had, and she guessed what he was thinking: the same thing
he'd told her many times. *You need to let him go.*

Now what would Russ say if she told him how things had
changed? How she could also *feel* their child, hold him? Only at
certain unpredictable moments. But still.

In the end she kept her silence and spoke a truth to herself.
I'll never stop being a mother. I'm needed, and not just by our son.

I'm needed. I'm needed. And I need.

36

Nilda pulled the lasagna, browned and bubbling, out of the oven and set it on the stovetop. Although the recipe called for fifteen minutes of resting time, she was ready to tear into it now.

She was grateful that the power had held through its baking, and so far no lights had flickered or dimmed in the storm. When they had the other day, that seemed more connected to some electrical issue—she imagined a burgeoning disaster in the wiring—than to the weather. Another good reason to be moving from this house.

"That smells good, Mommy." Sidney was sitting at the kitchen table, amid a spill of crayons, drawing pictures of Angus. Angus himself was nowhere to be seen, his bowl of kibble untouched in the corner. Last time Nilda checked, he was cowering under her bed, terrified by the storm.

"Let's hope it *tastes* good."

The lasagna was one of Sidney's favorites: 90 percent noodles and cheese, 10 percent tomato sauce. To her, jarred sauce would have been just as good as the sauce Nilda had made from scratch—another chore of distraction, one that had delayed their usual dinner time by more than an hour.

The sky flashed and exploded, rumbling the earth and the house. A hand to her pounding heart, Nilda approached the window, which she'd left ajar, just enough to admit a bit of fresh air. She looked for signs of a lightning strike, smoke or flames, and saw nothing more than the darkened yard, the pouring rain. But there was that banging again, from Graham's. She turned away from it and found Sidney staring at her.

"Can we *please* go close it? Water's gonna get into his house."

This was the second time Sidney had asked this, making Nilda regret that she'd mentioned Graham's door—front or back, she wasn't sure—as the likely reason for the sound. If she hadn't deleted his number from her phone, she might have texted him about it.

"No. Graham'll deal with it."

She guessed that wouldn't be anytime soon. Shortly after putting the lasagna in the oven, she'd dashed out for the mail, just in time to see him driving off somewhere. Then she remembered that his night classes were just starting up. And for some reason, one session was scheduled for Saturdays. Or that's what she remembered him saying.

Thoughts of Graham reminded Nilda of something she wasn't looking forward to: Soon, she'd have to tell Sidney they were moving again, giving some reason that had nothing to do with her suspicions about him. Yet in the time since those suspicions had become most acute, she'd thought as much about Alex as Graham. Or, rather, she couldn't stop picturing Alex's end. *He was just lying there, staring up at the sky.*

Sidney got up and started for the hall.

"Where're you going?" If Sidney were to bolt out the front door for Graham's, that wouldn't be at all surprising. Nilda recognized her own willfulness in Sidney, the same willfulness they'd both inherited from Jo.

"To the toy cabinet. I want the new crayons."

The ones on the table were pretty worn, and two of Sidney's favorite colors—spring green and violet—had gone missing.

The dryer beeped, sending Nilda into the utility room. She pulled the laundry from the dryer and began folding it. Then a sound stopped her. Not the banging from Graham's but a high, distant hum. She knew what it was: an invitation that filled her with dread.

Don't look. Just let it go.

Yet she was already heading back through the kitchen and

into the hallway, then into the dining room. In the corner the pedestal fan was running at its highest speed, just as it had when she found Graham's shattered vase. Now she found something else. In front of the window, on top of her mother's sculpture, were the remains of the model house she'd taken a poker to, then tossed down the cellar stairs.

The house that looked like Graham's.

That wasn't all. The remains were balanced on top of the model house from Sidney's room: one that looked like *this* place.

Nilda looked back to the wrecked house. Though its roof was caved and two sides were missing, the front of the thing remained. So did those spider eyes. They twinkled in the dimness, watching her.

Sidney couldn't have done this. Helen couldn't have either. She hadn't been here for days, living being or ghost.

Could the houses have moved on their own, driven by some kind of force? What, then, was that force? Or who? Nathaniel Farleigh? At various times in this house—when Nilda had studied the faces on the fireplace pillars and mantels, leaned in the turret chamber, or lain by the spare-room window—Farleigh had felt present, but only in the sense that something of every artist emanates from the work they leave behind. It had never been anything as blatant as the scene now before her.

A scene that didn't square with Farleigh, come to think of it. He'd grown to hate the house she'd smashed, even snuffed his cigars on it. Why, then, would he have anything to do with resurrecting it from the cellar, and placing it on top of the house that stood in for his own?

And why was her mother's sculpture the stage for it, once again?

This sparked a picture of Graham's shattered vase, the shards scattered across the floor. Behind them the red waves of her mother's sculpture had looked like a force of destruction, frozen in time.

At the time she'd wondered whether the shattering had been

a warning, from her mother. Was this a second, more urgent one, about the dangers of staying here? About the dangers of Graham?

Don't worry, Mom. We're getting out of here, as soon as we possibly can.

She wanted to voice these words, but wasn't speaking to a ghost to believe that she existed? Even now, despite the scene before her, despite what she'd imagined in the spare room last night, that felt like false hope, or a jinx.

A clattering sounded at the window, like pebbles striking the glass. Surely, nothing more than rain in a wind gust. Still, mild curiosity drew her to the window. So did the desire to get that wrecked house behind her, out of her sight.

She and Sidney could go to Toni's tonight; it had been a standing invitation. Yet Nilda wasn't as brave as Graham about driving in this weather, and the forecasts had warned of downed trees and power lines, flooded roads. Tomorrow, then?

Rain poured in the dimness between her and Graham's window, where the curtains remained drawn. As strange as it seemed, this was the first time it really occurred to her: She'd never see the inside of his house again. At some point this place too would—

The curtains stirred. Then a hand reached through them— too small, too pale to be Graham's. It pulled one panel aside, revealing who it belonged to: a slip of a boy, with curly red hair.

The boy she'd seen in the photographs. Alex.

He wasn't some vapor, on the edge of dissolving. He looked every bit as solid, every bit as real, as herself. And he was fixing her with a wide-eyed stare, as if terrified by something on his side, or hers.

Look away, she thought. *Leave*.

But she couldn't.

He pressed a hand to the window, as if he needed her, or wanted to tell her something.

She stepped back and grasped onto the sculpture, the only

reason she remained on her feet. Then she closed her eyes and imagined something that had always calmed her as a child: her mother working glass. In the light and heat of the furnace, Jo slowly turned the blowpipe and the molten, glowing glass. Everything under her control.

Mom.

"Mom?"

A boy's voice, so distant. Then darkness. Then nothing.

"Mom? *Mom?*"

The voice drew her back…

…her son's voice. The sound of it wrenched her heart.

She opened her eyes and there he was, looking so far away, so frightened. What was he doing over there?

She pressed her own hand to the glass and mouthed, *Wait*, afraid he'd vanish once again, his hold so loose on this world.

Running to the hall, she found the front door wide open. She dashed through it, into the rain, then up to the Emmerlys' front door, which was also ajar. In all the years she'd worked at the Austerlanes, she'd never set foot in their house. Neither had her son, as far as she knew. Following Mrs. Austerlane's lead, she'd warned him away from everything connected to that boy.

Now she rushed through the door and ran for the room where she'd seen him. But he wasn't there. In his place stood a girl in a rain-dampened dress. Nilda's girl.

"I need to show you something, Mommy."

Mommy? I'm not your mommy. Where in God's name is my boy?

Her vision dimming, she grasped hold of an easy chair. *Don't go under, not here.*

She closed her eyes and tried to calm her breathing. Slowly, a figure materialized in the darkness, a woman standing before a glowing furnace, turning molten glass.

Mom.

Opening her eyes, she found herself—and Sidney—in Graham's study. Sidney must have come over to shut the door, and then curiosity got the better of her. But Nilda? She had no memory of getting here, just a dizzying murk in her head.

"We need to get out of here, Sidney. *Now*." It was possible that Graham's class had been canceled due to the storm, and he was just out for an errand.

She grabbed Sidney's hand and started pulling her toward the door.

Sidney planted her feet, tried to tug Nilda her way. "I need to show you something."

Nilda felt a flush of anger, and fear. "Just *tell* me about it. When we get home."

"Alex said you should see it for yourself."

Alex. A memory of him came back to Nilda, not as a figure from the photographs but as a figure in Graham's window: the last thing she could remember before finding herself in this room.

"Was he here?"

Sidney nodded. "I don't know where he went."

Had he led both of them here on purpose?

"Okay," Nilda said. "Show me. But we need to make it fast."

Sidney pulled her to the far corner of the study, home of the roll-top desk Nilda had never paid much attention to, perhaps because the cover had always been closed. Now it was pushed back, revealing a stack of mail, a composition notebook, and a bottle of expensive-looking scotch, nearly empty. Next to the bottle was a nearly empty glass, fogged with a moss-green residue. The remains of one of his tonics? Even from this distance she could smell something medicinal.

Sidney pointed to the notebook, which was place-marked with a pen. "It's in there."

Graham's journal.

Dread of what she'd find in it froze her, yet there was no time to waste. Nilda opened the notebook to the marked pages and scanned the most recent entries.

...And here, I must confess something if only to banish the possibility

of acting on it: I'm starting to feel the urge again, for the first time in years. Maybe this is just a reaction to the possibility of losing her, and a love that feels exceptional. *…my rage had nothing to do with you and everything to do with the urge…it's making that movie play through my mind, of the delivery, the transformation, the ebbing. The only new thing is the star.*

The loop repeats and repeats, and it seems it will not stop until I answer the urge or kill it…

Tinctures 23 and 24: utter failures. 25? It makes the movie feel a bit more distant, but still it plays.

Reaching the last two entries, Nilda slowed down in spite of herself. She needed to take in all the words, make as much sense of them as she could.

If anything, the feeling is getting worse, more intense.

That's not all. Today, while working on 28, Papa Nix came to mind. (No accident, I'm sure.) I remembered I hadn't rid myself of all of it. Yet even if I went looking for it, which I won't, *delivering it would be nearly impossible given our lack of contact. Thank God.*

Papa Nix. Graham had told her that he didn't miss his father, said it was a relief that he was gone. Had Papa Nix been a means to this end? Something Graham had concocted in his lab?

Nilda remembered him warning Sidney away from the door to the cellar. That warning had a new significance, so did the lock on the door.

The final entry, dated today: *Can't stop thinking of her eyes at transformation, at ebbing: the dulling of that beautiful green.*

A shock rolled through Nilda. *My* eyes.

She remembered Sidney speaking with a boy's voice. Alex's? *He likes watching their eyes turn to glass.* A simple truth or a warning. Perhaps born of experience.

Imagining that change brings me to the edge, and in my mind (and body) I go over it, and over it again.

She read the final lines:

This has me thinking through methods of contact, making the tincture

efforts feel all but hopeless. Still, I must work, work, work on them, on
anything: an absolutely necessary distraction, if an imperfect one.

And as I work, I hold on to this very small comfort: that she bears
more than a small share of blame for my condition. If only she weren't in
her ex's thrall, if only she'd stayed with me, how much brighter the future
would be, for both of us.

Her hands trembling, Nilda closed the notebook on the pen
and put it back on the desk, not remembering exactly where it
had been and hoping Graham wouldn't either.

What were *methods of contact?* Ways to jump her? Or break
into the house? The second possibility chilled her. Sidney was
in danger too, and they needed to get to Toni's right away.
Washed-out roads be damned.

Sidney glanced between Nilda and the journal. "What does
it say?"

Thank God Sidney hadn't read it. But even if she had, she
wouldn't have been able to understand all the words, let alone
the larger implications. Nilda herself understood just enough
to be terrified.

She tried to smile, and then she lied. "It's nothing to worry
about. But we need to leave. This isn't our house."

Then she thought of what they might be leaving behind. She
stripped off her overshirt and, as quickly as she could, felt for
traces of rain on the carpeting, scrubbing damp spots from the
desk to the door. Fortunately, neither she nor Sidney had gotten
soaked on the way here. And soon, with luck, they'd be miles
away from it.

As he neared the house, he cut his lights, slowed his speed to
a crawl.

Chances were he'd find not a burglary in progress—or completed—but just the "threat" the security system had alerted
him to: an open front door, probably a result of the storm. Still,
he couldn't be too careful.

All the way here he'd cursed the fact that the alert had come long after he'd left for a class that had ended up being canceled, long after the security system had supposedly armed, having assured him that every door, every window, was closed.

Through the rain's blur, he detected motion ahead and braked his car to a stop. Two figures were bolting from his property, then running along the road's edge.

Nilda and Sidney, the sight a stab to his gut. He watched them run for their house, then vanish into it.

Pulling into his drive, he found the front door closed. Maybe this had been their doing, a gesture of neighborly kindness.

Please, let that have been their only *doing. For their sakes, as well as* mine.

Soon—unless the security cameras had also failed him— he'd know the truth.

Of course I was under the spell, and the wonderful part is that, even at the time, I perfectly knew I was. But I gave myself up to it; it was an antidote to any pain, and I had more pains than one.

—From *The Turn of the Screw* by Henry James

37

Sidney repeated the list back to Nilda: "Jammies, tooth-brush, undies, socks, shorts, T-shirts, sneakers."

"You got it."

"And Fuzzy."

"Of course, Fuzzy." Nilda lowered the pan of lasagna, now covered in foil and barely warm, into the travel bag. Her hunger for it seemed to have been sated by adrenaline, which fueled both her darts about the kitchen and the thoughts now racing through her mind. One of them was that no degree of hunger, no deficit in blood sugar, could have explained what she'd seen in the dining room: on the sculpture or at the window. Nor could it explain the blackout she'd roused from at Graham's. When it came to her experiences in this house, she'd exceeded the limits of logic, long ago.

Nilda opened the "goodie cabinet" and started grabbing snacks from it, tossing them into the travel bag. "Do you remember where your suitcase is?"

"Yep."

"Excellent. Now. If you beat me in packing, you get a choco pop for the road."

"Really?"

"Really."

The truth was, Sidney was going to take the prize in this competition, win or lose: a small compensation for Nilda's latest lie of expedience—that they needed to get to Toni's as quickly as possible to check her flood-prone basement. As a "treat," they'd do a sleepover there. Tomorrow Nilda would have to explain, somehow, that their sleepover was going to be extended, indefinitely. And eventually, Sidney would realize that she'd never see this place again. Or Alex, presumably.

For her part Nilda wasn't sorry to be putting Alex behind them, however good or kind he'd been in life, however well-intentioned his ghostly warnings—*were* they warnings?—had been. Unless Nilda was mistaken, he'd overtaken Sidney to deliver one of them, his voice issuing from her without her knowledge or permission, as far as Nilda knew. Though the ends might have been noble, the means troubled her and made her feel powerless on her daughter's behalf.

She tossed the last package of peanut butter crackers into the bag and zipped the top. "See you in five minutes?"

"Maybe sooner."

"Go for it!"

As Sidney rushed up the stairs, Nilda thought of Angus, who last she checked, was still cowering beneath her bed. Getting him out from under it and into the car was going to be a struggle. Though the thunder was down to a distant rumble, the wind and rain had picked up, gusts now and then rattling the windows and seeming to shake the house.

"Sorry, bud."

She wished that, for Angus, there was some motivational equivalent of choco pops: her and Sidney's name for the pudding pops that Helen had made a couple of weeks ago and that had dwindled down to one. Foolishly, Nilda had pushed the last pop to the back of the freezer, sensing that it might very well be the last of Helen too, in their lives, at least. But there was no holding on to what was gone.

Her phone buzzed, delivering another shot of adrenaline.

Graham—with questions, suspicions.

Retrieving the phone from the table, she saw that she'd been wrong, of course. It was a text from Clay:

Rick says the place is yours. Call me when you have a chance.

Thank goodness.

But the call would have to wait until they got to Toni's.

She needed to round up just a few more things for her duffel bag—socks, underwear, a couple of T-shirts, her toothbrush and toothpaste. Anything they'd forgotten they could borrow from Toni, buy, or live without.

Nilda headed to the utility room, where her duffel sat by the dryer, ready for the load to finish. From the top of the supply shelf, the radio blared on.

This day in history!

August third, nineteen eighty-one: Air traffic controllers go on strike despite warnings from President Ronald Reagan that they'll be fired. But that's just what happens, marking a turning point in U.S. labor relations.

Nilda had taken to keeping this radio on for most of her waking hours, never dialing away from the AM news station that someone—Helen? Eula Joy?—had selected God knows how many years ago. The content didn't matter, really. It was more about having the company of voices, which she could hear—sometimes just barely—from almost every spot downstairs, except the living room. They made her feel just a little less alone.

And on this day in nineteen sixty-six, comedian Lenny Bruce, whose controversial brand of humor landed him in hot water legally, was found dead in his Los Angeles home at the age of forty.

She shut off the dryer and started shoving the almost-done laundry into the duffel bag, not bothering to fold the T-shirts or roll socks up with their mates.

The overhead light dimmed. Then it started flickering, as if struggling to stay on.

The radio seemed to be struggling too. Or, rather, the announcer's voice had become immersed in static. Then it vanished entirely. Nilda rose to shut off the radio, then froze. A new voice was rising up through the static: a woman's voice, distant and pleading. Nilda strained to hear her words but couldn't make out a single one. Still, there was something so familiar about the voice, so personal. Like it was speaking directly to her.

A bang sounded from the kitchen. The door. She ran to the kitchen and found that, sure enough, it had blown wide open, sending rain in sideways, soaking the floor. The push-button lock—a cheapo she'd kept meaning to replace—had been no match for the wind. The latch bolt had torn through the jamb, splintering it.

Shit.

She had to get this door closed, and keep it that way.

The kitchen chairs, solid oak, were heavy enough to do the trick. She grabbed the nearest one and dragged it over. Then she shut the door with one hand, holding it closed against the wind. With the other hand, she dragged the chair still closer, tipped it back to brace the knob. Not perfect, but—

She felt motion and force before she heard a sound: a grab at her waist, a hand to her mouth. He dragged her from the door and shoved her to the wall, his hand the only reason her face hadn't gotten smashed in.

Graham. She knew him from the fit of his chest against her back, from the way his angles met her own. She knew him from his smell, now mingled with the dampness of the rain.

He put his mouth to her ear and whispered, almost gently. "Painting. Fucking. Your very existence. I tried to make every-thing better for you. And I *never* asked for anything in return. Now the terms have changed, I'm afraid."

Sidney. She'd be here any minute, any second.

Nilda struggled against him, trying to break free. But he only pressed her closer to the wall, tightened his grip on her mouth. It was getting harder and harder to move, to breathe.

From the utility room, just static. No voices at all.

She wanted her red sneakers, not these beat-up purple ones.

Under the bed. That's where she'd left them. But when she got down to look, all she found was a hair clip and puffs of dust.

She returned to the closet and poked her head in farther, looked into the darker parts. There they were, in the corner. She ducked in, grabbed them, and threw them in the suitcase. Then she saw something that hadn't been there, even a minute ago.

On the bed, next to the suitcase, was the music box and earphones. The Walkman. But there'd been no sign of Alex for days. Not even the smell of the outdoors.

"Alex?"

No answer.

She picked up the Walkman and sat down on the bed.

There's no time for this.

Yes, there is. If you take too long, she'll come get you. And she'll give you the choco pop anyway.

She put on the headphones and pressed *play.*

> *Hi, Future Me.*

Alex's voice.

> *Whenever—if ever—you listen to this again, be it two thousand and two or two thousand fifty-two, I wonder if you'll think, "God, this sucks," or "This isn't too bad for a twelve-year-old who knows, like, four notes on the guitar."*
>
> *Maybe you're a world-touring rocker now. Or maybe this recording turned out to be your one and only gig, and you're now an insurance salesman in Burlington, and you can't even remember what happened to this guitar. Either way, whatever you're doing, wherever you are, here's hoping you're having as good a life as you can. Same to anyone else who might be listening, though I can't imagine who, or why.*
>
> *Here's to the future. And here's to the first song.*

Strumming first. Then he started singing one of the songs they'd listened to together, head to head, sharing the earphones.

His voice reminded her of the water from the creek: clear and bright. Different from her dad's but just as good. Like before, she started singing along with Alex, holding notes with him whenever she could, feeling the power of their joined voices.

The first song ended and another one started.

She listened on. She stayed.

❧

For some time, he made no moves, just kept her pressed to the wall, his hand clasped to her mouth. Yet now his breathing was even, slow. As slow as when he'd held her close in his bed, nearing the edge of sleep.

Maybe he was having second thoughts. Maybe—

No. He knew what she'd done, what she'd seen. There was no way out for her. Or Sidney.

Sidney.

She struggled against him, weaker this time, her vision graying, her legs failing. Once again, he pressed closer, squeezing more air from her lungs. Then he froze, wanting to draw this out, it seemed. This ending he'd desired for so long.

Can't stop thinking of her eyes...the dulling of that beautiful green.

The poison for that dulling was somewhere—a pants pocket? His reach for it might be her only chance to push back, break free. If she lasted that long.

The static sizzled up, louder. She tried to stay tuned to it, hoping this might keep her on her feet, keep her in this world. As if sensing her slide, he thrust a knee between her legs, keeping her pinned to the wall.

Something emerged from the static: that woman's voice. Nilda detected a two-syllable plea, a question. As she strained to hear it, the volume rose.

"Nilda? *Nilda?*"

Her mother.

Nilda called out to her, or tried to. His hand stifled her cries, making them unintelligible.

Night knitter, night knitter, I'll never know why
You've made it your duty to cover the sky

Her mother singing.

No. None of this was real. If it were, wouldn't she have sensed a shift in his attention? A new alertness to the radio?

She was hallucinating out of weakness. And a lack of oxygen?

With a blanket so thick and so dark in its hue
That only the moon and the stars can break through

Imagined or not, the voice was strong and clear—to her. And the words brought back another darkness: of her childhood room at bedtime, when her mother sat by her bed, stroking her hair, soothing her, and singing this very same song.

Enough light to satisfy possums and owls
Who go on the hunt with their hoots and their howls

He shifted his weight and slipped his arm from her waist, bringing her back to this world.

Something was happening—not just whatever he was doing, or about to do. All along her arms her flesh prickled and hummed, as if she'd become tuned to the radio signal, the singing, and the wind whistling past the door. She felt…euphoria, then a warm puff of breath by her ear.

"Just wait, you'll see." Her mother's voice, at a whisper.

Mom.

She tried to turn to her, fighting the hold of his hand, feeling the rage of the wind. It electrified her, with joy.

A gust thundered closer, as if answering her call. Then came the blast to the door. It slammed open, hurling the chair across the floor. Graham had eased his hold on her, and she sensed him looking the same way she was, toward the wind and rain gusting through the doorway.

Her mother was nowhere in sight, but she'd started back up with the song, her voice as strong and clear as before, and seeming to come from everywhere. Now a second voice came through on the wind, rising above it, drawing closer.

Helen's voice, singing along with her mom.

While I remain safe in your needle-made night
Hoping for dreams that will only delight

But bad dreams will come, and you know this is true
Knit me right, knit me right, knit me right through

On the last note, Helen stepped through the doorway, her hair and raincoat soaked, her face marble pale in the dimness. She looked their way, seeming not at all surprised, or the least bit fearful of Graham. In fact, she fixed him with a look that was almost tender.

She took a step toward them, Graham still in her sights. Then she took another. "Shhh, my little one, shhhhh."

Did she see Alex in him?

And did Graham see her? Once again, he'd frozen still.

Helen stepped closer, her tennis shoes squelching, her coat dripping rain on the floor. "Shhhhh, my dear, shhhh. Everything will be just fine, my sweet wee love."

Though the words weren't meant for her, Nilda felt them in her blood, like a rush from the kindest of sedatives. Like that old feeling of her mother stroking her hair, as she sang her gently to sleep.

"Shhhhh, my love. Let go, let go, *let go.*"

And that's when he released her, or when she broke free of him, somehow. Whatever happened got swallowed by darkness, and when Nilda emerged from it, she was on her back, looking up at Helen, or at whoever—whatever—Helen had become. She'd transformed into a giant image of herself, her head nearly grazing the ceiling. The image was flat and wavering, like a movie projected on a windblown screen. But those eyes weren't part of a movie. They regarded Nilda with what felt like tenderness, care.

"Shhhhh," said Helen. "Shhhhh." Once again, she lulled her to sleep.

38

How very small he was now. In her hands he took up no more space than old Joe, her first. His bones every bit as fragile.

His eyes? Wide open. Terrified.

"Shhhh," she said. "Shhh." The same thing she'd whispered to Joe, and countless other roosters, countless other hens.

Rituals weren't to be trifled with.

She turned him over, stroked his back gently. For in the grand scheme of things, he was just as helpless and deserving of mercy as those chickens had been, despite the necessity of his end.

"Shhh," she said. "Shhh." With every stroke of his back, her hand crept closer to his neck.

Before she could get there, piss soaked her palm, streamed down her forearm. Before she could get there, he was gone.

But bad dreams will come, and you know this is true
Knit me right, knit me right, knit me right through

39

Rain. Wind. The floor beneath her back. The ceiling before her eyes, with its familiar cracks and stains. *I'm alive.*

But there was no sign of Sidney, or Graham.

Nilda struggled to her feet, then froze. There he was, slumped at the foot of the wall where he'd pinned her, soaked with rain and smelling of piss. The only expressive thing about him? His dopamine T-shirt. His eyes were fixed in a gaze that saw nothing. His body was as still as the toppled chair between them, the chair the door had knocked clear.

Also between them, a syringe: what Graham must have been reaching for, until—

An image flashed into her mind: Helen as a giantess, shushing her—him—into oblivion.

No. That couldn't possibly explain Graham's death, but what could?

There was no time to think that through. She bounded down the hall, and up the stairs.

Without a knock of warning, she barged through Sidney's door. And there she was, sitting on the edge of her bed, listening to…a Walkman? Something Clay had slipped into a moving box? Whatever the reason for this distraction, Nilda was grateful for it.

Sidney didn't remove the earphones, just kept listening to whatever was playing through them. The look she turned on Nilda seemed a preview of teenage annoyance.

That suggestion of Sidney's future. Or the fact that she was fine. Or just her very presence. All these things, and others she'd never be able to put a finger on, made Nilda burst into tears.

Sidney stripped off the headphones, tossed aside the Walkman, and ran for Nilda. When she threw her arms around her, Nilda hugged her back, as tightly as she could. She buried her face in Sidney's hair, breathing in that smell still tinged with milky sweetness. All too soon, it would fade out for good.

Sidney pulled away and looked up at Nilda. "What's wrong, Mommy?"

How to answer this question? As Nilda led Sidney back to the bed, her mind spun with possibilities, none of them good. She sat down close to Sidney, still holding her hand. "Graham had an accident, downstairs. And he's really hurt."

Sidney's eyes widened. "What happened?"

"He fell."

Thankfully, Sidney didn't ask for more details. "Is he going to be okay?"

Nilda couldn't bring herself to say no. "I'm not sure. But there's something you can do that would be a really big help. I need you to stay up here until I tell you you can go back downstairs, okay? I don't think it'll be too long."

"Why?"

"I need to call some people for help, and some of the things they'll need to do...it's grownups-only stuff. Do you understand?"

"You mean it's gonna be scary?"

"Possibly." Nilda gave Sidney's hand a squeeze. "But everything'll be okay. I promise."

Sidney didn't look reassured.

"Do you think you can do what I asked you? It's really, really important."

Sidney nodded. "Are we still going to Toni's?"

"I think so. But not for a while."

She headed to the door, then looked back at Sidney, Helen's words rising to her mind, and echoing the ones Nilda had just spoken. *Everything will be just fine, my sweet wee love.* If only Nilda could really believe this. She smiled at Sidney and left.

Downstairs, Nilda paced the hall, phone in hand, not quite

ready to dial 911. What the hell would she say? He'd attacked her, no doubt. But she had no idea how to explain what had happened to *him*.

Once again, the image of Helen rose up in her mind, and she pushed it aside.

What if I *killed him, and I just don't remember?*

This question sent her where she least wanted to go: back to his body. There, she looked for signs of injury or other clues, fearing that something might spark a memory or moment of recognition. Nothing did. All she saw was what she'd seen before: a dead-still Graham with glazed eyes, his face a blood-less white.

That face. She remembered when she'd first studied its lines, reminded of that painting of Narcissus, down to the Roman nose, the full lower lip, the rounding of the chin. Death hadn't changed a single feature, nor had what he'd done to her, or tried to do. But a slain wolf could be beautiful too, even if it had leapt for your throat.

Turning back to her phone, she knew what she needed to do. Call Toni. She found her number, hit *dial*, and waited.

Pick up, pick up. *Please.*

And Toni did, on the second ring. "Hey, Nilda! What's up?"

The sound of her voice was all it took. Once again, Nilda broke down, thinking how close she'd been to losing every-thing. Sidney, worst of all.

"Oh, sweetheart, what happened?"

"I'm okay. So is Sidney, but—" She struggled to get the words out. "But Graham, he's—" She couldn't speak. She could barely breathe.

"Take your time. Take all the time you need."

Nilda did. And once she'd collected herself, once she started talking, she didn't hold anything back. She told Toni how Gra-ham had broken in, how he'd tried to inject her with some-thing—something to knock her out, she guessed, or poison her. She told her everything she'd come to suspect about him, and everything she'd discovered in his journal. And she told her everything about Helen and Alex, down to her belief that they were ghosts. Then she tried to put into words her last memories of Helen, struggling to figure them out even as she spoke.

"When I woke up from that vision of her, or whatever it was, Graham was dead. And the *how* of that, I just can't get my mind around it. I think it would have been physically impossible for me to kill him, unless I got hold of a weapon. But there's no sign of that, and no sign of a mark on him. But the alternative to *me* killing him…"

Nilda had no idea what that alternative might be. Helen lulling him into a permanent sleep, if such a thing were even possible?

She shared these thoughts with Toni. "If Helen suspected that he played any role in Alex's death, she would have had a motive. Maybe this was revenge, delayed."

Silence on Toni's end.

"You think I've lost it, don't you?" More likely, Toni suspected that Graham had drugged her, causing her mind to run wild and conjure thoughts of ghosts, and that final vision of Helen. That suspicion wasn't unwarranted. After all, Toni had been right that Graham's tonics weren't as innocent as Nilda had presumed.

Yet Graham hadn't drugged her, not tonight anyway. The syringe was full. And in a larger sense, Nilda didn't believe that any of Helen's agency—any of what she'd desired or done, any of who she'd been, or might continue to be—could be assigned to Graham, or to some potion of his. He was unworthy of Helen, and everything about her.

"No, I don't think you've lost it. I think you just had an incredibly traumatic experience. And I'm glad you're telling me everything about it."

Feeling restless, Nilda wandered into the kitchen, where she'd left the tote with the lasagna and snacks. Once so strong, her appetite had vanished, and the lingering smell of the lasagna sickened her. "Whatever the truth is, I need to call 911. And I have no idea what to say when I do. I can't blame this on a

ghost." Nilda came back to the explanation that had filled her
with dread before. "Maybe I *am* responsible. Somehow."

On Toni's end the sound of distant giggles, Mae's and Livia's. The sound of a normal life. "Even if you are responsible—
which I seriously doubt—it was self-defense, Nilda. He had to
be stopped, and I'm damn glad he was."

"So what do you think I should say?"

Toni went silent, as if mulling things over. "You're right
about leaving out the Helen stuff. I'm not saying I don't believe
you. But it's gonna be a hard sell for most people."

No doubt *most people* included the police.

"That doesn't mean you have to lie. Just keep things simple
and to the point. Say Graham broke in and attacked you, made
it so hard for you to breathe that you fainted. When you came
to, he was dead, and you have no idea why."

Toni's advice, and her mention of self-defense, eased Nilda's
anxiety, but only so much. She imagined police finding Graham's death suspicious and bringing her in for questioning. She
imagined the questioning taking a really bad turn. Not wanting
to be alone with these fears, she shared them with Toni.

"I think you're getting ahead of yourself. But if the police *do*
wanna bring you in, insist that you have a lawyer present. I'm
sure Rosie can help."

"Really?"

"Really. I'll call her as soon as we get off the phone. Then
I'm gonna catch the first return flight I can. Jack and the girls
can live without me for a day."

Nilda didn't put up a fight about this. "Thanks so much,
Toni."

"Of course."

Once again, Nilda felt close to tears, this time out of gratitude.

"One other thing. Don't touch that syringe. If it has fingerprints from him, that could be pretty incriminating."

Fingerprints seemed likely. For some reason—incompe-
tence surely not one of them—Graham hadn't bothered to

wear gloves. Maybe he'd imagined poisoning her with whatever was in the syringe—Papa Nix?—and then making her, and any other evidence, disappear.

Almost certainly, Sidney would have been part of that evidence had Graham not been stopped.

In her mind she saw Sidney heading down the stairs, wondering why Nilda was taking so long. She saw her walking toward the open door and the blowing wind and rain, getting closer and closer to Graham—

Nilda pulled herself out of this movie of what might have been. Sidney was safe. Toni was coming home. And then there was the memory of her mother's voice: singing over the radio, then whispering in her ear. A voice that had felt as real, and as comforting, as it had in life.

William Fletcher Tenneman, who was recently appointed headmaster of the Fairmoore School, has been placed on leave pending an investigation into allegations that he sexually assaulted or harassed students during his twenty-three-year tenure as a highly praised, award-winning teacher at the school.

As reported previously, allegations against Tenneman were initially made public over social media, in response to a painting, critical of Tenneman, that was displayed earlier this month at the Sky Tent Music and Arts Festival. After the festival internal documents from Fairmoore were leaked to the *Sun*, revealing a history of complaints against the headmaster: allegations of both sexual harassment and sexual assault. The documents also include copies of letters from Fairmoore officials to some of the complainants, in which the school denied the allegations and, at times, threatened legal action in response to them.

Fairmoore officials have declined to comment about whether they investigated any of the allegations at the time they were made, or about whether any disciplinary action was taken against Tenneman as a result of them. Today the school released this statement to faculty, staff, and the press: "Due to the seriousness of the allegations against William Fletcher Tenneman, he has been placed on paid administrative leave, pending a full review of the facts and circumstances regarding the complaints made against him."

In a statement emailed to the *Sun*, Tenneman said, "I strenuously deny these baseless charges and look forward to seeing the truth come to light."

Fairmoore graduate Ardley Cohen, who has been active in the social-media exchanges about Tenneman, said that he assaulted her eight years ago, during her junior year. According to Cohen, after she reported the assault to school authorities, "absolutely nothing happened. I hope that things are different this time and that there truly are consequences. But we have to keep the pressure on the school to see that they do the right thing."

Cohen said that the painting of Tenneman inspired her to come forward on social media and to connect with other alleged victims of her former teacher. "He and Fairmoore have tried to silence us for far too long. Now we're reclaiming our voices."

Another Fairmoore graduate, Toni Westford-Liu, said she was assaulted by Tenneman twenty-one years ago and threatened with a lawsuit after making two complaints to the school. "This time," she said, "I'm not going to go away quietly." Westford-Liu added that she is prepared to take legal action against the school if Tenneman isn't fired, "at the very least."

—"Fairmoore Headmaster Placed on Leave" by Pruitt
Moss, *The Halifax Sun*, August 29th, 2019

40

The chorus of night bugs. The smell of citronella oil. The darkness relieved only by moonlight. The wine buzz that had melted Nilda and Toni into their respective recliners.

Over her three weeks at Toni's, these evenings on the back porch had come to feel like a ritual to Nilda, a necessary one. But tonight would mark the last of them, for now. Tomorrow morning Nilda would be driving to Boston, where Sidney, Clay, Angus, and most of the stuff from Farleigh House were waiting for her. Later on, she and Clay would move the stuff out of storage and into the month-to-month rental: the second floor of a triple decker. Though the new place had a back porch, it would never be anything like Toni's, with its screened-in, summer-camp feel. But Nilda was grateful for a fresh start, as uncertain as she was about what might follow it.

Toni let out a long breath.

"You okay?"

"Yeah. Just playing the same old tape in my mind."

"The Ardley tape?"

"Yep."

Since the festival and social-media blow-up, Toni, Ardley, and a few other victims of Tenneman had become comrades-in-arms against him and Fairmoore. Toni had come to feel especially connected to Ardley. As she'd put it, "Maybe because I see my old self in her, and my girls in her. I just wish I could have done more to fight him. Before he could hurt her, or any-one else."

This regret, which Toni had expressed to Nilda several times, as if on a loop, was the Ardley tape.

Toni took another sip of her wine. "You don't have to say what I know you're about to. But I appreciate the sentiment."

Nilda was about to say what she'd said every other time: that Toni had done—and was still doing—all she could to fight Tenneman. That until recently, all the cards had been stacked against her, and against every other young woman he'd harassed or assaulted. That any guilt should be borne by him and Fair-moore alone, not by their victims.

Nilda raised her glass. "Let me say this, then: *to justice.*"

Toni clinked her glass against Nilda's. "To justice."

Nilda sipped her wine and eased back in the recliner, again wondering what had become of her painting of Tenneman. Maybe someone from Fairmoore had confiscated it, the first step toward a defamation suit against her, by the school or by Tenneman himself. Despite her faked registration for the festi-val, she'd have to be a prime suspect as the artist, given her for-mer acceptance of the portrait commission. Then again, it was possible that neither she nor the painting was on Fairmoore's or Tenneman's radar right now. They had plenty of other trouble to deal with.

As a comfort, she called up the mental pictures that had

soothed her since the festival: the painting moldering in a garbage dump, the painting bursting into flames.

Toni leaned toward Nilda, her glass extended. "One more, just for good measure: to the M.E."

Nilda clinked Toni's glass. "To the M.E."

Last night's toast. With it, they celebrated news they'd gotten earlier that day: the medical examiner's finding that Graham's manner of death had been "natural," leaving no possibility that Nilda could be held responsible for his end. The M.E. had found the immediate cause of his death to be ventricular fibrillation: cardiac arrest, in layman's terms. As Rosie had put it, when relaying the news: "Sometimes, people just drop dead."

Thanks to some connections in the M.E.'s office, and in law enforcement, Rosie had been the main source of information about the investigation surrounding Graham and his death. Autopsy reports weren't public information, and Nilda's last contact with the police had been on the night of Graham's death, when they'd asked her just a few questions, not in the setting Nilda had envisioned—a concrete-block room at the police station—but at her kitchen table, Rosie at her side. Since then, the cops hadn't exactly been forthcoming about their investigation—understandably, Nilda supposed.

Yet, through Rosie, Nilda learned the contents of Graham's syringe: "some herbal stuff" and potassium chloride, which can cause cardiac arrest and go undetected in autopsies. But the M.E. had found no injection marks on Graham's body, and only his fingerprints had been found on the syringe.

Through Rosie, Nilda also learned that investigators had raided Graham's place, confiscating stores of potassium chloride, "miscellaneous concoctions," and also his journals, which, in Rosie's words, contained "some pretty disturbing stuff." Nilda wondered what poisonings—imagined or realized—Graham might have described on those pages. His father's? His college roommate's? Alex's? Others she couldn't begin to imagine? But there seemed little point in building a case against a dead man, and maybe, in the end, the journals and everything else the cops found would just get shelved. Whatever happened or didn't happen with the investigation, the most important truth remained: Graham Arthur Emmerly would never harm another soul.

A thunk sounded on the screen before them: the landing of an okra-sized bug—too big, too fuzzy-bodied, to be a moth. In silence they watched it spread its wings, skull-pale in the moonlight. Then, before either one of them could remark upon it, it flew back into the night.

Nilda took another olive and started nibbling around the pit. "I have a theory." It wasn't a new one. She'd gotten it shortly after Graham's death but had kept it to herself, guessing that spoken aloud, it might sound every bit as preposterous as it quite possibly was. But now, something—maybe because this was her last night at Toni's, maybe because of the appearance of that otherworldly bug—made her want to share it. "Helen scared Graham to death."

Toni stared ahead in silence. Then she said, "That seems plausible."

The flatness of Toni's voice suggested otherwise. She would never say what she probably believed: that Helen had been nothing more than a hallucination of Nilda's. At times Nilda almost believed this herself. Then the memories would come back to her: of the ordinary Helen, who'd cooked and cleaned and, at times, offered advice; then of the giant, wavering Helen, whose head had nearly grazed the ceiling. Both versions of her had seemed every bit as real as Toni.

When it came to the night of Graham's attack, it felt as if the memories of Helen had eclipsed nearly everything Nilda could recall about what he'd done. She remembered the door banging open, and the clasp of his hand on her mouth. But she couldn't recall a word he'd said to her, or much else.

A few days before, her curiosity about this had led her to the internet, where she'd found articles about dissociative amnesia, an inability to recall things associated with a traumatic experience. Maybe that was as good an explanation as she would ever get.

Toni set her wine glass, now empty, on the table between them. "Have you seen any more of her?"

"Helen?"

"Yeah."

It seemed that Toni was trying to play along, to be a good sport about Helen, and Nilda's experiences with her. "No. The only place I'd ever seen her was in that house, or someplace else on the property. But even if I went back there, I doubt I'd see her again."

"Why?"

"I have no idea. It's just a gut feeling." Nilda thought of one supposed *raison d'être* for ghosts: that they lingered on Earth to accomplish some mission, vanishing for good once the deed had been done. If Helen had suspected Graham of killing Alex, her mission had certainly been accomplished—if Nilda's theory behind his death had been correct.

"That must be a relief, huh?"

"I'm not sure. I'm not sure about anything when it comes to her, or that house."

Living there, Nilda seemed to have been situated in a hazard zone of crosscurrents: of grief—Helen's, made material, and her own; of desire mingled with malice—Graham's; and of artistic influence and expression. She'd been living within the creation of an architect who'd made it his mission to influence the mind through his work. And then there was her mother's presence through her art, especially *Revenge in Glass*. Perhaps all these things had influenced one another, in ways Nilda would never comprehend. Together, they'd been powerful enough to affect her physically and emotionally.

For the first time in weeks, Nilda thought of *The See-er*. Perhaps that show's star would be able to make more sense of all this. But Nilda had no desire to contact her, or even to tune in for another episode. She'd had her fill of this sort of mystery.

She placed her olive pit on her napkin, alongside the others.

"You know what else? I never felt like I lived up to my name in that place, certainly not when it came to Graham."

Seeing Toni's blank look, Nilda offered a reminder. "I mean the *translation* of my name. Ready for Battle?"

"Ah yes." Toni went quiet for a moment. Then she looked Nilda in the eye. "I'm gonna have to disagree with you. I mean, the painting that kicked Tenneman's ass? You did it in that house—or in that studio. Close enough, in my book. Your mother would have been so proud."

Nilda hoped so. She thought of *Revenge in Glass*, again wishing she'd learned more about who had inspired her mother's own act of vengeance through art. Maybe, if her mom had lived long enough to learn of Tenneman, and of what he'd done, she would have been willing to say more about what had driven her work on the sculpture.

Toni toyed with her napkin, looking lost in thought. "What was that thing she'd say, when she really connected with your work?"

Nilda had no answer. Though, surely, the memory was buried somewhere in her mind, she couldn't grasp it now. "Remind me."

"I *think* she'd say, 'I *feel* this.' She'd have that same reaction to your painting, I'm sure."

This moment with her mother seemed lost to Nilda—Toni's words sparking no mental images of it, no memories of her mother's presence, no emotions. All there was was blankness.

Dissociative amnesia? It couldn't affect *good* memories, could it?

Or maybe it could. The sound of her mother singing that night was growing fainter and fainter, the memory of it harder and harder to retrieve—so much so that Nilda had started trying to recreate the sound in her mind, never successfully. It was becoming like a story of a story of a story, passed—with ever greater imperfection—from one teller to another.

"Nilda? Are you okay?"

"Yeah." She tried to remind herself that she'd been through

a lot, not so long ago. Surely, with time, the old memories—the good ones—would resurface. "I just miss her."

"Of course you do. She was a wonderful, wonderful woman."

A saying of her mother's came back to Nilda, like a warm whisper in her ear. A reminder that Jo was still very much with her. A relief.

Everything will be just fine, my sweet wee love.

Historically significant fixer-upper features 12 rooms (incl. 4 bedrooms and 2 1/2 bathrooms) with over 3,500 sq ft of living space. Quirky yet charming detailing throughout. Property is priced well below assessed value and is being sold as is with no seller concessions.

—Listing for Farleigh House

41

Nilda tossed the last of what had been under the kitchen sink—used scrub pads, furniture polish from the Eula Joy era, three almost-empty canisters of scouring powder—into the trash bag. The effort revealed yet another possible job to tackle: the stained and soiled contact paper lining the bottom of the cabinet. She grabbed the cleaning spray then put it down. This mission was about clearing the last of the detritus out of this house, not about making it spotless.

Her phone buzzed on the counter. Incoming from Allison, she guessed. Flipping over the phone, she saw that she'd been right. She tapped open the text:

How are things going?

Nilda saw this for what it was: not idle curiosity but a nudge. She knew that the buyers wanted to "show off" the place to some friends later today, and Allison, crack real-estate agent that she was, had promised them she'd make it happen.

In her reply Nilda cut to the chase:

I'll be out of here in an hour, give or take.

Although the buyers' offer had been lower, just slightly, than the only other serious bid, Nilda had accepted it. Because in Allison's words, they were "besotted with the place," her tone suggesting bafflement.

Nilda didn't want to know why the buyers—a young couple—were besotted. Nor did she want to learn about whatever plans they had for the place. It wasn't seller's remorse so much as a lingering possessiveness, an unwillingness to imagine how others' futures might unfold here. Nilda had felt this way about every other place she'd lived in, formed some connection with, and left behind, by choice or circumstance. She'd feel it about the rental in Boston too, when she moved out of it next week. And she'd feel it about her new place in Providence, whenever the time came to depart from it: God willing, years from now.

Nilda pocketed her phone and left the trash bag by the back door. Then she headed for the dining room: her final destination on the cleanup tour.

Months earlier, in her rush to get the stuff in this house moved to Boston, sent to Goodwill, or trashed, Nilda had overlooked not just pockets of junk but also some possible keepers. Among the latter: the champagne coupes that had been shoved to the back of the built-in china cabinet in the dining room. When Nilda discovered them, she imagined Eula Joy raising one, poker-faced, in answer to a toast. Now they felt like one memento of this house, of Eula Joy, worth keeping. None of her great-aunt's other possessions had made it to Boston.

Entering the dining room, she felt a weighted ache in her chest, melancholia. Not the first time she'd experienced it in this house on this day. Surely, this had something to do with the new barrenness of the rooms, and the shadows cast by the slanted autumn light, dying even as it peaked. Yet she sensed that the greater share of her sadness came from the fact that these were her last moments in the living space, the creation, of Nathaniel Farleigh, with whom she'd come to feel a greater connection since leaving this house.

For one thing, he'd helped break her spell of painter's block. Shortly after the move to Boston, she painted three variations of the portrait she'd done of him. Now she was in the middle of two abstract paintings inspired by her time in the leaning chamber. As she worked on them, she at times approached the out-of-body feeling she'd experienced in the chamber, that moon's glow eclipsing her thoughts. Balm for the soul?

No. Quite the opposite, sometimes. Yet she tried to keep those words from Farleigh's journals in mind, words she'd written out—with a few changes—and taped to the wall by her easels:

> *If an artist feels she must steer clear of discomfort, in her thinking and in her work, what revelations are possible, for herself and her audience?*

Her phone buzzed again. *Please let it not be Allison.*
Thankfully, it was Toni.

Did you get the lighter fluid?

Nilda texted her back:

Yep. Wish me luck.

A string of prayer emojis appeared in reply.

On her way to the china cabinet, she paused at the bay window, looked into what had once been Graham's study, those curtains no longer barring it from her view. Now the room looked as empty as this one, the once-laden bookshelves bare. She hoped the entire house had been cleared of Graham's possessions and potions, leaving a blank slate for whomever might move in next. Some distant relative he'd never spoken of? Or a complete stranger?

May nothing linger there to trouble you. Or pull you into the unfathomable.

Odds were, they'd never learn about what Graham had done, or attempted—in that house or beyond it. Not from any breaking news. The last thing Nilda heard, from Rosie, was that the police had all but given up on investigating Graham's history, and she wasn't surprised or sorry about that. It was long past time to put him to rest, in every sense of the word, and she'd be happy to never hear another word about him.

It didn't take long to get the champagne coupes wrapped in newspaper and packed into the last remaining moving box: small enough to tuck under her arm, which she did. Then she took one last spin around the room, realizing that this was it. She was about to leave this room, this house, behind. For good.

In the farthest corner, she spotted a black streak on the floor, from a shoe, it seemed. Something the easy chair must have blocked from her view. As she studied the mark, an image, a motion, flashed through her mind: Sidney running for something, and skidding to a stop to catch it.

But she'd never seen Sidney do that here, certainly not in the space where the chair had been. And why was this non-memory bringing her to the edge of tears? Sidney was fine. She was just outside. Playing with Angus, the last Nilda had seen.

A flash of alarm sent her out of the house, onto the patio. Straight ahead, Sidney was running through the yard, Angus at her heels, waiting for her to pitch the ball clutched in her hand. A chewed-up, spit-sodden thing. His favorite.

This sight, this relief, broke Nilda down. But she did her best to pull herself together, knowing she needed to keep things moving, get them on the road. There was just one more thing left to do.

She called out to Sidney, trying to sound joyful. "Ready to start that fire?" The sadness lingered, cracking her voice.

Sidney answered by dropping the ball and charging to the patio. Surprising herself, Nilda threw her arms around Sidney and held her close, rocked her. Then Sidney started to wriggle, and Nilda released her, once again yearning for the old clinginess. *If it ever annoys you again, pinch yourself. Hard.*

Nilda fetched what she'd left in the house: the champagne coupes and the bag of trash. She set the coupes on the patio and, trash bag in hand, led Sidney to the top of the drive, where Allison's maintenance team had left a dumpster for whatever came out of the deeper clean the agent had planned for the house and yard. Nilda tossed the trash into the dumpster and, with Sidney, headed to the middle of the drive: the temporary home of the fire barrel she'd rolled out from her old studio and placed on cement blocks, as instructed by the internet. Today's kindling: a few old moving boxes, folded to fit in the barrel; some paper waste she'd crammed on top of the boxes; and on the ground near the barrel, the very reason for all this effort: the thing Nilda most wanted to burn.

Things, actually: the collapsed roof of the model house, mostly stripped of its shingles; what remained of the back and sides, with their snuff marks from Farleigh's cigars; the innards; and the part she hated the most—the front panel with its spider-eye windows. In the light of day, all of this looked more like junk than it ever had, the glint of those windows dulled. Yet Nilda's drive to do what she'd described to Toni hadn't diminished.

She'd never forget her first sight of this house, this thing, on Sidney's bed. Or its appearances on *Revenge in Glass*. Even if the forces behind its surfacing had had the best of intentions—to warn her about Graham—the house itself felt too corrupt to be left behind, even in its dilapidated state, even in a dumpster. But it wasn't just that. Nilda needed to obliterate it, for her own sake as much as anyone else's.

With Sidney she'd tried to keep the explanation simple: *I wanna burn the bad kid's house. So it doesn't scare the new people.*

Remembering her exchange with Toni, Nilda fetched the lighter fluid she'd purchased on the way here, and the butane fire starter Toni had lent her. Then she led Sidney several paces back from the barrel.

"Stay here, okay? Just till I get things started."

Never a Girl Scout, never a camper, Nilda had no experience starting fires and had picked up the lighter fluid out of insecurity. Now the "Danger" warning on the label gave her pause. She squirted the barrel with two weak shots then struck a flame to the top of the kindling: a piece of junk mail. The flame burned through this and seemed to vanish, smoke its only trace. Nilda moved to light another spot, then stopped. A fire had started, a small one, and was working its way through more junk mail. Within a few minutes, the kindling was ablaze, the smoke overtaking that bittersweet smell of the air, apple-ish and edged with leaf must.

Sidney stood beside her now. Realizing they didn't have

much time before the kindling burned itself out, Nilda handed her the smallest piece of the house, then took up a piece for herself.

Catching Sidney's eye, she said, "This is as close as I want you to get, okay?" They stood a couple of yards away from the fire.

Sidney nodded, her eyes aglow with something that seemed more than firelight. She'd gotten that same look when Nilda told her of her plans to burn the house, making Nilda wonder whether some pyromaniacal blood flowed in her daughter's veins.

"Now watch this," Nilda said. With an under-handed pitch, she tossed her piece into the fire. Sidney followed suit, and from here they took turns, until they got to the parts that were too big to be tossed: the roof and the front panel. Nilda took charge of these, ending with the front panel, which sat at the top of the barrel, all the better for her to watch it burn.

As she did, she thought of the other model house, which wouldn't be going with them, as much as Sidney had wanted it to. Nilda had put it back in the hideaway spot in Sidney's old closet, sure that Farleigh had left it there for a reason, and hoping it would stay put for good.

Nilda took Sidney's hand, feeling the need to mark this occasion with words, something like a toast, or a prayer. She gave it her best shot. "Goodbye to bad things. Hello to good ones. Hello to fresh starts."

Sidney didn't say anything. The fire seemed to have consumed all of her attention. Still, this couldn't be just about what Nilda felt, and needed. She tried to draw Sidney out. "What are you looking forward to the most?"

Sidney didn't hesitate to answer. "Seeing Daddy."

She might have meant this evening. Nilda would be dropping her off at Clay's place for another overnight, and Sidney would be staying with him for the next few days. Then again, Sidney's words might have been a reminder of the promise that Nilda and Clay had made to her, that even after the move to

Providence, Clay would continue to be a regular presence in her life.

And in Nilda's? After taking Sidney to Clay's for overnights, Nilda would sometimes stay for dinner. Sometimes, she'd linger long past it, she and Clay slipping into his bedroom after Sidney was fast asleep, or so they'd assumed. More than once, Sidney had asked Nilda if she and Clay were getting back together. The only thing Nilda could think to tell her was that she and Clay would always care about each other. The bigger truth: Nilda still loved him, and maybe always would. Yet her wariness of recommitting to him felt every bit as great as that love. If the two of them were to have any future after the move to Providence, only time would tell.

Now Nilda brushed her hand through Sidney's hair. "You know we're gonna make that happen."

Before them the fire raged, the house front's lower half consumed in flames. Above the flames, through the smoke, those windows remained, or what was left of them. Their glass blown, they were now mere voids, like socket holes in a skull. Nilda thought of their real-world counterparts, in Graham's room, of how she'd turned away from them, never suspecting that a far greater danger lay next to her.

The fire popped, shooting up sparks and ash.

"Like Swirly World!" Sidney's nickname for one of the new abstract paintings: swirls of color against darkness, and flecks of orange and yellow. Like sparks.

"Yes," Nilda said. "Like Swirly World."

Her work on this painting, and on all the other new ones, had had nothing to do with drinking some special concoction. More and more, she questioned the influence of Graham's tonics, and of Graham himself. The truth was, she'd always had—and would continue to have—the ultimate agency over her art, no matter how out of control other aspects of her life could feel.

Thank God for that.

And thank God for something else: Whatever Graham had said to her that night, whatever he'd done to her, seemed to have vanished from her mind entirely. She remembered the bang from the kitchen, and running to the blown-open door. She remembered coming to on her back. But everything in between? It seemed to have been scrubbed from her mind, as if her mother had come to the rescue with one of her homemade cleaning solutions.

Like that grime never existed.

"Yes, Mother, *yes*," she said, almost conjuring the smell of vinegar.

Sidney seemed not to have heard the words, but Nilda had only whispered them. And it was all about the fire now, the flames having pitched to a roar. They had overtaken all of the house front, and seemed intent on sending it heavenward, in that uprushing column of smoke.

Nilda wedged the box of champagne coupes into a corner of the trunk, hoping they'd survive the trip home. Then she shut the lid.

"Sidney? Angus?"

In seconds they came running from a final round of playing in the yard, Angus with the ball in his mouth.

Nilda grabbed the ball, tossed it into the back of the car, and wiped the spit on her jeans, now so soot-stained that there was no point in sparing them this indignity. The soot was a consequence of her half-assed attempt to clean out the barrel and not leave a fire hazard behind. After the flames had burned down to embers, she'd hosed down what remained in the barrel and tossed the biggest chunks of it into the dumpster. One of them: the front of the model house, now sodden, carbonized, barely recognizable. *Good.*

Nilda opened the door behind the passenger side and called out Angus's cue: "Up, up!"

He leapt onto his seat, circled, and sat. Ready to hit the road. So was Sidney, it seemed. She'd opened the door on the other side and was climbing into her booster seat.

By the time Nilda had rounded the car to buckle her in,

Sidney had her Walkman in hand, and the headphones in place. Since the move to Boston, she'd listened to the thing so much she'd worn out one of the tapes that had come with it, her favorite. In response Clay had started making her replacement cassettes, all with songs from the eighties and nineties, like the original. It included a generous sampling of tunes by Tom Petty, one of Alex's favorites, apparently.

"Can you get that?" Sidney was pointing to the floor in front of her, where Nilda found one of the cassettes. Next to it, half-shoved under the driver's seat, was Fuzzy, no longer attached to Sidney almost every minute of the day. The toy was more matted than fuzzy these days, and now so deeply soiled that Nilda's sponge cleanings no longer made any difference. If Sidney had lost all interest in the thing, Nilda might have tossed it into the trash: a day that, perhaps, was not far off. Surely, the person who'd given it to Sidney—Nilda couldn't remember who—would never be the wiser.

Nilda handed Sidney the cassette and took the wheel, started up the car. Backing out of the drive, she kept her eye on the fire barrel, not wanting to give the house a final glance, not wanting to experience another wave of sadness.

She didn't. In fact, she was as ready for the road as Sidney and Angus had seemed. Ready to be gone from this place.

Within minutes the house had all but vanished from her mind, her senses overtaken by the waning light, by the leaves drifting down from the trees on either side of the road. Orange, gold, red.

So familiar, this road, this light, these trees. Maples, mostly? Yes.

Yes.

She was back. She was *here*.

And never had the wheel felt more sure in her hands. Steering the two of them through the curves and straights of the road, she found it hard to believe she'd preferred to leave the driving to Russ.

The two of them.

She looked to the rearview mirror, to the backseat, and there he was, nodding his head to his music, his red-gold curls catching the light.

My dear, sweet boy.

She looked back to the road, feeling more hopeful than she had in years. *Goodbye to bad things. Hello to good ones. Hello to fresh starts.*

DISCUSSION GUIDE

1. How do Nilda's feelings about Nathaniel Farleigh and his architectural works evolve over the course of the novel? In the end, what are your feelings about him and his work? Do you see him as a positive force or something more complicated?

2. The friendship between Nilda and Toni seems to be a grounding force for both women. In what ways do Nilda and Toni complement each other?

3. Mothering and grief seem to be woven together in the novel, from both Nilda's and Helen's perspectives. How do the absences of Jo, in Nilda's case, and of Alex, in Helen's case, affect the two women and their relationship? Consider, especially, how these losses affect them as mothers.

4. In various ways the novel considers how art can be used to exact vengeance. What advantages might art have over other forms of revenge?

5. In the climax scene, Helen seems to show some sympathy for Graham, even as she seals his fate. Why? Is her sympathy at all warranted?

6. Do you think that Helen is consciously malevolent, or is she more like a force of nature, driven to do what she believes is best for Nilda, and ultimately for her son and herself, perhaps heedless (or unaware) of any toll this might take?

7. What do you think about the ending of the novel? Are there reasons for hope for Nilda despite what is revealed in the final passages? Why or why not?

ACKNOWLEDGMENTS

I am deeply grateful to Jaynie Royal, Pam Van Dyk, and everyone else at Regal House Publishing. Their dedication to their authors, and to producing books of the finest quality, has been unfailing, and I am incredibly lucky that *The Inhabitants* found a home with them.

I never would have been able to complete this novel, and improve my early drafts, without the help of many. I'd like to thank those who commented on those drafts or provided moral support throughout my writing and revising process: Sally Bunch, Ellen Darion, Beth Gylys, Karen Henry, Chris Juzwiak, Audrey Schulman, Grace Talusan, Gilmore Tamny, Ellen Thibault, and Patricia Wise.

I am also grateful to the Mass Cultural Council, which has helped to support my work and the work of countless other Massachusetts-based writers and artists.

Once again, I'm incredibly thankful to my husband, John, who continues to be an inspiration to me. A thoughtful reader and editor, he smartly critiqued many aspects of the novel.

Finally, I will be forever grateful to my brothers, Grant and Neil, and to my late parents, Barbara and Nelson, who were early supporters of my desire to tell stories and to create my own books: handwritten, staple-bound, and illustrated, and often featuring haunted houses or castles, or spectral visitations. All this is to say that the seeds of *The Inhabitants* were planted years ago, and I appreciate the early nurturing that they received.

To learn more about Beth Castrodale and her books, visit her website at bethcastrodale.com. If you subscribe to her e-newsletter, you'll receive a free ebook (Beth's literary mystery *Gold River*). Just visit bethcastrodale.com/gold-river.